GOLD
IN THE
COFFINS

I0652416

DOMINIC CERTO, KSJ AND LEN HARAC, PH.D

HARMITA PRESS

This is a work of fiction. The events and characters described herein are imaginary and are not intended to refer to specific places or living persons. The opinions expressed in this manuscript are solely the opinions of the author and do not represent the opinions or thoughts of the publisher. The author has represented and warranted full ownership and/or legal right to publish all the materials in this book.

Harmita Press

ISBN: 978-0-578-15516-6

Library of Congress Control Number: 2015900274

PRINTED IN THE UNITED STATES OF AMERICA

ACKNOWLEDGEMENTS

WE WOULD LIKE TO ACKNOWLEDGE AND GIVE THANKS TO **THE MARINES OF HOTEL 2-7** AND ALL U.S. COMBAT VETERANS OF THE VIETNAM WAR, AND ALL WARS, WHO SERVED PROUDLY AND RETURNED TO FACE NEW CHALLENGES HERE AT HOME. WE EXTEND OUR THANKS FOR THE WORKS OF "**OPERATION HOMEFRONT**" AND "**THE WOUNDED WARRIORS PROJECT**" TO SERVE THE VETERANS COMMUNITY.

WE WOULD ALSO LIKE TO ACKNOWLEDGE AND THANK THE **ESSEX COUNTY CHIEFS OF POLICE ASSOCIATION** AND THE **ESSEX COUNTY SHERIFF'S DEPARTMENT** FOR THEIR COMMITMENT TO LAW ENFORCEMENT AND THE SAFETY AND PRESERVATION OF OUR COMMUNITIES

FINALLY, WE WISH TO THANK BOTH OUR FAMILIES FOR THEIR SUPPORT AND LOVE, FOR WITHOUT THEM NONE OF THIS WOULD BE POSSIBLE.

TABLE OF CONTENTS

FOREWORD

By

–Beth Sarafraz, NY BLUE NOW MAGAZINE Managing Editor/Writer, with articles published in The New York Times, New Jersey Monthly Magazine, Boxing World. Eastside Boxing.com, The Brooklyn Eagle, The Brooklyn View, The Bay News, The Newark Star-Ledger, NY Cop.com, The Jewish Press, and other publications.

Dom Certo and Len Harac have co-written a compelling account of successful businessman Donnie DeAngelo's treacherous journey through the land-mined maze of Wall Street trying to take his restaurant and coffee company public. DeAngelo, accompanied by his all-for-one and one-for-all band of Vietnam Marine Corps buddies, finds himself tracked by FBI, the mob, and other law enforcement types who may – or may not – be on his side, and seems headed for bankruptcy, jail, or worse. Despairing so deeply that he considers suicide, despite the unshakeable support of his devoted Columbian-tough wife, DeAngelo must come up with a way to endure, survive and hopefully prevail against all the odds. First, however, this bright but naive son of blue-collar Italian immigrants must figure out what the hell is going on and why the big honchos investing in his company seem to want the business to fail. And in doing so what provocative course of retribution and justice do they pursue.

Mirroring real life accounts of corruption scandals at the

highest levels of our nation's business sector, the book reads like nonfiction behind the scenes kiss and tell all about the American Dream's greed and glory mix. I was up all night race reading to the very last page – and then I had to remind myself this was a work of fiction, but so thoroughly crafted and written that I was sure this story shoulda, coulda, woulda happened to someone out there, for real – but that someone shoulda, coulda, woulda taken the hit and the story to his grave. As a published nonfiction writer myself, I give high praise to this debut book by Dom Certo and Len Harac and await more world-class work by this high-powered writing team.

CHAPTER 1
MAN OF THE YEAR

Ironic, Donnie DeAngelo thinks to himself, as friends and supporters gather by the bar at DeRosa's. The old Italian restaurant is a New Jersey fixture for celebrating big events. On this wintry night in December, the Italian American Police Association is giving him its Man of the Year Award.

DeAngelo's charitable contributions and achievements in the business community have been measured and deemed worthy by those attending this tribute to him: the mayor, the chief of police, numerous cops, FBI agents, and others in law enforcement and government positions. DeRosa's is packed, a warm testament to DeAngelo's popularity.

"Ironic," DeAngelo mumbles to himself, as he thinks back on his early days of struggle. He sees the flashes of explosions that came close to taking his life in Vietnam. He remembers the blood-spattered faces of innocent children crying for their dead parents while covered in dirt and human waste. He recalls the stream of bodies wrapped in bags and shuttled onto a big copter. Could he have saved one more life? Was war a badge of guilt? And once again, he yearns for an escape from the agonies of doubt and self deprecation. He knows he was given a precious second chance, and that many others weren't so lucky.

DeAngelo wonders whether his determination to better the lives of his family and friends was worth the many moral compromises he had to make—which involved working with people despised by almost everyone in the room.

His blonde hair and blue eyes make people think he might be Irish or Scandinavian, but DeAngelo's lineage is pure Sicilian. His father, Joseph Pasquale DeAngelo, a hardened World War II Marine, married Marie Pasquale after the war in a small village wedding outside Messina, Sicily. Joseph was proud, brave, principled, and hardworking, supporting Marie and their five children with the salary earned at his construction job in New Jersey.

Donnie was the oldest of the children. Joseph never spared the rod in disciplining him, wanting to ensure his eldest grew up to be a leader achieving more than he had. Perhaps in response, DeAngelo engaged in mischief throughout his adolescence. He would hold his own in street fights so well that he became an avid boxer and would later win his division title while serving with the Marines.

Joining him in those hijinks were his high school friends—Tommy Ryan, Craig Andersen and Big Lou Williams. After graduation, they all served in Vietnam together. Each of them ended up saving the lives of the others numerous times. They'd shared laughs and terrors, and grown as close as any family.

When they returned to the U.S., though, they didn't receive a heroic welcome. The country was divided and bitter regarding anything military.

DeAngelo had struggled, working in construction while taking college courses at night financed by the GI Bill. It was a tough way to support a wife and two children. He and his young pre-war bride decided to divorce and raise their two children living apart, but providing alimony and child support payments was tough on Donnie. When DeAngelo was laid off in the dead of winter and his two children were screaming for new shoes, he decided it was time for a different career.

He'd approached his closest friends from Nam—Craig Andersen, Big Lou Williams, and Connie Ryan, the widow of Tommy—for funds to start a vending machine business, with the aim of growing it into a restaurant chain. They were glad to loan him the money. He'd sworn to no longer accept mere scraps from a life filled with sweat and debt.

But New Jersey mobsters weren't so accepting of DeAngelo's ambitions. He'd quickly learned they considered vending machines part of their turf, and that he'd therefore unwittingly entered into another war zone.

But DeAngelo was no pushover. Between his father's beatings, his experiences taking care of himself on the streets of Newark, and his battles as a Marine, he'd learned to never back down. When wiseguys threatened him, he just smiled and told them, "There's plenty for everybody."

That wasn't what they wanted to hear. DeAngelo found his vending machines destroyed, and his drivers harassed and beaten, always with a calling card that warned him to back off.

DeAngelo's bold resistance met its match on a cold December night. After a long day, he was walking back to his car from the New Jersey Institute of Technology, where he'd just picked up the cash from his machines. Out of the corner of his eye, he'd noticed another car pulling up. DeAngelo had lived through enough to be able to smell danger. He'd opened his car door just enough to put his hands on the dumbbell bar he hid under his seat. After the war, DeAngelo had vowed to never carry a gun again. But that didn't mean he wasn't ready for a fight.

The other car drove up to him. He turned slightly and heard the driver say, "Tonight you're finished, asshole." Before the driver or his companion could get out, DeAngelo growled and slammed his dumbbell into their windshield. The glass shattered and collapsed on top of the driver. DeAngelo screamed, "You want me? Come on, fuckers!" He wildly smashed the remaining windows, as the two men inside cowered.

When he was done, the men started to move to open their now-windowless doors. Then, a campus police car appeared from a side street, attracted by the noise of smashing glass. The men sped away.

The incident did not go unnoticed. Newark wiseguy Tony Capanaro was a Genoa captain, who disliked any encroachment on vending routes managed by his crew. He wanted DeAngelo to disappear. But DeAngelo had some powerful friends. His aunt-godmother was an attractive Vegas showgirl who had married into one of the big Mob families. Over the years, he was a regular at their birthday parties, barbecues, and family events. The Mob guys grew to like DeAngelo. A "sit-down" was arranged, and DeAngelo agreed to certain conditions. After that, he was left alone.

DeAngelo's business started booming. He added more routes. In a few years, as he'd planned, he grew his business to include restaurants.

He branded his locations as "Brickman's Bistros," an epithet in tribute to his father's hard work as a mason, and blended it with a Hollywood-like atmosphere. His staffers were well-trained, and he maintained a culture championing hard work and rewards for excellence. As a result, his people were loyal.

DeAngelo built his business from a few restaurants to fifty. Brickman's Bistros became famous throughout the industry, earning him cover page stories in many industry magazines.

DeAngelo even started his own gourmet coffee company, which manufactured and distributed high-end coffees to his own restaurants, as well as others. He knew his product, and would travel to Colombia to buy the best beans, at the best price. He knew how to deal with the Colombians, and they respected his hard, but fair style of business. It was in Cali that DeAngelo met the beautiful Anita Bedoya and her two boys. Anita would eventually become his second wife.

Thinking of Anita snaps DeAngelo back to the present. He spots her beaming with pride, as politicians and fundraisers give speeches to sing his praises and then grab slices of pie.

He still finds "Nita," as he calls her, to be stunning. Her long, black, wavy hair surrounds an angelic face. Her hourglass figure is flawless, and her shimmering tailored designer dress makes her even more ravishing. Anita had softened him over the years, molding him into a loving father and husband. Stern in her judgments, she has a tendency of being over protective and suspicious of most people, making Donnie's life even more a challenge. What seems like a character flaw is really only a result of her experiences.

Anita had a difficult past. Two of her eight brothers and her first husband who fathered her two boys had been killed by members of the Colombian cartels, simply for being in the wrong place at the wrong time. She'd even lost her two sons, for a time, to the cartel guerrillas. But she had the courage to stand up to the cartel bosses, and earned their respect.

When DeAngelo met her, the attraction was immediate and mutual. Their passion flared into a commitment that brought her and the two boys to a safer home. Anita learned quickly the ways of affluence, but never lost touch with her true identity.

DeAngelo stares at Anita as if to say, "You're my real prize." In turn, Anita feels proud of him—not for his award, but for his love, his tenacity, and his keeping his promise to take care of her and her children.

Soon all eyes glance at DeAngelo. The Master of Ceremonies, Chief Celona, is winding up the evening and getting ready to introduce him for his acceptance speech.

Taking the opposite action of most award recipients, DeAngelo loosens his tie and unbuttons his suit jacket. He usually follows fashion rules, but tonight he wants a look that matches the irony he feels inside.

Finally, Chief Celona utters the magic words: "I am proud to present our 2000 Man of the Year, Donnie DeAngelo."

The crowd responds with enthusiastic applause, whistles, and shouts. DeAngelo smiles and goes up to the podium, looking like a winner. He lets the applause continue, relishing the moment, even though he feels like an imposter. His mind's eye remembers the cries of fatherless children he is unable to save, after the siege of a barbarous battle in a small village near Danang. And again he is reminded of his failures.

He spots Craig, Big Lou, and Connie; the three friends who helped make everything possible. He points to them, smiles, and they respond by toasting him with beer. Connie is glowing, loving Donnie like a brother. Big Lou, a big black brother from another mother, roars with laughter. Craig, legless from the war, is grinning with pride and joy.

Finally, the applause dies down. DeAngelo accepts the plaque and official handshake.

"I know this award is a mistake," he says. "But I try to not disobey the law—at least, not anymore." Everyone chuckles.

DeAngelo pulls his pockets out from his suit pants, showing that they're empty. "I started with this. And if it wasn't for those two men and that lady there," he says, pointing to Craig, Lou, and Connie, "they'd still be empty, and coming from a much cheaper pair of pants." The audience laughs, and directs their applause to the three smiling people.

"I will be brief, before someone decides this really is a mistake," DeAngelo continues. "In life, we are lucky to have a second chance. I've been lucky to have more than that. Good things come in three's. For me, these are my wife and children, my friends, and my purpose. They are all very dear to me, more than I can ever express."

DeAngelo looks around the room. For a moment, he seems lost for words. He takes a deep breath, smiles at his wife and friends, and then begins again.

"Loyalty, bravery, commitment, and integrity aren't just words. They're a responsibility to the people we love and cherish. If we ever fail to honor them, we let go of who we are and become dangerously lost."

A respectful silence hangs for a few seconds, feeling, to DeAngelo, like hours.

He swallows and stands tall, holding his award.

"I accept this award for those people in my life who made it what it is. Without them, I'd probably be a homeless Vietnam Vet, walking the streets stumbling and muttering to myself—which could still happen if I don't get my wife back home in time for the finish of the Colombian soccer championships."

DeAngelo waves goodbye, making repeated "thank yous" to the crowd.

As he steps down from the stage, he spots a face he neither expects nor welcomes—someone from his dark past.

"There he is," DeAngelo mutters to himself. "Bitter irony, about to hit me in the face."

CHAPTER 2
"JUST A FAVOR"

The face in the crowd is Frankie Cavallo, a known Genoa street boss. The Genoas share an uneasy truce with the Cantinos, and Frankie is always in the middle, but liked by both.

Cavallo had been a former Miami Dolphin tackle, well known for his two Super Bowl winning games in the 1970s. He'd had a bit of celebrity, being a home-grown boy who'd helped carry the Dolphins through back to back wins, so his prison time, acquittals and blemished past means little— especially to the celebrity sycophants and even to some police.

Cavallo is a hulk of a man, with a face that means business. His boxing-like features and wit make him a crowd pleaser, but he is also a notorious "button man" for the Genoa crew. At six foot, four inches and a solid 250 pounds, he presents a solid wall of threat to anyone who questions his ability to enforce a 'special request.'

Frankie is known to play with small businessmen who get in trouble and need his help. Later on, they might unfortunately find out that accepting his help results in his taking over their businesses—if they're weak and afraid.

But, Frankie also has a warm side that shows when it comes

to family. He adores his grandchildren and wants them to be taken care of. His wife, Alicia, a dedicated Latina, whose family originates from Puerto Rico, speaks fluent Spanish, adores Frankie and always waits out his prison time faithfully—whenever something, or somebody, puts him away. Fortunately for Frankie, his crimes usually amount to small time racket offenses that plead down to a year or two of time. Frankie never cares about the time, though. He says he visits all his friends, gets to play cards and workout—on the state's nickel. He keeps his family out of his business and makes sure his son and daughter live, happily unbridled, with suspicions of his crimes.

Cavallo had been a tough kid growing up, with little or no family, but he was like another adopted son to Donnie DeAngelo's aunt.

As his eyes follow Donnie leaving the podium, having achieved local stardom, he sees Donnie gaze his way—with trepidation. Cavallo, alone, casually makes his way over to Donnie, who is just a few feet from his chair. Donnie nods, smiles, and detours over to Cavallo.

"Don't you think this is the last place you want to visit?" Donnie whispers, as he leans towards Cavallo's ear.

"Why? Many of these guys are my friends—and sometimes, business buddies." Cavallo's bravado oozes confidence and wit. "You know, Donnie, I'm proud of you and your Aunt Kay would be proud, as well," he says, patting Donnie on the shoulder.

Donnie's Aunt Kay had been a Vegas showgirl in the early 1960s and a half-sister to his father. She'd been an attractive, outgoing feature act at some of the top shows in Vegas and later married a Palomo crime boss with a strong family ethic. He'd semi-retired his business and moved back to New Jersey to settle down. While handling his rackets and business, he'd met fate with a heart attack and left everything to the care of his widow, Kay. Kay, no lightweight herself, had learned, over the years, how to move around in more places than just a kitchen, so she'd kept his crew honest and working.

When Frankie Cavallo had been a local adolescent getting in trouble, she'd taken him in and treated him like another member of the family. Frankie had behaved himself around Kay and the family, but learned a lot from her crew. He'd adopted Donnie's aunt as a second mother—just as Kay had adopted him as another son. Through the years, Frankie and Donnie had crossed paths, but never in business.

"Listen, Frankie, leave her out of it! Don't tell me you came here just to congratulate me." Donnie looks back at Nita and his friends, who watch him making conversation with Cavallo.

"Donnie, I'm glad for you and proud of you. We go way back–"

"Yeah, and?" Donnie seems anxious to return to his wife and friends.

"I need a favor," Cavallo says, short and direct.

"I knew it, Frankie. Look, I'm totally straight and–"

Cavallo is quick to interrupt. "Nobody's totally straight. C'mon Donnie, you're talking to me—Frankie. I suppose you had nothing to do with moving against the Betrano brothers when they tried to take some of your business in Newark?"

"Frankie, I've been straight. My business is straight and my family is straight. What is this favor?" He avoids an answer and shows impatience.

"My son is a real estate broker and he can help you with the business."

"Your son? C'mon, Frankie, you're setting up your son as a front man. Quit playing around."

"All right. Look, I have some connections, but I don't

have to be involved. He can help you add some locations for your vending stops. You know a lot of these locations are union driven."

"He can help me? He can help me?" Donnie repeats himself in anger. "C'mon, Frankie, these are all your whipping boys, and all you'll do is have him front for you."

"So what, Donnie? It's clean! You pay him a commission, nothing comes to me and everything is nice. You grow, he makes a living, and I smile in pride as my cousin does better. C'mon, are you so clean that you're stupid? This is honest business, no bad stuff."

"Listen, Frankie, I gotta go, people are starting to notice, and not the people you or me need to notice—okay? We'll see and talk about this later." DeAngelo doesn't wait for a reply. He hurries back to Nita.

Once back with Nita and his friends, he gets back to more pleasant conversation, but his thoughts are still on Cavallo and what he will do. The anxious moments dwindle away as his friends— Craig Andersen, Big Lou, and Connie Ryan—wave Nita and him to come over to the bar area, where a lively conversation is taking form.

"Hey, Doc, are we allowed to stay friends, now that you're a big shot?" Andersen sometimes calls DeAngelo 'Doc,' referring to their time in Vietnam. He especially calls him that when he wants to show respect to DeAngelo.

"I don't think so. It's about time I moved up to a better social circle." He lifts his head as if in pride and winks at Big Lou.

Big Lou, ever the silent deep thinker, rarely speaks, but when he does, his big base tone, a trademark of his Nigerian father, carries the message. "Well, if he does, then I think I will just have to kick his ass, because he's stuck with us! He's saved our asses, given us a home and acts like the papa, so he is one stuck sumabitch. Excuse my language, Ladies!" Big Lou tilts his head toward Connie and Nita.

They all laugh, but they know how DeAngelo had struggled to make the business work and take care of his friends. With the money they'd given him for his business amounting to their only savings, he'd parlayed it all into a lucrative business.

He'd given Andersen and Big Lou an apartment in the office building he'd purchased, never taking rent. He'd paid their bills, furnished their home, and made sure they wanted for nothing.

As for Connie Ryan and her child, Sonny—DeAngelo had never forgotten his friend, Tommy, and therefore, when his widow and child needed a home, Donnie had made the down payment and helped Sonny through school and college.

Yes, they'd become friends—but more than friends, they'd grown into a family , living for each other. Bound by history and by life, itself, the survivors and fighters had become the embodiment of loyalty to the end—whatever and whenever the end would be.

Andersen never looks for sympathy. His legless body and the scars from the war are not going to dampen his spirit this night. He spins around in his wheelchair and manipulates the device like a boy spinning a top. He is exhilarated over his friend's success and devotion. He is also six or seven beers ahead of the rest of them.

Craig Andersen is a hero in every sense of the word—boyish yet jaded in appearance and personality, with a dark side that everyone knows will come and go. He'd been a combat-trained sniper who never backed down from any mission. Friends in the same Company, the four men each looked for each other. Andersen had lost both legs from a 'bouncing betty' booby trap mine, while trying to save both Lou and

Donnie when they'd become trapped under fire. It wasn't the first time that one of them would risk his life to save one of the others. Each had his own moment doing exactly that, and they'd all showed the same care for their friend's widow. So, Connie Ryan has three big brothers to look after her and her son. Her little Irish smile sparkles wide, her freckles blaze red from the alcohol and party exhilaration.

"You know, I wish Sonny was here."

Her smile recedes and her eyes water. "Donnie, I know he would love to be here too, but he told me to wish you his best and to tell you that when he comes home, he'll drink you under the table." She giggles briefly. "Those were his words, not mine."

DeAngelo chuckles and holds her for a moment. "Listen, Connie, he's coming home soon. His time in Afghanistan is short, because I understand his Seal Team Unit is being reassigned to Virginia. He only has a few more months and then he's totally out." He pulls her close and kisses her on the cheek. Then Nita pulls close to her and, in a delicate gesture, takes her from Donnie.

"ARE WE THE BEST OR WHAT? OOOOHRAH!" Andersen screams the Marine Corps battle cry and the others join in with harmony to bring back the party atmosphere. They all laugh and toast their friend and brother.

Not so enamored by DeAngelo's celebrity is an attractive woman FBI agent named Jenay Tobias, who wastes no time in approaching DeAngelo.

"Mr. DeAngelo, congratulations! That's a fine honor, I'm sure you're proud." She extends her hand to both congratulate him and introduce herself. "Jenay Tobias, I'm with the FBI. Can I speak with you for a moment?" She points her head away from his friends, gesturing that they should speak privately.

DeAngelo eyes the tall woman, shapely and attractive, but definitely dressed and manicured for police business. Her hair is bundled tightly, her makeup very subtle. She flashes an attractive smile when tossing innuendoes, but she also studies her prospect like a recruiter doing an interview. Her voice, pleasant and soft, is very distinctive and her pleasant brown eyes compliment her brunette hair.

DeAngelo is reluctant to carry on the conversation. One confrontation a night is enough. "Sure, but can we do this another time—you understand?"

"Of course! I just wanted to introduce myself. You know, you seem to know important people on both sides of the aisle. But that's for another day, so let me leave you to your family and friends, and again, congratulations."

She walks off as quickly as she'd appeared, leaving Donnie with a flirtatious inviting smile. But coming from an FBI agent, nothing seems inviting to Donnie. He wonders for a second if Cavallo was engaging him in something more provocative then he had planned . Whatever sizzled in that pretty FBI mind was enough to make him anxious and concerned.

CHAPTER 3
NITA'S PAIN

DeAngelo, starting his day with an early morning coffee and a mountain of paperwork, is suddenly greeted by a hulking figure gazing down at him.

"Hey Donnie, I hope you don't mind. Your secretary said it was okay to come in since we're cousins." The scarred face, flattened nose and broad shoulders belong to none other than Frankie Cavallo, the Genoa Capo at odds with the Cantinos, and former childhood friend who had been taken in by Donnie's aunt when they were teens.

"Frankie, we're not cousins and you should let me know when you're coming to see me. What's up?" DeAngelo is courteous, but finds as at the awards ceremony unwelcome.

"Donnie, is that any way to treat an old friend? Don't you remember how you used to look up to me when you were just a little kid? Don't you remember who taught you how to play football?"

"Frankie that was a long time agoand you're not exactly my aunt's protégé or a member of the Miami Dolphins anymore. You're a guy who's been in a lot of trouble—and you seem to stay that way."

Cavallo, back in the day, really had been on the Dolphins team until he'd torn a ligament in his leg, and then later, on in his shoulder. His strong arm tactics got him noticed and hired, opening business doors for the Mob, but he'd soon became an undesirable partner, even for them, in family business.

Cavallo, on the down side of sixty, is likable, affable, and popular enough in many circles, but all that charm, wit, and professional football experience is only a front to hide his duplicity and corruption. Cavallo has a warm loyal side that he shares with only a few people. He is generous to some, treacherous to others. Because of his affection for Donnie's aunt, who'd given him a home and made him part of their family as a young man, he thinks of Donnie as a cousin, a cousin who wants to grow, a cousin who might not refuse an offer.

"Listen, Donnie. You do a lot of vending business, you have these upscale cafes in a lot of big corporate locations and you sell a lot of coffee. Well, I happen to know a lot of business guys who can use you." Cavallo pulls up a chair and makes himself comfortable.

Donnie leans back in his chair, away from Cavallo.

"Frankie, thanks—but no thanks. I'm running a very straight, legit business. If I hook up with you, the Feds will be on my case. I don't need that, and neither does my family." DeAngelo is abrupt, anxious to end the discussion.

Cavallo smiles. "It wasn't always like that, Donnie," he remarks. "I heard you used to be a tough guy and didn't take any shit, building those vending routes of yours. In fact, some of the big guys said they really respected you and told others to lay off."

"They respected me because I didn't cave in to them and I was always fair. Whatever I took, I took clean and wasn't afraid to keep it."

Cavallo interrupts. "I guess it didn't hurt that Aunt Kay was adored by Johnny Barone and it didn't hurt that he owned almost all of Jersey? C'mon, Donnie, let me join your family, I'll make you a lot of money."

"Frankie, I'm going to tell you one more time—the only family I represent is my wife and kids and I do everything straight. And that's the end of it."

"Okay, okay, so you're straight. That's good, but listen, you deserve to build your business for your family and your friends—I understand you got a couple of old war buddies you look after. Well, this can work, nothing criminal, nothing to give you trouble. I can help bring you locations and business and no strong-arm stuff—I promise, strictly friends. And I do it through my son. You know Richie. He's a former school-teacher, now doing real estate and he's as clean as they come. If there's any finder's fee or commissions, you pay him, nothing goes to me. Look, I've got two beautiful grandkids and I want to see their father give them a break, not like I was."

Cavallo eyes soften and his smile begs for attention more than fear.

"I mean it, Donnie! I love my grandsons, and my boy, and I wouldn't mind paying back a favor to your aunt. I'm getting old and tired of this life. I've put aside some money and—"

"I don't know, Frankie. How can I be sure this will be straight, and I don't get tangled up in all that family bullshit?" DeAngelo stands up and begins pacing toward the window, looking out to the street.

"Donnie, I swear it's straight. I already put aside enough for my wife, Alicia, and I would never fuck up my kid's life, or my grandson's. What do you say? I'll just be in the background and make a few introductions, but my son will handle all the deals in a straight way, with you as the boss. What do you say?"

Donnie stares at Frankie, looking for a hint of truth. He pauses, then tells him, "Okay, maybe we'll try something. Give me a list of what you had in mind and I'll take it from there."

Cavallo jumps to his feet and embraces DeAngelo with the strength and energy of an older man who seems to have mellowed. But, not to be fooled, DeAngelo maneuvers Cavallo to the door and tells him they will be in touch.

No sooner is Cavallo out the door, than DeAngelo is on the phone with his aunt's attorney, Billy Feorio. Feorio has been with Donnie's aunt for years, as she acquired more business from her deceased husband's connections and banking interests. Aunt Kay is sweet and loving, but not to be treated gingerly. She had taken over her husband's business and family interests when he died of a heart attack at a family pool party. She ran that business as if he had never left and earned respect from even the toughest of the wiseguys.

Not knowing much about Cavallo's history in the last few years, Donnie decides to take a temperature reading. After salutations and family updates, DeAngelo asks about Cavallo. Feorio pauses and tells Donnie he'll get back to him, but that pause in his voice is a heavy precursor of what DeAngelo expects to hear.

It doesn't take long for DeAngelo to get a call from Feorio. "Donnie, your aunt says to stay away from Cavallo. He's hot and they're watching him. So be careful."

"Okay, thanks, Billy." DeAngelo puts the phone down slowly and takes a sip of his coffee. He ponders his personal vision for the future—building a mega company that will support and comfort his family, Andersen, Big Lou, Connie and Sonny Ryan, plus his employees, a company that will lift him up from the streets of Newark and the rice paddies of Vietnam and make him into a man of substance and accomplishment.

He has spent his whole life taking care of others. The grueling demands of the business, with its ups and downs, always made him vulnerable to failure, especially with the fluctuations of the market, the aggression of competitors, and the onerous expenses to sustain the business. But the dream never lost its halo, even as he muddled through the bills, expenses and proposals. He'd always known he had to make the business grow and become secure. Failure was not an option.

DeAngelo puts aside his visions of success. Monday is a busy day, with new orders piling up. Better to do the rounds and visit with each department. His Vice President, Mitchell Atchinson, sidles up to Donnie for his regular senior staff review, thus giving him a snapshot of developments.. Atchinson, the son of English Irish immigarnts, is short, slender, balding, talkative, and not well-liked by most of the employees, but DeAngelo trusts him. The company is growing too big, too fast to make changes, so Atchinson, still young and aggressive, remains—a recipient of luck and staying power.

The front of the building is clerical and sales. Donnie walks through the double doors in the back, into the warehouse, production rooms and coffee roasting-packaging area. He sees his wife, Nita busy with orders and training a new utility attendant. She smiles and turns back to her duties.

Nita's work ethic is intense. A mother at fifteen in Colombia and a widow by sixteen after her husband met with a Cali cartel bullet, she is obsessed with giving her two boys, Anton and Geraldo, a better life. As the only sister in a family of eight boys, she'd faced death and self-sacrifice more than most, in the backwoods of Cali, with another brother brutally murdered by the cartels. In spite of the tragedies, she grows more radiant and beautiful on the outside, with her will to survive deepening, on the inside.

Domingo, Nita's youngest brother, had been resident manager at the largest resort in Cali, called 'La Princessa,' where Donnie would stay when doing business. The two men became friends, with Donnie trusting Domingo with many of his arrangements.

Domingo, an attractive young man but a stern manager, was mentored and loved by Don Vito Santiago, a Sicilian-Colombian Mob leader who had pulled away from drugs and opted for the resort business. In this way, he had been able to provide a home away from home for all the cartel bosses and crooked politicians who loved the amenities, women and disco of "La Princessa." Don Vito, a hard, old-school Sicilian like his father, had a doting amiable side, like his Colombian mother, and took to Anita's family like his own.

Scarred in more ways than just the physical kind, he'd built the largest, most lavish resort in Cali. It boasted sumptuous suites and even an underground waterfall, plus rooms and tunnels, which served as convenient escape aids for the cartel bosses, when they needed to retreat from the "*Junglas*"—the Colombian Security police.

DeAngelo had developed a friendship with Don Vito, on his business trips. Looking the other way, not being interested in Vito's Mob connections had resulted in a closeness between them. They laughed together about their experiences in business. Together, they'd shared a feeling of admiration for both Domingo and his sister, Anita.

Vito had been pressed to tell Donnie: "You know, the big guys want Nita, but she hates them and what they stand for. They want her, but she turns from them. They respect Domingo and me. We take care of them. I know their business and I protect them. I don't like their business—it destroys. Women and gambling, that's where I made my money. But, they need me, so they leave her alone. She is a good woman. If you want a good woman, take her out of here."

Vito and DeAngelo had remained friends through every visit. Donne would eventually gift Vito with a gold-engraved cigarette lighter that said *"Amistad Es Un Vinculo...Su Amigo, Donnie"*—"Friendship is a bond, your friend, Donnie." Vito, a heavy smoker, had always used the lighter and bragged to everyone about it being a gift from his American friend, Donnie.

With each trip, Donnie and Nita had grown closer, until finally, he'd decided to bring her and the boys out of danger, to a better life. Within a year, Donnie had hired the best immigration attorney and a former federal judge to make the process go quicker. In short order, Donnie had become a father again and Nita's dream had come true. Together, they built a life that underlined commitment, loyalty and love.

The boys, Donnie's adopted sons, became young men of honor, doing well in school and at home. He'd loved and treated them as his own and they'd looked to him as a real father. Nita, ever the good wife and strong business manager, had given Donnie endless love and support in this, his second marriage. He'd worked hard to be a good father for his two children from his first marriage as well, but now they were grown and on their own.

Like Nita, DeAngelo became a father at a young age. His son, Jason, was the firstborn, followed by Caroline, when DeAngelo returned home from the war. Both are loving and beautiful children who make their father proud. He'd adores them both and wanted more for them than a mediocre existence, so he'd worked two jobs while finishing college and working toward his dream of building his own successful business. His hard work, courage, and determination—along with the seed money from his three friends—made the sapling grow into an oak, and all of his children into responsible adults.

DeAngelo has a lot to appreciate and he knows it. He was given a pass by the mob and even befriended them when things got dirty. He never wanted his family or friends to see that side of him. He wanted them safe and prosperous. He wanted for them what he never had. Smiling to himself, he decides to take the business further. Despite his growth, he knows the moves by competitors and the growth he has chosen will be costly. He knows he must continue to grow to feed the horse, or the race will slow to an ugly finish. He phones Cavallo for a meeting and together, they work out a plan to add business—but only on DeAngelo's terms, meaning straight up, legit.

Within a few months, business starts to increase as together, Cavallo's son and Donnie engage in new locations and more stops. Things go fine until one day a well-dressed woman and man walk in, flash their badges and announce they are FBI and wish to see DeAngelo.

DeAngelo, obviously anxious to address the situation, greets the attractive woman and somber looking gentlemen, bringing them into the conference room. There, behind closed doors, they converse.

"What's this all about?" He looks to the woman he remembers from his award dinner, then back at the man.

"Mr. DeAngelo, I'm Special Agent Jenay Tobias, we met before, and this is my colleague, Richard Jennings. We're here to investigate your involvement with Mr. Frank Cavallo." Both agents stare silently, offering no further discussion. Jenay Tobias, an attractive woman in her thirties, is all business in a gray tweed suit and bundled hair. Wearing very little make up, she borders on beautiful, if not for the too-stern demeanor. Tall, almost meeting Donnie's height at 5 foot 10, she casts an imposing presence with only a few inches between their faces.

"Well, I'm not too familiar with Cavallo, I really do business with his son." DeAngelo motions for both agents to sit, since the atmosphere is tense. Responding to his gesture, they sit quietly and Tobias, the obvious team leader, begins.

"Mr. DeAngelo, do you have any idea who you're dealing with? Frankie Cavallo is a known Mob enforcer. He's already been to prison for a number of things, and he's not a nice guy. Is this what you want for your business?"

"You don't seem to understand, Ms. Tobias, I'm only considering working with his son, and to my knowledge, his son is just a former schoolteacher and now a real estate agent. He will merely do sales for me. Frankie Cavallo is an old acquaintance, but we have no business together." DeAngelo remains calm as the agents glance at each other back and forth.

"Mr. DeAngelo, you realize I can subpoena you and bring you in for questioning? We have a major ongoing investigation, and we will put Mr. Cavallo behind bars, I promise you. I don't think you want to join him." She speaks with authority and conviction, refusing to blink.

"Ms. Tobias, I assure you nothing of a criminal nature is going on, and I would love to help you."

Tobias removes a card and hands it to DeAngelo.

"Mr. DeAngelo, I will be in touch with you further and I may ask you to come in for questioning. Do you have a problem with that?"

"No, I want to be as forthcoming as possible." DeAngelo takes her card and offers to lead them out of the building.

Once they leave the building, DeAngelo wipes some of the sweat from his forehead. Before he has time to think over his risks, he hears a shrill scream coming from the back of the building. The scream is blood curdling and coming from Nita.

DeAngelo rushes to the coffee production room where he

finds Nita, surrounded by the women from the office, scream-ing, "*NO, MI HERMANO!! NO!!*" *No, my brother, no!*

DeAngelo makes his way to the little group surrounding her. One of the women stops him and tells him, "Her brother, Domingo, was shot and killed—we passed the phone to her when we heard it was a call from Colombia. She's hysterical. Leave her with us for a second, and then you can help her."

DeAngelo is in shock. Promptly he calls Don Vito in Cali. He discovers that Domingo was shot in a cartel war. He loves Domingo and had always promised to bring him here with his sister, because Domingo wanted no part of the mob, but life in Colombia meant dealing with the cartels was a necessity, not a convenience. He feels great pain for not doing it sooner, but for now, he needs to be with Nita and give her comfort.

After a few minutes, he makes his way to Nita and hugs her. She cries while falling into his arms, mumbling in broken English, "They kill him, like they kill my other brother and the kids' father. He's a boy, he's a good boy, he's—" Before she can finish, she screams again. Donnie tries to pull her close, but she pulls away and buries her head in a handkerchief that he gives her. DeAngelo suggests they go home, and together they leave.

In the days that follow, Donnie stays close to Nita and her sons, comforting her and cradling them all with love and atten-tion. He offers to take her to Colombia, but he knows it's not a good time—with the FBI watching and the business in jeop-ardy. Nita convinces him to stay, so reluctantly he makes plans for her to go alone but with the protection of Don Vito. He speaks with Vito, who promises to watch her and protect her. He arranges to have her met and protected by family, as well. He knows with Vito and family she will be insulated and safe. Vito assures him he knows that Domingo was at the wrong place at the wrong time and that Nita is not in danger.

After arranging Nita's trip, DeAngelo returns to his office, only to be served with a subpoena by the U.S. Attorney to appear before the Federal Grand Jury. Not wasting any time, he calls Cavallo for a meeting. Cavallo suggests the Limelight Diner, owned by a friend. Once there, Cavallo points to a booth in the back where they can talk. They take the booth and DeAngelo wastes no time.

"Is this place safe to talk?" DeAngelo peers at every part of the diner.

"Yeah, this is an old business partner of mine. He has this place swept and he's here almost 24-7. Relax, Donnie, you're gonna get old fast."

"Frankie, do you know this Jenay Tobias?"

"Yeah, she's been after me for years, but she's got nothing. She thinks she's gonna make a big bust—she's got nothing." Cavallo makes an order and Donnie only asks for coffee.

"Well, she says she's putting you away and is convinced I'm in with you. I told you this was not a good idea, son or no son. And now, I have this subpoena to appear before the Grand Jury!"

"Look, Donnie, they do that to scare you. They'll bring you in to intimidate you, corner you, and make you feel like if you don't give them something they'll bring you before the Grand Jury, and if you lie, they'll put you away. But, it's a scare tactic. Do you know what percentage of people actually go before the Grand Jury? They serve hundreds and maybe a couple, they will actually call. After they grill you, they will let you go. Just tell the truth. You didn't do anything wrong."

"Well, they seem determined and I feel like they've been following me."

"They probably have. But, you don't have a racketeering charge, and you're not doing anything wrong, so don't sweat it.

Look, drink your coffee and don't grow old."

The conversation carries on for a while, but DeAngelo is not confident that Cavallo is right. When the meeting ends, they hug briefly and each goes his own way. DeAngelo knows the relationship has to end, but he faces a bigger problem—the Grand Jury subpoena.

★ ★ ★

Friday, in dismal rain, DeAngelo makes his way to the Federal Court House in Newark. He is ushered into the waiting area of the U.S. Attorney's office where he sits in uncertainty, awaiting a call. It doesn't take long before Jenay Tobias comes out to greet him.

"Hi, Mr. DeAngelo, follow me, please."

They make their way to a conference room, where DeAngelo faces Tobias with two colleagues and the U.S. Attorney, who introduces himself as William Petersen and suggests that DeAngelo cooperate with Tobias. Then he leaves and Tobias begins.

"Mr. DeAngelo, I already told you about Mr. Cavallo and things I'm sure you already know, so I want to go further. We have dozens of witnesses who will testify about Mr. Cavallo and he will be indicted. You can either cooperate or face the grand jury and perhaps perjury charges."

"Ms. Tobias, I am being truthful, as I haven't even sought counsel or brought an attorney to this meeting."

"Mr. DeAngelo, that will do you no good, you are not allowed an attorney to be present on your behalf for the Grand Jury. You're on your own."

"Well, what exactly do you want from me?" DeAngelo

holds his hands out, in a show of innocence.

"Look, Mr. DeAngelo, you have an impressive war record, and you're a well-respected man in the community. You have a nice family and appear to run a clean business, so you should be on this side of the table with us, not defending Cavallo."

"But I'm not! I'm telling you the truth!"

As if deaf to the last statement, they continue for hours with specific questions all leading to extortion, racketeering, theft and strong arm tactics that DeAngelo is expected to confirm, but none of which transpired. It is a circle that goes round and round. Tobias and her colleagues are agitated and upset. They try a different tactic in the hopes of frightening DeAngelo into a confession. Tobias nods for her partner to come with her to the area outside the door, but near enough for DeAngelo to hear them talking. Tobias does all the talking in a loud enough whisper for DeAngelo's ears. At the same time the US Attorney returns to the conference room to ask brief questions but allowing DeAngelo to hear Tobias's conversation with her colleague.

"I want that doctor of Cavallo's brought up on perjury charges. I don't care how long he's been practicing, he's lying to us and I'm not playing around. Talk to Petersen and get him charged, enough of this nonsense with these people."

Tobias returns to DeAngelo with her partner, expecting him to feel intimidated by knowing that a respected doctor can be charged, just like him—if he doesn't cooperate. Still, he stays true to his belief that he did nothing wrong. The US Attorney tells Tobias he will be outside arranging some orders. DeAngelo knows the attorney will be watching from a remote position. Tobias nods and turns to DeAngelo "Mr. DeAngelo, this is my last offer to you. If you will agree to wear a wire and help us, we will forget this grand jury today and provide you protection, support and immunity from any prosecution."

"Prosecution for what? I haven't done anything and I'm not wearing a wire."

Tobias stands up and takes him to U.S. Attorney Petersen, waiting by the exit of the conference room.

"Let's take a walk." Petersen escorts DeAngelo on one side, as Tobias takes the other side. They take a walk down the hallway that seems endless and arrive at a standing sign in front of double doors. The sign says: GRAND JURY IN SESSION.

Now DeAngelo knows, there are no more games. He will be escorted in to the Grand Jury for heavy interrogation. With one last look at Tobias and Petersen, he enters the chambers. Both the US Attorney and The FBI believe DeAngelo will crack under the strains of consistent tactical implications and the impact of the grand jury during a grueling day of questioning DeAngelo is told to take the stand and sit facing the Grand Jury. Unlike in a court case with a jury to the left, the Grand Jury is right in front, facing the person being questioned, so they can observe every answer. The U.S. Attorney is off to the side, in a sort of bully pulpit. There is no attorney for the witness; he must answer every question. In addition, no counsel on the witness's behalf raises any objection to any question the U.S. Attorney poses to the witness. After being sworn in, DeAngelo can see that the jury is studying him like a new movie. He notices that many are dressed casually, some even with sweatshirts that have UNION stamps, like Teamsters or Teacher's Union. The grand jury atmosphere seems casual, but dark. The room is poorly lit and almost dreary. After being sworn in and answering the basic introductory questions, the U.S. Attorney wastes no time in turning up the heat.

"Is it true, Mr. DeAngelo, you seemed very upset and bothered by the FBI entering your building?"

DeAngelo pauses, and then looks at the Grand Jury. "Wouldn't you, if two FBI agents charged into your office, holding up badges and saying FBI, where's DeAngelo?"

The jurors release a somewhat suppressed laughter, clearly antagonizing the U.S. Attorney.

"Mr. DeAngelo, no comedy please. This is a serious matter, and there are serious charges for an indictment." He continues. "Is it true that Mr. Cavallo called you on several occasions, 'The Man,' and that he wanted to be a part of your family?"

"I don't know about 'THE MAN,' but I do run my company, and my aunt did help raise Mr. Cavallo when he was a teenager."

"Then you know about his criminal background?"

"Well, I know he played for the Miami Dolphins and I know he was a grandfather who loves his family–"

"Mr. DeAngelo, I will ask you again. Just stick to answering the questions. Nothing more."

Upset and determined, the U.S. Attorney continues for the next three hours, but DeAngelo remembers what Cavallo had said: "Just tell the truth and you will be fine. If you change the truth, that's when they will try to take you down. A lie is a lie and makes everything a lie. You did nothing wrong, so stick to what you know is true."

And so he does, for the next three hours, to the utter frustration of the U.S. Attorney. When all is done, he leaves the grand jury chamber, only to face Tobias and the U.S. Attorney, who turns on Tobias.

"This was a total waste of time. I told you he couldn't help us. Now I look stupid." Petersen walks away from Tobias, and Tobias escorts DeAngelo back to the exit area. As they reach the exit door, Tobias smiles.

She puts her hand on DeAngelo's shoulder, telling him,

"You know I will get him—with or without you, and I believe you, but if you're smart, you will stay away from his kind. You're not his kind."

Days fly by and then, DeAngelo receives a call from Cavallo to meet. DeAngelo feels it's not a good idea, but agrees reluctantly, to make sure he cuts the cord. The usual place is fine. Once outside the diner, DeAngelo sees Cavallo, who hastens toward him. DeAngelo feels a litte unsure about Cavallo's intentions, but he stands unmoving in front of the diner. Once Cavallo faces DeAngelo, he embraces him and kisses him on the cheek. DeAngelo wonders if it's the wrong kind of a kiss—precursor to a grave. Standing erect with head withdrawn, he hears Cavallo bellow out words of praise.

"I TOLD YOU! I TOLD YOU! Just tell the truth and nothing will happen. You did good, Donnie. You really did good. And you did nothing wrong. And you said nice things about me. Not too many people say nice things about me, especially under the heat of a Grand Jury and an obsessed prosecutor."

DeAngelo is stunned and speechless. He'd expected a much worse greeting and outcome to their meeting. Instead, he is treated with affection and appreciation.

Cavallo looks directly into Donnie's eyes and tells him, "I know you're straight, and stay that way. You've got a good business, a good family, and I appreciate you treating me like you did. But, you need to move on and stay away from my kind. Listen, no one will ever bother you, I made sure of that. You're a stand-up guy, and now I know why the big guys like you. If there's anything my friends or I can ever do for you, just let me know. I may be in prison, but I'm not dead."

DeAngelo finally opens his mouth and questions Cavallo. "How do you know everything?"

"Listen, there were enough union guys in there to start a committee, and I have my sources. These people are on a witch-hunt, and they may get me. So what? Big deal! I have enough friends inside and at my age, I like to play cards and just work out a little, so how's it so bad? I'll miss Alicia and the kids, but they can come visit. I'm getting too old to let shit like this bother me."

"Frankie, I feel bad about this. I'll make sure your son and grandson receive their share of the business deals they helped make happen. We're doing well in some of the—"

Before he can finish, Frankie cuts in.

"That's fine, Donnie. My kid said you sent him a check. I appreciate that and so does he and my grandson. I told you it was honest stuff and you don't have to worry about it. You got a good company and you deserve some of the business. You know, Donnie, there's gotta be good and bad in the world, otherwise it's a boring place. And if there was no bad, you'd never know what good is. My kid's good, you're good and I'm a bad guy—but not that bad." He smiles and looks around the parking lot before he continues.

"But listen, you stay away from me unless you need something. I got a big fight on my hands, and they're still gonna be watching you. My kid's going back to teaching, so the little money he made will help out, and he appreciates it. But, I told him to stick to teaching and forget about doing any more deals, because they're watching him too, even though he's innocent and means well."

There is a moment of silence between the two of them, and then Frankie speaks again.

"But, remember, stay away from me and my kind, you don't need trouble. Watch your back, and take care of yourself and family first—and fuck everybody else."

Frankie lets out a loud laugh. He hugs Donnie again and whispers in his ear, "Remember if you need anything, let me know."

CHAPTER 4
PRICE OF COMBAT

"Mr. DeAngelo, you have a call from St. Mary's Hospital. It sounds important."

"What's it about, Deanna?" DeAngelo has just wrapped up a meeting with vendors and is about to have an a la carte lunch of cold pizza in his office before his next meeting.

"I think it's about Mr. Andersen, sounds serious."

Already concerned about Nita and her trip to Colombia, he is anxious about another problem.

"Okay, Deanna, I'll take it." Donnie always remains close to Craig Andersen, one of his three closest friends from the war, as Andersen fights his own private battles against depression and a failed marriage. No amount of alcohol drowns the agony of a lost soul fighting for an identity that is slipping away. This is the case with Craig Andersen—a crack Marine sniper with so many combat action awards in defense of his Marine brothers, but unfortunately the mere mention of his Silver Star, Bronze Star or Purple Heart only reminds him of what he sacrificed, not his bravery. His sacrifices are more than he can handle: the loss of legs, the compassion of a wife he adored and the independence of being his own man. For now, he can be his own man, staying within the care and protection of Donnie DeAngelo.

Donnie had given him an apartment in his building and pays his bills, same as he'd done for Big Lou Williams, his other Marine brother. He'd done as much for Connie Ryan, widow of the third of his closest friends, Tommy Ryan, a helicopter pilot who served with Donnie in Vietnam. These three friends had helped Donnie start his business enterprise with their modest life's savings. Donnie would never forget that, pledging to himself and to them that he would never abandon any of them. He could only hope his friend was all right.

"This is Donnie DeAngelo." He pushes away from his desk, prepared to leave.

"Mr. DeAngelo, we have a Mr. Andersen here, who was brought into our emergency room. It seems he fell out of his wheelchair and down some steps and he's badly bruised, but I believe he can be released."

"Oh, thank God. So he can come home?"

"Yes, but he's very intoxicated, and mumbling about his wife and won't speak to anyone but you."

"I'll be right down."

The hospital is only minutes away and before they can bring Andersen to sobriety, Donnie rushes through the door. Andersen is difficult and abusive to the staff, barking about women being selfish and no one having character. Upon spotting DeAngelo, Andersen completely changes mood and turns euphoric.

"Doc, Donnie! My buddy! OOOH RAH! Take me the fuck out of here! The enemy is engaged in trying to make me sober!"

"Craig, watch your language, Buddy. There are women here and we don't want to give them the wrong opinion of Marines."

"OOOH RAH! Damn right. Sorry, ladies." With slurred

speech and a wobbly head, Andersen makes an attempt at courtesy. As soon as DeAngelo appears, he signs papers and heads out the door with Craig.

Andersen sleeps on the way home. All the while, Donnie looks over at his lifelong friend and protector. He covers the legless torso with a blanket and once he is at the building, he carries Andersen, cradled like a child, to the elevator he had built especially for his use. He manages to open the door and bring Andersen to his shambled apartment—then to his bed. He covers him again and dims the light. He walks around broken liquor bottles, glasses, and a cracked frame hanging off a picture of Andersen and his wife. He eyes what appears to be legal papers on the bureau and finds divorce papers from Andersen's wife. He stares at the black and white documents with its many dripping daggers of innuendoes and attacks and then neatly folds it and slips it into a drawer. He turns slightly to insure his friend is fast asleep, and then heads back down the elevator to his office. On his way there, he uses his cell phone and calls Big Lou.

Lou Williams, better known as Big Lou because of his size and stellar college football record as defensive lineman for Penn State, had once showed promise for a shot at the NFL, until a bad injury had torn apart his knee, leg and his back. But, his injuries were not enough to keep him out of the Marine Corps and away from his childhood friends. So, when the action in Vietnam hit a frenzy, he'd joined just behind Ryan, Andersen and DeAngelo. Never anything small with Lou – he'd become an explosives expert while doing the work of an '0311' or the common MOS of 'grunt in the bush.' Big Lou had known mines, booby traps, artillery support and had been the expert of choice when claymores were required for an enemy engagement. Lou had been popular with all company commanders for his 'right on' direction and execution. He'd been in demand more than he liked, until one day when Lou had found himself surrounded by his own artillery support – which had failed to follow his call-in coordinates. That had been followed by an accidental dump of napalm. Between the two, he'd not only suffered damaged eardrums, but the incident had left him with migraine headaches that had intensified after his discharge.

Lou, a quiet man with a heart , has few friends, and little family—except for Donnie, Andersen, Ryan's widow and her child, Sonny.

"Lou, do me a favor, Craig's under the weather and not good. He took a fall and I just brought him home from the ER at St. Mary's. Can you come upstairs and look after him? He's not going to be in a good mood. His wife just served him divorce papers. I'll come up later. Please make sure he stays off the bottle, so hide the stuff. You're big enough to handle him."

DeAngelo laughs as Lou tells him that with no legs and a hangover, Andersen is still a lot to handle.

"Well, do the best you can." They finish the call and DeAngelo hurries back to his office for a staff meeting.

In the conference room sits Mitchell Atchinson, his chief operating officer, who has been with him for almost five years, a vice president of operations, three district managers, and a director of sales. The meeting is long overdue, as everyone is anxious to discuss expenses, growth, and new markets.

"Donnie, we are growing, but so are our expenses. We have to get serious." Atchinson is not well-liked by the employees because they feel he distorts facts and uses his relationship with DeAngelo to get his way. Lately, DeAngelo has been wrapped up in dealing with his three friends and some of their problems. Andersen has a short fuse and a life that hangs by the second. Lou spends all his time in tests at the hospital for his hearing and migraines and at Connie's home, which had nearly gone into foreclosure, but was saved, thanks to DeAngelo. In spite of all the setbacks for Donnie and his friends, the company continues to grow, but so do the expenses.

"Listen, Donnie, the only way we can get this company to where it should be is if we get financing or investors and grow. We have a great product, we service ten states, our cafes and bistros get rave reviews, but we're swimming in new expenses, and we need more startup funds for new locations. Why don't you take a break from your three friends? They're draining you and besides, we should be getting a decent rent from Andersen and Lou, instead of the $200 a month you charge and then pay yourself. We could easily get $1200 a month and have them pay their own utilities, not to mention that elevator you installed for Andersen. They all eat free at our expense, and even with Lou, you—"

"That elevator is a disability elevator that meets code for anyone we rent to who's disabled. And don't mention my friends again. That's none of your business." He stares down Atchinson to end the discourse and move the meeting forward. DeAngelo is known to be pleasant even in the toughest of meetings, except when it comes to his friends—that territory is not to be explored. DeAngelo carefully reviews documents for signatures and then hits buttons on his calculator, as he flips papers. Annoyed and worried about Andersen, he drops the papers and addresses the group.

"Look, I understand we need some course of action, and I have all the numbers. I have meetings over the next few weeks with investors and bankers. You're right, we're doing well, that's our calling card, so I'm sure we'll get there. I'd like everyone to give me a break today, dismissing them. Give Mitchell your reports, and Mitchell, you write me a summary brief. Leave it on my desk if I'm not here."

"But Donnie, I need to go over–" Before he can finish, DeAngelo holds up a hand.

"Just write me a brief and I'll review it. Some of this stuff can wait. Just holler if the walls are falling, okay?"

"Okay, boss, whatever you want. I hope whatever is bothering you turns out okay."

DeAngelo points to the door, signaling to Atchinson that he needs the space.

Pressing his fingers to both temples, DeAngelo remembers Domingo and not getting him out in time. He remembers his wife's screams of immense pain, upon learning of her brother's horrible death and is relieved she has returned. He thinks of Andersen and the pain he endures in his compromised life. Then there's Lou, strained by the effects of shattered eardrums and severe headaches; and now the business, growing, but facing a watershed of good and bad. It all seems a bit much until DeAngelo is interrupted by his new administrative assistant, Deanna, who is Connie Ryan's sister.

"Mr. DeAngelo—"

"Please, Deanna, you're not still new, just call me Donnie, please."

"Donnie, my sister really appreciates what you did for her and Sonny. If it wasn't for you, they could never have re-financed the house. I just want to tell you that, as a family member. And I know you and Mr. Andersen are always there for her and Sonny. In fact, Mr. Andersen does so much to get Sonny through college and to mentor him, that Sonny wanted to be a Navy Seal and now serves courageously"

"I know, Deanna. And Sonny is like another son to Craig and me, and we both know Lou loves him, as well."

"Yes, I know. But his mother is worried about losing him

now that he's in Afghanistan. She says it was hard enough losing his father. She couldn't stand losing her only son."

"Deanna, Sonny is a big, strong, smart kid. He's not going to do anything stupid, and the military needs their Seals—they don't give them up lightly."

"I hope you're right, thanks, Donnie."

"Thanks, Deanna, and stop worrying. Tell your sister I will stop by later, after I check on something." Donnie smiles at her as a sign of understanding.

"Mr. Andersen?" She smiles back.

"Yes, Mr. Andersen."

CHAPTER 5
TO BE OR NOT TO BE

After struggling through a long night of anticipated tribu-lations, DeAngelo faces a new day and the prospect of meeting investors at a CEO forum held monthly, in New York City. DeAngelo looks the part of a successful CEO—impec-cably dressed, manicured, and tanned; he favors custom-made suits and designer ties. DeAngelo never forgets his beginnings and the struggle his parents shared to give him a better life. He's a get-along executive who prefers to maneuver amiably within a circle of successful individuals from whom he can learn and develop in his own journey to the top.

The ride into the city is the usual nose-to-nose rush of cars, their occupants eager to bite into the Big Apple. Frustrated from the trek, he arrives at the Wall Street Inn and is directed to the Bull Room, where there is a gathering of other well-dressed executives. Most of them are CEOs who attend the monthly forum to exchange ideas, meet business partners, and listen to high powered speakers with something to offer. Today's featured speaker is Wesley Goelner, CEO of Triangel Brothers' Assets, Inc., a billion dollar investment banking firm, started by three Swedish brothers, that prides itself on IPOs

(Initial Public Offerings) and Reverse Merger IPOs.

DeAngelo quickly finds some of his colleagues and glides through the customary niceties, making small talk about business and new developments. He's quickly relieved of the obligatory conversing when they call the start of the meeting and introduce the honored speaker, Wesley Goelner.

Goelner, no lightweight contender in the Wall Street Olympics, began managing hedge funds after earning a notable reputation as a pit bull broker. A graduate of MIT Sloan School of Management, with a Masters from Stanford, Goelner has the required pedigree, but more than that, he exemplifies the language of the Wall Street huntsman. He's glib, brilliant, and cunning and at 6 feet 5 inches commands attention. He looks upon the plucky game of speculation as one-upmanship. Known for his largesse in developing a relationship with a new individual tied to a desired project, he quickly transforms from blithe Santa Claus into an obsessed stalker. Relentless, he never gives up on an opportunity to gain wealth and glory at someone else's expense. Cloaked in the disguise of mentor and keeper of the Promised Land, he engages and works his prey until the latter is ensnared. Sometimes they both triumph—student and mentor—if everything goes perfectly; but if not, he still always wins. His motto, often quoted by colleagues, goes: "I don't get in the game unless I win." Unfortunately, his first goal is singular; the bi-product is mutual gain.

The crowd in attendance is captivated and Goelner takes them through the merits of working in the public arena, ultimately to emerge from the backroom of private ownership. He focuses on the concept of reverse merger IPO's—how the process is quicker, less costly and offers the same outcome as straight IPO's. Goelner's outgoing personality, Beau Brummel appearance, and wit hypnotize all the spectators—but especially

DeAngelo, as he faces the challenge of his business and his need to grow it.

Once the speaker is done and the crowd applauds, DeAngelo hangs around near the podium, where he's approached by an old colleague, Fred Cunningham, a distributor of packaging equipment, who Donnie knows from his coffee business. Cunningham comments on the talk, and how he personally steers clear of any public ambitions.

"Donnie, I like my business private and it's mine. I don't bet in poker or on the horses and I don't gamble my business. But Goelner is a pretty sharp guy and very convincing. He and my brother are good friends and old school chums. Want to meet him?"

"Sure. He's an interesting guy. Some of what he talked about I liked—"

Before he can finish, Cunningham calls Goelner over to Donnie and introduces him.

"Wesley, great speech. You impressed my friend, Donnie DeAngelo. He owns Brickman's Bistros—you heard of them? In fact, he has one here in midtown."

"As a matter of fact, I have. I've eaten in more than one. I've been to one here in the city and another one in Boston, and I think I saw one in the Tampa airport."

DeAngelo grins and nods.

"You know, you have a pretty nice business. You were packed at each location."

Cunningham puts his arm around DeAngelo and continues. "Yeah, my friend here also owns a high end coffee business and distributes to some of the best coffee shops besides his own. He's a humble guy and a war hero—don't underestimate him."

DeAngelo is uncomfortable with the subject. "Fred, since

when did I hire you as my PR guy?" DeAngelo takes over the conversation. "Fred means well, but I'm no hero and my mom and pop business struggles like any other business."

Goelner jumps in. "Why struggle? You seem to be growing. Every bistro I've been in is busy, and the coffee business is hot right now."

"Well, growing is expensive, some do well, some don't, and we're always faced with the upfront costs and start up for each location, as well as the demands of my employees, and my goal to give a return to my investors."

Goelner becomes the diplomat and lays his hand on DeAngelo's shoulder.

"Can I call you Donnie?"

"Sure."

"Donnie, you don't have to work that hard. And if you're making money, why not let the public share in your dream and bear the expense while you grow?"

DeAngelo hesitates for a moment, and then returns to the idea.

"Sounds nice, but I don't know."

Before Goelner can finish, Cunningham excuses himself. "I'll leave you two to big business, I need a donut."

"Look, Donnie, are you profitable?"

"Yes, but—"

"Donnie, are you still growing?"

"Yeah, but we're struggling with the costs and the demands, and the—"

"This is something that will make all of that go away. Why don't you take my card and let me take some time to look at some of your numbers and structure, and maybe we can find you the elixir of the gods?"

"And the fountain of youth?" DeAngelo grins.

They both laugh and DeAngelo trails with, "Okay, I'm game."

Goelner wraps it up with his closing remarks. "In the meantime, send me your company statement from last year, some overview, and we'll talk more."

They shake hands and separate, smiling. As DeAngelo makes his way to the door, he stops to say goodbye to Cunningham.

"Fred, just want to say goodbye and thanks for the introduction. You know, he's a pretty interesting guy."

"Donnie, he's everything he wants to be and more. My brother once told me that Goelner is the kind of guy who can charm your pants off, but never let your guard down with him. He's smart, but he's all about Goelner."

Before long, DeAngelo is back in his office with an anxious Atchinson, waiting.

"Donnie, did you go through all that stuff I gave you?"

"Yeah, I signed the requisitions for new equipment and the two new leases in Jacksonville. I don't like some of the numbers in South Jersey."

"I know, but its part of doing business. I also have a lead on doing our brand in Vegas."

DeAngelo cuts in. "Are you crazy? I'm already up to my ears in costs with what we have and the new acquisitions. Vegas is too far and too expensive. I like the east coast."

Atchinson is visibly agitated. Disliked by most of the employees, he sugarcoats all the problems, leaving overworked middle management to clean up the rubble. Atchinshon likes to keep a wall between DeAngelo and the management.

He likes to maneuver his power, squeezing the payroll to his own advantage.

A balding, middle-aged, skinny, and out of shape operator, he'd worked as a consultant to coffee companies and other bistros before meeting Donnie at a convention. They'd become acquaintances and later, friends, with Atchinson helping Donnie to cut his coffee costs and expand some locations. Eventually, an aggressive Atchinson moved his way into Donnie's favor and inner circle to the point of managing day-to-day operations, as Donnie worked to help his friends and give his family more time.

DeAngelo trusts Atchinson, but Atchinson is out for Atchinson and uses his friendship with DeAngelo to serve his own purposes.

Atchinson keeps on track with conversation about growing the business.

"Look, Donnie, if we could get an investor, a good investor, we could make this thing big. We're already in all the food magazines and the customers love us."

"Mitch, what do you think about going public?" DeAngelo looks directly into Atchinson's eyes. "You know, doing an IPO? But in this case, it would be a reverse merger IPO where we would take over a shell public company and become them. At least that's how it was explained to me."

"Are you serious? Why would you say that?"

"I was approached today at the CEO forum by a guy who runs Triangel Brothers Inc."

Before he can finish, Atchinson is on it.

"Triangel Brothers? I know them. They're big! I just read about them doing a deal with Crown Mitchell Industries. They bring companies public or infuse capital."

"Well, this guy—his name is Wesley Goelner, he's the

CEO—he thinks we would be good for a reverse merger IPO, but I don't know–"

"Donnie, that might be exactly what we need. You know, that might put us on top. You should follow up." Atchinson is excited and jubilant, even pushy. DeAngelo decides the conversation should continue.

"Mitch, I spoke with Jim Fredericks, and he's not too excited about this and thinks it could hurt us as much as help us. He's not so sure, but gave me a lot of the facts."

Fredericks, DeAngelo's corporate counsel for many years, is a good friend. They enjoy each other's company and share similar interests. Their wives are friends, as well, and the two couples always share a monthly dinner to let the wrinkles iron out and keep the friendship warm.

Fredericks, a brilliant tax and business attorney, had teamed up with Donnie early in his business, contributing to his growth through prudent decisions. He keeps Donnie on track and supports him in his struggles, protecting his interests like a brother. Jim Fredericks is a leader in his community, a good father, husband, and a great friend. Fredericks, like DeAngelo's employees, shares little affection or respect for Atchinson, but always defers to Donnie and his belief in the man.

DeAngelo continues.

"You know, Mitch, Nita and the guys—Craig and Lou— aren't so sure either. I thought they might like the idea, but they seem to prefer staying private and keeping the business under my control. But, they don't know for sure and only want what's best for all of us. Nita's back from Colombia, but she's still shook up about her kid brother Domingo, as well she should be. And she's very protective and private. You know these Colombian women are mystical and she is warning me that she senses danger with this deal."

"Donnie, you would still be CEO and own the majority of shares, but at least you'd have unlimited funds to do whatever you need and you could do well—really well. You're running the company, not Fredericks or the guys, or even Anita. They put their trust and confidence in you and this could be something good for everybody."

DeAngelo looks back into Atchinson's eyes.

"Mitch, it's not just about me, it's about the guys, and the employees, and everything we put into this. What if we lose or crash or—I don't know, I'm not so sure."

"Donnie, I've worked with companies that have gone public, and they did exceptionally well. I was an interim CFO for another food company that did it; the owners became rich and the company tripled its size in no time. Don't be shy, work with Goelner. I'm sure he has a great plan, so we can all benefit. I know you don't care about getting rich, but you could help Andersen, Lou and Connie, and even bring some of Anita's other brothers here and give them a future. And the employees would gain, as well."

Atchinson is convincing, but his generous concern for everyone hides his main concern—the future of one person—himself. Everything Atchinson does is about Atchinson, but he always disguises it in the company's interest.

DeAngelo puckers his lips and stares out the window, then turns back to look at Atchinson.

"We'll see, Mitch. I'll think about it."

CHAPTER 6
ONE STEP FORWARD, TWO BACK

"**L**enore, make sure everything is covered on that list and let me see it before you send it over to Triangel and Goelner."

Lenore Reynolds is an experienced private and public controller of both small and large companies. After becoming collateral damage from an IPO that fell apart, she found her way to Brickman's Bistros on the referral of a friend. From the moment Lenore and Donnie first met, the chemistry was good. Lenore is vintage Wall Street boiler room, but she prefers private. Tall, thin, with glasses and zero sex appeal, she is none-the-less appealing as a manager and confidante to Donnie and anyone else she befriends. Always knowledgeable and thorough, she embraces projects, always multi-tasking with quiet subdued expertise.

"Donnie, are you sure you want to do this? You have a nice, quiet, private business. Are you going to give all that up to have so many people watch your every move, and hold you responsible for any mistakes? You're won't be your own boss anymore."

DeAngelo is pacing as Lenore goes through her list. He hesitates to answer because he is anxious, but the words fly out.

"Lenore, I have no choice. We are strapped and although we do a great business, we're falling behind. New leases, start-up costs, escalating payroll—it never stops and I'm afraid we're going to get caught with our pants down."

"This is not a silver bullet, Donnie. You could hit big or you could lose everything. You're dealing with wolves. These people have no conscience and if you're not moving that stock up and showing stardom, they will abandon you and plunder your assets.. And if you make mistakes, they will turn you into a punching bag and knock you out. Is that what you want?"

Donnie smiles at Lenore, knowing she always wants the best for him.

"Lenore you're a sweet woman, just give him what he needs, please."

"Okay, it's your company."

Donnie makes his way to the office only to find more piles of papers, bills, and notices that push him harder toward a new idea. He pushes the heap of paper to one side and phones Goelner, assuring him he'll have his checklist covered by noon. After a series of phone calls, emails, and overnight packages, the process advances. By the end of the week, almost every item is covered and reviewed.

Goelner is ecstatic and assures DeAngelo he is a perfect candidate for the reverse merger IPO. It doesn't take long for Goelner to locate a public shell corporation that Donnie's company can purchase, merge with, and ultimately assume a public identity. Then, following an adequate name change, a new registration and process of due diligence with the SEC, which is like jumping through another series of hoops, a new company emerges. It is seen as new stock to be traded on one of the smaller exchanges, like the OTC—Over the Counter, or as a small cap stock on AMEX—American Stock Exchange. Once the price warrants it, it moves to one of the bigger exchanges like NASDAQ or the "Big Kahuna" and the Blue Blood of trading—the New York Stock Exchange. After all this is done, you know you have arrived.

The process is time consuming and cumbersome, but Goelner assures DeAngelo that the filing and registration process doesn't stop growth, that through a process of conditional debentures, Triangel can advance money to DeAngelo's company to make acquisitions and grow. In addition, there are the costs of acquiring the shell and the onerous costs of going public. All of this, however, can be financed through Triangel, with the loans secured by DeAngelo's assets. Although DeAngelo is hesitant to put up his building and the company as a guarantee against the IPO, Goelner assures him that the loan agreements and financing arrangements to fund all the costs and acquisitions are written so that they allow enough time for the company to be registered, and upon registration, the debt is traded for stock in the new company.

Goelner points out that ninety percent or more of the companies that he registers pass muster and become public, especially after the due diligence completed by the accounting of Triangel. He provides Donnie referrals from several successful IPOs that he has transacted and gives him verbal guarantees that they would not waste their time or money if Brickman's Bistros did not pass muster. Once public, the program of pushing the stock, combined with additional debentures to the new public company for more acquisitions, produce a win-win result. The stock price goes up, the investment firm gets repaid in accelerating stock, the shareholders gain, and the loans go away at no real money cost, just more stock. As growth escalates, more stock can be issued or converted to preferred stock, thus protecting key shareholders.

The process is complicated, but has all the attraction, or more appropriately, the illusion of a no-lose, get-rich venture. In the very rare instance of a "glitch" or failed registration, the company has benefited in the growth and acquisitions that can pay back any loans.

As DeAngelo learns the process, he immerses himself in the intricacies of the new company identity and regulations. He finds every book and webinar on Sarbanes Oxley Compliance—the U.S. law that set new or enhanced standards for all U.S. public company boards, management, and public accounting firms. He attends every meeting with his appointed public attorneys and accountants for the compliance requirements and he reads every book available on all related subjects until the wee hours of the night. This is a new responsibility for Donnie DeAngelo, besides running his company. He needs to become a public CEO, with all the demands of public regulations. This leaves no time for family, friends or relaxation, only hours dedicated to learning and applying his new responsibilities to running a growing company.

Once embarked on the new endeavor, Goelner encourages Donnie to grow and buy small but prominent companies in his field, promising an even quicker jump to stardom for Donnie's company. Donnie complies and in weeks, he is closing purchases of small promising companies that expand the company's size. He uses the debentures to acquire enough money for down payments, with the balance to be paid off by more debentures, should the SEC registration take too long. But, the debt mounts along with the costs of compliance. Within months, there seems to be a curious quicksand-like entity formed of growth and debt tied to a brass ring that seems within reach. Donnie remains positive, but many nights are sleepless and filled with anxiety.

★ ★ ★

The headquarters of Triangel Brothers Assets, Inc. are nothing short of opulent. Glistening fountains decorate the entrance, with floor to ceiling art works, sculptures and a uniformed security personnel presence behind long marble desks, greeting each person entering.

Wesley Goelner, well known by every guard and employee, speeds through the lobby as if being chased by predators, never failing to ignore every salutation afforded him by any passersby. Once inside his encampment, he is addressed by his assistant, Ben Ridgefield, who is accompanied by Tony Caputo, the third in line.

"Good Morning, Wesley! How about some coffee?" Ridgefield makes a move toward Goelner's bar.

"Yeah, give me a coffee, black, and bring me all of DeAngelo's files. Hurry up!"

Ridgefield is quick to pass the torch to Caputo, telling him to get the files. While Caputo hurries to collect the paperwork, Ridgefield takes a seat and questions Goelner.

"Is there something wrong?"

Goelner reads through papers from his briefcase and ignores the question. Ridgefield tries again.

"Wesley, is something bothering you?"

Before Goelner can answer, Caputo brings in a stack of papers and hands them to Ridgefield and leaves. Ridgefield passes them on to Goelner. Goelner speaks while he reads.

"How are we doing with comments from the SEC on DeAngelo's filings?"

"Not bad, Wesley. He only had about a dozen his first go around and we answered them. There was an issue with one of his acquisitions, and they seem to be asking for audited returns going back at least three years, but the acquisition meets the guidelines and shouldn't require audited returns. But I got to tell you, one of his debentures is coming due and his legal and accounting fees are getting up there."

"So, have him get another debenture to cover the first debenture and to pay off Rosenthal and Berneti." Goelner continues to ignore Ridgefield as he flips papers and reads reports.

"Don't you think he's getting in a little deep? I mean, Wesley, he's up to five million— between the debenture principal, fees, interest and all the professional fees to get him public. How do you want me to explain another debenture allowance and advance, as he's past the due date for settling the first one?"

Goelner pauses for a moment and lays down the papers. He sips his coffee and smiles while, at the same time, glaring at Ridgefield, who has the look of bewilderment.

"Look, Ben, my loyal minion, I don't do these deals to lose money. Either he gets registered and trades, allowing us to make a fortune; or he fails and I take over that monstrosity of a building in Hoboken, his company, that big house of his, and anything else he owns. Either way, we get a big fucking building and a nice sized company for pennies on the dollar. But you better start to make friends with his guy—what's his name?" Goelner searches for the name of DeAngelo's assistant and vice president.

"Oh, you mean Mitchell Atchinson?"

"Yeah, that's the guy. He's a weasel, but he runs a big chunk of the operation, and I understand he was CFO of a small public company. He'll play ball if we have to move in on DeAngelo. Just feel him out. Plant some seeds and feather his nest a little. In the meantime, I'll keep DeAngelo on track. He might make it and we'll all be happy. Won't that be nice?"

Ridgefield pauses for a moment, then poses another question.

"You know, we pushed him into some of these acquisitions and almost promised him that the timeline on these debentures would not be a concern. You don't think he has a case?"

"A case of what? Beer? Wine? Soda? What? We do it all by the book and with paperwork to back it up. Look at all this shit!" He throws up some of the papers for DeAngelo's filings, then continues.

"I've got the SEC lawyers, the secured papers, the witnesses, and the purposeful intent. I've kept him alive and have been very generous. Either way, we win. So quit bothering me with this shit, I've got a dozen other deals going on. Get him public, or take his shit. Now go and do something productive."

Without hesitation, Ridgefield gathers the papers up, nodding in agreement as he exits.

Goelner leans back for a moment and stares out the window. He holds his fist beneath his chin, closes his eyes in deep thought, then opens them and grabs the telephone. He calls DeAngelo.

"Donnie, listen, it's Wesley. Yeah, good to hear your voice. Hey, you know your debenture is coming due, and Rosenthal and Berneti are nagging me for some of your professional fees. I don't want you to worry about them; you need to manage that growing kick ass company of yours. Since I believe in you, I'm going to redo the debenture agreements, pay off the old one, and pay your accountant and attorney so we can get your ass public. That's the least I can do. You're my guy and I don't let my guys down. So I'll have Rebecca email you the new agreements and you just get them signed and sent back asap. Gotta go. Hang in there, big guy!"

The mindset of the speaker on the other side of the phone

is not so exuberant. DeAngelo holds the receiver, and as he sets it down, ponders the terms of the new debenture and the mounting professional fees. He also considers the balance of payments on the acquisitions and the continued growing interest on the debentures. With little concern for anything else, he heads over to Lenore's office. Once there, he fails to speak and just stands erect, thinking. Lenore knows Donnie well—his moods and his needs—but always gives him room to let her into his world when the moment requires strong, but feminine empathy.

"Lenore, can you give me a list of all our debentures, the due dates, the interest and all our professional fees?"

"Donnie, are you sure you want that? Why don't you have another cup of coffee and give me some time to put it together?"

"Yeah, sure, I'll be in my office. Thanks, Lenore."

"Donnie, I told you going public is no walk in the park. It can be a windfall or it can be a downfall. Why don't you speak to Mr. Fredericks? He's a great attorney, but he's also your friend, and I know he can help you."

DeAngelo smiles, knowing Lenore's good intentions. He leans over and tells her not to worry, that they will be okay. He turns to leave, but Lenore interrupts his departure.

"Oh, Donnie—"

"Yeah, Lenore?"

Lenore looks down, away from Donnie's fearful eyes.

"One other thing. Mr. Andersen called and he sounded— well, let's say, a little out of it."

She frowns as she pushes out the words and looks up at Donnie standing in front of her, while she remains seated. His eyes are concerned, but tired. He looks like he hasn't slept and is mired in problems.

"Well, what did he say?" Donnie always has an open heart

for Andersen, no matter how many bats are flying about him.

"He said, tell my good friend I need him to come see me. He said something about the VC creeping up again, and he needs a good backup man, and to send Doc. Does he need a doctor?"

"No, Lenore, he used to call me Doc. But right now, I could use one. Don't worry, I'll go over and see what's bothering him."

CHAPTER 7
TOO FAR TO WALK

In his dimly lit, sparsely furnished studio apartment in Hoboken, New Jersey, Craig Andersen rocks back and forth aimlessly. Sitting in a vintage Bentwood rocking chair, he remembers the day he lost his legs.

Craig's cold gray eyes are fixed upward, and his wavy gray hair falls loosely around his forehead. His boyish swagger belies the wrinkles of passing decades. The years have passed slowly, but his recollection of the events that shattered his life remains clear.

It had been a hazy, damp monsoon day on October 14, 1968. The Viet Cong and North Vietnamese Army had launched a brutal campaign against the 7th Marines in Da Nang.

The Marines had a strong wing in Air Group 16 (MAG 16) and the NSA Naval Hospital. They'd secured Marble Mountain, named for its marble that shimmered in the eastern sunlight. From there, they launched platoon maneuvers and killer teams.

The nearby landing zones of Ross and Baldy took in the dead to be shipped home, and the wounded to be fixed up at a naval hospital ship or a convalescent center at Cam Ranh Bay.

NSA Da Nang had a headquarters command and nearby airport to support the pipeline that gave the war plasma. The enemy launched only an occasional distant mortar round or sporadic firefight. The main terror of their attacks was the parade of casualties that hit triage, and the crippled copters that returned from medevacs and assault missions.

Andersen, an ace sniper, had been about to receive a Bronze Star for valor at MAG 16. The honor meant little to him. While being exceptionally good at what he was trained to do, he felt a part of himself turning colder every day.

Andersen organized his emotions into two areas—for the wife he left behind, and for the three best friends who shared the war with him.

Tommy Ryan, a medevac pilot, was a former schoolmate and had furloughed him to the NSA hospital. DeAngelo, a Navy Corpsman serving with the Marines, and Big Lou had both saved his life numerous times.

These were Andersen's brothers-in-arms. Each of them was going to pick up a Bronze Star for holding position at Hill 280 while fighting over 200 Viet Cong. They were celebrating together before returning to the bush and life's edge.

Ryan was the rat pack leader and he called the shots. He and his wife Connie had been together since high school, always staying close to Donnie, Craig, and Lou. When Connie gave birth to a little boy named Sonny, Craig was named godfather, but all three men were considered his uncles.

Ryan bunked with his partner Frank Costa, who was a little smaller in stature, but his equal in hijinks and bravery. Costa was dimpled, green-eyed, and youthful, with brown hair in a short Marine cut. He was Ryan's co-pilot on flying missions.

They'd all had a night of drinking to do before their decorations the next morning. Ryan had brought the guys together in his Quonset hut to catch up on old times.

But, before they could open bottles and start the party, Ryan received an order to take a run past the northern area of Marble Mountain, where there was enemy activity and sounds of anti-aircraft fire. For Ryan, there was no greater thrill. He decided to have the boys come along so he could show off his piloting skills.

"Okay, ladies, we have a dance to attend," he said.

"All of us?" DeAngelo asked.

"Bet your ass! When's the next time I'll get a chance to follow up on some enemy shit and have a corpsman, sniper, explosives guy, and Frank to back me up—all bronze stars heroes!" Ryan laughed, and everyone laughed with him.

"Then let's do it!" Costa opened the door, and they all followed Ryan out to the LZ.

Once they reached the chopper area, everyone was scrambling. More than a few birds were heading off to answer the SOS. Ryan jumped into his Huey, and the boys came fast behind him. Ryan was quick with his engines and first in the air, headed straight for the area under siege.

Ryan was daring, and loved stunts. When the action called for an impossible maneuver, he'd make it happen.

As they headed for Marble Mountain, there was smoke in the horizon from anti-aircraft artillery and small arms fire. This was not the usual heavy ground fire. Ryan pointed his bird straight for the smoke, and as he did, the noise from the LAWS below became much louder. As the men inside the bird looked down, something caught Ryan's eye in the sky above. It was a Navy A4 Skyhawk wobbling and dropping altitude. Ryan could see it was hit by anti-aircraft fire.

"Hey, that's a fucking A4! What the hell is it doing out here?"

All eyes turned to the wounded bird fighting to stay in flight. A4 Skyhawks were primarily used in bombing raids much further north, and usually supported by an aircraft carrier. They were seldom seen in action this close to MAG 16.

"The pilot better ditch, because that baby is going down." Ryan headed for the jet. He heard radio contact from other chopper pilots in the area coming to provide support, but Ryan wanted the catch.

"Look, he's ejecting!"

They saw the pilot shooting out into the air, while enemy fire surrounded him. Ryan radioed back to the other chopper pilots.

"Don't get too close, there's too much fire. I'm going in to get him. I have a crew, so we can bring him in."

The A4 crashed into a marsh south of the base. There was a bellow of fire and smoke from the huge explosion.

Ryan and his friends turned to watch a parachute open and the pilot drop into the high grass area about 500 yards to the west. "We have to go in fast and bring him back," said Costa, "or we're all wasted."

Ryan pointed the chopper up to gain altitude. "Hang on!" he said. "I've gotta get out of the line of fire. Do any of you know what an auto-rotation sweep is?"

Before they could answer, Ryan laughed, turned the chopper over, and accelerated downward, circling as if it was about to crash. Costa smiled as his three passengers looked like they were on a roller coaster drop headed for dirt.

Ryan commanded, "DeAngelo, you're the corpsman. When I get close to ground level, go with Williams and get that guy. He might be hit, or in a fog. Andersen, make sure Charlie doesn't ambush them." Ryan fought to control the chopper's downward momentum. "Come on, you motherfucker. Hold tight for me!"

As the chopper came dangerously closer to land, it abruptly leveled off. When it was just a few feet from the ground, the three Marines jumped out.

DeAngelo and Williams sprinted to the drop site. They could see the parachute in the grass. As they made it to the jet pilot, they could see he was still in his ejection seat and hooked to his parachute. He was bleeding from the ear and nose, and incoherent from shock.

"Let's cut him loose! He's out of it!" DeAngelo pulled out his K-Bar, and cut the seat from the chute and then from the pilot. Williams did a 360, looking for the enemy. There was fire coming from AK47s and occasional mortars, and it was getting closer.

Williams helped DeAngelo lift the pilot. As they began to run with him back to the chopper, the gunfire and explosions increased. Mortar shells burst all around them. They stumbled as the pilot and high grass slowed them down.

Andersen could see them in the distance, running and ducking from gunfire. Then he spotted Viet Cong getting closer. He left his position near the chopper and headed towards his friends. "Come on, you crazy sons of bitches. Move it!"

Andersen fell to his belly to avoid incoming fire and stabilized his Remington Prolly M40 to make every shot count. He began to pick off VC as they closed in. With the precision of an expert sniper, he hit every soldier he fired at. Some of them fell only a few feet from DeAngelo, Williams, and the dazed pilot. "Move it, you slow motherfuckers!" Andersen yelled. "There's more of them coming!"

As they grew closer, they struggled even more. Nervous for his friends as the enemy surrounded them, Andersen jumped forward to help them as they came closer. But, as he lunged forward, Andersen's foot broke the camouflaged wire of a Bouncing Betty. The VC-made mine popped up and exploded a few feet from the ground. The shrapnel tore into his leg and torso, and thrust him into a dirt-and-straw covered hole with poisoned punji sticks.

Andersen was in agony. Williams scrambled to his side. They looked in horror as they saw his legs were impaled on and shattered by the sharpened sticks. Andersen was covered in blood and dirt. He bellowed horrible sounds, reflecting the agony of his wounds.

In a quick movement, DeAngelo took the weight of the pilot to free up Williams. "Get Craig, and let's get the fuck out of here!"

Williams dropped his weapon and leaned into the pit. With his large, muscular arms, he quickly pulled the spikes out as Andersen screamed in pain.

Once Andersen was free, Williams hoisted him over his shoulder as if his friend was weightless and scrambled for the chopper. DeAngelo and the pilot were already there.

"Hurry up," yelled Costa. "They're right behind you!"

As the VC moved to within a few yards of the chopper, Williams and DeAngelo laid the two wounded men on the floorboards of the Huey, and then jumped in themselves.

Ryan took to flight. Bullets and airbursts from RPG rounds came from all directions.

Suddenly, one bullet struck Costa directly into his forehead. He bounced back from the impact. Then his eyes went wide and frozen, and he slumped, motionless.

As the men ascended, they saw masses of VC swarming in and firing at them. Bullets continued to pepper the aircraft. One entered Ryan's chest, then another. He took deep breaths and swallowed hard, fighting to pilot the craft.

Ryan maneuvered the chopper in circular sweeping motions. Some rounds scraped the sides of the ship. But, he darted off to MAG 16, and safely away.

DeAngelo held the jet pilot, who was bleeding and unconscious.

Williams held Andersen, who was bleeding and moaning.

"Are you okay?" Williams asked.

Andersen shook his head. "I'm dying! And I can't feel my legs!"

The chopper landed abruptly and forcefully in MAG 16 short of the LZ, almost crashing. The landing was so hard that the bird's landing skids were jammed against the bottom of the chopper.

The airwing rescue team scurried to pull Andersen and the pilot from the chopper. They found blood splattered everywhere. They also found Ryan with his hands on the controls and Costa slumped over next to him. While the landing was a success, both pilot and co-pilot were dead.

CHAPTER 8
SONNY'S STAR

Dear Uncle Craig,

Only a few more days till another deployment, but it's a getaway from these fucking Taliban bastards. I guess we despise them just as much as you hated the Viet Cong. Yesterday, we lost a Seal Team brother to an IED after setting up perimeters for tracking Taliban movements. He was a new guy, and young. Never spoke much, but was always showing off the same pictures of his wife and little girl. They're sending him home in a body bag, with a Bronze Star. But, medals and sympathy won't help his wife and baby. I can't imagine how they're going to put him together for his homecoming—he was blown apart into a million pieces scattered all over the place. Funny thing—he'd been telling me I'm too serious and to lighten up, saying I have too much of a mean streak. He didn't know my mean streak is the stone replacement for a beating heart. That way, if they try to take my heart, they get nothing—only a rock.

Mom says you've been having a rough time, but that Uncle Donnie is always there for you and Uncle Lou. She says Lou has bad headaches and his skin is bad from all the Napalm hits you guys took in Nam. It's crazy, this shit war is in the desert and your shit war was in the jungle. Maybe the next one will be in the North Pole! I'd sign up for that, always wanted to see a polar bear. Seriously, I worry about you, Lou and Mom. Please watch out for her. She's never found a man like Dad, so she made me her whole world. No complaints, it's a beautiful thing to be all that to someone you love.

Well, I've gotta get back to being a grunt. I should be home soon and I expect you, Lou, Donnie and me to put away some serious brew. Can't wait for a bed with sheets and pillows and food that's not in a can.

I miss you, and I pray for you because I could never pray for myself. I'm hopeless and I like it that way.

Thanks for being a second father to me and for giving me inner strength—something no amount of physical training can do. You, Big Lou and Uncle Donnie make me proud to serve my country. The three of you kicked ass, came back, stuck together, and gave Mom and me hope and love.

With all my love,

Sonny

★ ★ ★

Dear Sonny,

There's a good-looking blonde here at DeRosa's who says you can share her bed anytime, but I don't think you will do much sleeping. So, get all the rest you can while you're there, because when you get back, you'll be busy banging and drinking—two award winning sports that you seem to know well.

Sonny, there's always a war to fight somewhere. Sometimes, the enemy in front of you is easier to take out than the one inside. All we have is our self-respect and the people we love. I'd be dead by now if I didn't have you, your mother, Big Lou and Donnie. That's my family, my reason to live and keep going. If you guys hadn't been around, the enemy inside of me would have made sure I ended the pain a long time ago. But, you and your Mom gave me purpose, especially after Bonnie called it quits and took off. I guess I would've done something like that, too, if I had to be seen stuck with a legless, bitter old Marine. I need this fucking wheelchair and crutches, or I'm just a doorstop—and a drunken one at best. Ooohrrah!

Anyway, enough self-pity, that's my 30 seconds worth of it for today.

I'm sorry about your friend. John Wayne never taught us how to deal with losing our amigos, just how to walk tall and kick ass. I wonder why they leave that part out of movie scripts? You never get over the friends you lose, NEVER! They stay with you for a lifetime— sons, fathers, husbands, and brothers to other people who become, in wartime, your brothers and your friends. I'm grateful Big Lou and Donnie made it back. We are all kicking ass with Donnie's business and we just may hit a gusher, since Donnie is going public. I think I'll get a limo, just so I can have a bar and some guy with a hat open the door and pour me a drink! Ooohrrah!

Listen, Sonny, you stay out of harm's way. But if it comes down your path, smile at it—because you're gonna kick its ass. You always intimidate fear and make it shrink with a smile. It makes you a bigger, stronger man. Stay true to your soul. Stay brave and fearless and when you cry inside for a lost brother or a dark moment of fear, don't be ashamed. Those inner tears will put out fires that can consume you—if you don't let them flow.

Know that I love you and will watch out for your mother and pray for your safe return. You are the son I always wanted, the son who makes me infinitely proud.

God Bless you! Oooohrrah!

Love,

Uncle Craig

★ ★ ★

Andersen pauses for a moment before he seals the envelope that will carry his sentiments and support to the man he calls his adopted son. He reaches for the 5 x7 framed picture of Sonny, his mom and the three best friends when they first moved into the building they now call home. Sonny is a smiling teenager trying, with his arms extended, to somehow embrace everyone. Andersen smiles and nods as he places the picture back on the table beside his wheelchair. He looks around the room, then reaches for an old, but well-preserved Mass card with a prayer on it for Sonny's dad, Tommy Ryan, at his final service. He remembers how the brave pilot fought to return Lou, Donnie, and him to safe surroundings right before he died. He gently tucks the Mass card into the envelope, licks the flap shut, and leans it against the framed picture of Sonny.

Within seconds, there's a knock at the door. As usual, Lou enters without waiting for Andersen to answer. Big Lou is short on conversation, but when he gets excited, he begins to ramble.

"Hey, man, I'm so pissed! I got these damn clinic and doctor bills, plus all these tests, and the VA won't cover it! It's fuckin $3,350 ! They say they didn't approve it, so now they're sending this shit to me! Donnie told me not to worry, that he'll look into it and no matter what, he'll see it gets paid. You know, if they screw around with it, Donnie will pay it—and that pisses me off. I feel bad, but what can I do? These motherfucking headaches are driving me crazy and lately, I see these little fuckin spots too. I don't want to be a drain on Donnie; the guy's already paying all our bills. Do you ever see a rent, utility or any motherfucking bills come to us? No, because the guy takes care of all this shit. I tell you, if this company goes big and we make some nice money, we gotta send that guy on a vacation with Nita. He never stops, just keeps on going—like that bunny with the drum."

Lou pauses long enough to study Andersen and sees he is not paying attention.

"Hey, man, why you looking so serious? You been drinking again?'

Andersen slowly raises his head to gaze at the big man who he sees as a brother.

"Listen, Lou. You take those headaches serious and fuck the VA! God only knows what all that Napalm shit did to your insides. All those explosives you were playing with back in Nam might've done some real damage and the goddamn government better take care of you."

"That's what I say, Craig, but the government said some of the tests they did before didn't show anything. But, man, that was two years ago and these headaches have been getting worse. Now I'm seeing little black things, like the mosquitoes we used to get flying all around us in the bush."

"Well, talk to Donnie, I got my own problems." He pushes himself up from the wheelchair and points with his head to his leg stubs.

"Man, *that* guy has enough problems. He looks like he hasn't slept in days, working on this public thing, and he still feels bad about Nita's brother. I'm gonna try and get him out for a drink or sumthin and make sure he gets some rest."

Lou eyes the letter addressed to Sonny and then takes the picture next to the letters.

"Hey, Man! I remember this day! We was all excited about moving into this place! Donnie had that big party and made sure we had nice digs. Look at Sonny! He was a skinny pimply little guy then."

"I wouldn't say that to his face now." Andersen raises an eyebrow and looks intently at Lou.

"Yeah, he's a big athletic dude now and a bad ass Seal. You

know, I got a friend from Nam who was just about eighteen when we were there. Now, he's one of Sonny's senior COs and he says Sonny is one bad ass dude. Sonny is his point guy for most of the nasty shit they get, and he says Sonny will take out anybody—just for fun. Imagine that, little Sonny is now DA MAN! I'd rather just make love, not war, but shee-it—if I had to take out some asshole, I would do it."

Andersen forces out a laugh and spins his wheelchair to face Lou.

"Lou, our days of taking anyone out are pretty much over. We can barely take care of ourselves. I'm half a man with a bad drinking habit. You're a retired jock with brain problems. Donnie is a workaholic tied to his business, Nita, and us. Some killer team we make!" He chuckles and then laughs loudly, as Lou stares him down.

"Well, speak for yourself, you old fucker, I'm still in my prime! Check out these arms."

Lou lifts his arms in a double bicep pose and shows the nineteen-inch arms that never went away. At 6'4" Lou remains solid and shows little sign of aging; only the tired eyes and graying hair give his age away. He smiles and kisses both biceps, then speaks.

"So, speak for yourself, old man, this boy can still play!"

Andersen acknowledges the spirit of Lou's words and his obviously impressive physique. He smiles at Lou and tells him, "Am I supposed to be impressed? I can still kick your big black ass!"

Lou leans forward and lets loose with laughter.

"Craig, you are one funny son of a bitch!"

The two men laugh, then Andersen reaches for a bottle of scotch on the table where he'd put the letters. He holds up the bottle as if it's a trophy and looks to the ceiling as he begins a toast.

"Let's drink to Hotel Company and Echo Company and the 7th Marines and Tommy Ryan and—" Before he can finish, Lou takes the bottle in his big hand and holds it steady. He sees the desperation in Andersen's face and speaks softly, but with conviction.

"Craig, you really wanna do more of this shit? You've had some long nights and you need to slow down, man. You gotta be in shape to celebrate when Donnie makes all this money."

Andersen pulls the bottle away from Lou, telling him, "I don't need money, what am I gonna do with it? Buy a new wheelchair? Maybe some phony legs to pretend I'm a real man? I can't even fuck anymore, I have no desire. The only reason I gave Donnie the money was to help him and us. It's his dream and the money wasn't doing nothing for me, but knowing Donnie, he could do something with it. And I trust him. He's always been looking out for us, in Nam and now. I'm happy to see him make it. Connie will get a break, and you and Sonny will have some fun, but I'm washed out."

Lou eyes Andersen with sorrow, then puts aside his obvious empathy and tells him, "Stop it, man! We care about you. You have people who love you and we have fun, so stop this shit, man. You make your life what it is and not just because you missing a couple of legs. You still Craig Andersen inside and out. You got a soul, a brain and attitude, so don't be going down that pity trail—'cause I will kick your ass!"

Lou makes his words ring loud and clear. They hang in the air like a rain cloud about to burst.

The men smile at each other and Andersen extends his arm offering a handshake to Lou, who pauses before he takes Andersen's hand. The silence is broken by a shout raised in harmony from both men: "Ooohrrah!"

CHAPTER 9
A BAD HAND

Things move along well, and DeAngelo is engaged in numerous acquisitions and new contracts. Aligned with the restaurant and contract business, his vending and coffee distribution flourishes. But, although he has advanced his kick-start, or seed money, for many of the projects he's engaged in, he's met with more than a few obstacles. He is understandably nervous about the supporting funds he needs to pay off the balances on the acquisitions. In addition, the long process of audits by the PCAOB accountants charging burdensome fees, gives Donnie some cause for concern.

For now, he focuses on the management of his business and employees. Working late is never a problem for the vigilant CEO. DeAngelo is a positive force in all his methods—he tends to be an optimist, but with a keen sense of instinct towards unpredictable danger or accidents. This was the case in Vietnam where, as a young Marine corpsman in the heat of combat, he'd moved as if invincible to danger, but always sensing when the danger might prove fatal. In those cases, he'd been more careful—not immobilized by the threat—but more conscious of his actions directed towards avoiding total disaster. Sensing a high-risk situation never delayed his need to act—it merely put him on full alert.

In business, Donnie knows where to make his moves and when to pay attention. He begins to feel uneasy about the delays in his audit and in the mounting debt from new acquisitions. His inordinate professional fees and looming painful penalty fees make him a little wary, should he ever default or be late on any acquisition or other note. He registers his concerns, but moves forward in acquiring new assets for the company and hiring additional employees to serve a growing demand for increased customer service. As he studies the requests by his department heads for new equipment, and the previous bills created by his professional team of accountants, attorneys and consultants, he dials up Goelner for more funds.

"Wesley, I need some additional funds from the contingent reserves to facilitate these purchases, add equipment, and pay these insane accountants and attorneys."

"Not a problem, how much are you looking for?"

"At least $1.5 million for the deposit on the Marco chain in Florida, plus another $750,000 dollars to pay the late fees on Rossman and that asshole attorney you recommended. And my payroll is escalating."

"Hey, Donnie, your attorney, Fredericks is not cheap either!"

"Wesley, Jim is reasonable compared to your guy! He actually does work and really cares. I don't mind paying him and he's a good friend. Besides, he and I are caught up."

"Okay. You'll have the money in your account tomorrow. Just sign some papers, which our accounting and legal will email to you today. By the way, the SEC is looking hard against my contingent reserve program, but don't worry about that, now. I have plans if they over-regulate it or want it stopped, so that we can continue, anyway."

"Stopped? You think they would do that?"

"They may. They have some new young attorneys who feel our contingent reserve program dilutes new IPO stock and jeopardizes the ownership of the original owners. But that's foolish, you and I know that."

Donnie reflects for a moment, registering the cavalier comments of Goelner. He senses the kind of danger that he would've acted on in Vietnam, but as the problem of funding persists, he chooses to move forward and hope for the best.

"Yeah, I hear you, but I'm concerned about what you're telling me here. I'd like to meet with you soon, because I have concerns. I'd like to know more."

"Sure, sure, Donnie, anytime—just call and you know I'm here for you."

The phone conversation ends on a hopeful high note, but the doubts linger in DeAngelo's mind. Burdened by the thought of a funding watershed disaster and being in a helpless position to act or control the extenuating circumstances, he pulls out a bottle of his favorite scotch, pours three fingers, and toasts to his circumstances: "Here's to life, my friends and the completion of these fucking audits!"

Suddenly, his office door bursts open, and standing before him is a radiant and seductively dressed Nita. She smiles and flips back her hair, confident that she is done up to entice and remove Donnie from his entanglements.

"Put that down, *Papi*, I'm not going to have a drunk with me tonight. I decided to come and buy you dinner, and if you're good, to seduce you." Nita takes the glass from Donnie's hand and leans closer to whisper in his ear. "You don't need this. I know what you need."

She melts his defenses as she smiles with the look of a cat begging to play. Nita's charm and Colombian beauty are in full gear. Her beautiful chestnut eyes sparkle as she flashes a soft smile and touches his face. He knows in a moment he is hers for the night and the worries and demands of the business can wait. He smiles back at her and gives her a formal invitation.

"How about dinner at *Mesa di Amor*? You can have your favorite desert, *aroz con leche*, rice pudding, *y mástarde que puedotener mi postre favorite*, and later I can have my favorite desert—you."

Donnie's Spanish has improved over the years. He has worked at it in order to make his new bride and her boys comfortable, to show his commitment to them and to their new life. He also enjoys speaking it when heated moments like this fire up his desire.

After a slightly rushed dinner with a few cocktails to celebrate, the attentive couple returns to their large suburban home. Finally, they put the rigors of business and all the other problems behind them. They are home from the battle and anxious to feel happy again. Nita quickly checks for the boys, but they are away at soccer camp. Donnie assesses the situation's erotic possibilities and takes her from behind.

Nita is old school Colombian. She likes a forceful man who takes control, loves the animal side of sex mingled with a dedicated suitor's ardent love. Donnie wraps his arms around her and leans her forward. He nibbles at her ear and feels the wrenching pull of arousal well up inside of him as he paws at her large, firm breasts. He yanks down the light satin blouse exposing her braless chest—Nita needs no woman's harness. Her firm skin betrays her age, and her passion is as ferocious as when they first met.

Donnie strips away her blouse entirely and has her bend over the oak railing that decorates their entrance. He yanks her skirt and tiny g-string from her body. Nita has a rounded bottom—large enough to grab, but small enough to manage. Donnie enters her quickly and vigorously and finds her responsive—her moist vagina eager to receive his hardness.

Nita loves to scream and enjoy the moment. She loves to bury her nails in any part of Donnie she can grab, often leaving marks he later needs to hide with long-sleeved shirts. They fuck each other in every part of the foyer. Then, he carries her up the stairs to the bedroom, to finish in a missionary embrace, so he can watch her pretty face. They finish and laugh out loud, knowing they're acting like kids. Exhausted from a long day and a passionate evening, they fall into each other's arms and drift off into slumber.

★★★

The week flies by and DeAngelo is at the Triangel Brothers building, on his way to Goelner's office. He is overwhelmed by the lavish and ornate surroundings—every hallway garnished with striking oil paintings and dramatic sculptures, rich Italian marble floors in white and gold echoing every step taken to the grand entrance of the CEO's suite. The secretary opens one of the double doors to allow Donnie an imposing view of Goelner in waiting, looking like a lion about to roar and partake of fresh meat. He tells Donnie to take a seat.

"Listen, Donnie, these fucking SEC attorneys have clamped down on my contingent reserve program of allowing advances to you for a trade of your stock at a discounted share price. This has worked fine for me for the last two years. The companies participating liked it too, but now they've decided to put a hold on it, so we can't do funding that way anymore."

Donnie's face turns pale. He feels like the danger he'd instinctively sensed is now imminent. "That can't be! How the hell will we continue and meet our obligations? This will crash the company! Why would they do that?"

"Oh, some crap about how the constant trading of stock for funding will dilute the stock and allow an investment firm to take over the company—but that's nonsense! The stock usually grows, new preferred stock gets issued, and in the end, everyone makes money anyway. It would take forever for me—I mean for the investment firm—to dilute the stock and take it over. You have so many shares as principal stockholder that you have nothing to worry about." He takes a breath and sees doubt in DeAngelo's eyes. "Calm down, old friend! We have another option."

Goelner walks around his desk to sit at the chair beside DeAngelo. "I can give you conditional debentures that you can use for your acquisitions, bills, and whatever operating capital is necessary. You just have to meet some paper standards and nothing will change."

"Yeah, but that's a loan, not a trade of lower priced stock. We can't afford any more loans! Look, I've even put in more of my own money, reduced my salary, and deferred other things owed to me by the company. I will end up broke and the company will be in too much debt." His mouth remains open, lost for words, searching for answers.

Goelner is quick to answer, quick to lower the alarms sounding and the red flags rising up. "Look, they are debentures repaid with stock, just like the contingent reserve. Nothing has changed that much! We're just using different titles and different delivery methods—you'll see."

"But, I'm also not trading because of the stupid delays in the audits your accountants have imposed. If I don't meet the debenture deadlines, I'm certain I will incur penalties, fees, and worse since you are a secured creditor."

"Donnie, Donnie, if you're not listed again to trade by the time they become due, I will give you extensions – or, we'll refinance. You'll be fine and you'll be trading by then. I can get you there."

DeAngelo pauses, takes a deep breath and stares at the ceiling before responding. "From your lips—"

"Yes, my friend, I know. Don't worry, we didn't do this to lose money! You have to trust me."

"I get a creepy feeling whenever someone says that, unless it's my mother or my wife."

"Well, look at me like extended family! Now, go back, keep doing what you're doing, and I will fund it."

DeAngelo gives Goelner a skeptical glance before leaving. He comments on the attractive and opulent office, in a tone of indifference knowing his instinct is on high alert.

After a hectic commute from Manhattan, DeAngelo finds his longtime attorney, Jim Fredericks, waiting in his office. He is surprised, but greets him with a smile, because Fredericks always has a way of making Donnie feel better about any dilemma.

"What the hell are you doing here, Jim, looking for a check?" DeAngelo always plays tongue in cheek with guys like Fredericks.

"Hey, that's not even nice! In fact, I haven't billed you for a lot of things since you started this diabolical venture. And have you forgotten that we planned this meeting?"

"We did?" DeAngelo stutters, trying to remember.

"Yes, and it's good that we did! Listen, Donnie, you are really putting yourself in jeopardy! Lenore tells me you are using a lot of your own personal money to keep this thing going. Why? Aren't they funding you?"

"They are, but they always get tied up in Sarbanes Oxley compliance requirements, making my audits drag. When they pass a deadline point, I'm not allowed to trade. Now, I've got to meet payroll and other things, not to mention we have this new way of funding with conditional debentures in lieu of stock."

Fredericks, Donnie's longtime friend and attorney—though not his active attorney for SEC compliance reports of the company—knows enough to warn him. A seasoned business and tax attorney at the top of his game, Fredericks commits to clients he likes, some of them becoming his good friends. "Listen Donnie, that's another word for LOAN and you don't need any more loans! You're up to your ears in debt, and you're recklessly draining your own piggy bank. I've been with you for almost twenty years, and you and I have had some good times, but this is not one of them."

They both laugh for a few seconds, remembering moments of bravado when business hadn't seemed like all work and no play. Donnie offers Jim a drink of scotch from his sidebar, but Fredericks declines.

He stares at Donnie, seeing the ambiguity and apprehension in his eyes. "I'm going to tell you one last time. Watch out for Goelner and stop using your own assets to keep this dream alive. This is your friend and counsel forewarning you."

DeAngelo nods, forces a smile and stands to see him leave.

CHAPTER 10
CALL OR BLUFF

"Hey, Dad, Caroline and I got together with Geraldo and Anton. We were thinking we'd do something for you and the guys on Veteran's Day, since we're not sure how long you old dinosaurs will be around."

Jason smiles with the sarcastic wit that is always endearing to Donnie. He is the oldest of Donnie's children, his first-born. Tall, stocky and sporting a classic Van Dyke beard, Jason likes to keep the atmosphere light. His father is usually a good sparring partner, but today is not a great day for a volley.

"That's nice, son. I think the guys would like it, but I'm dealing with a lot right now and I'm not sure if I'm up for it."

"Listen, Dad, since I've been with Hendricks and Blane and their crazy furniture deals nationally, I've had nothing but headaches trying to coordinate a reasonable national program that makes sense. They've made me Vice President of Bullshit—and there's plenty going around. You need a break from all your bullshit, too. Caroline called Geraldo and Anton, we all got together and we think this is a good idea. So what do you say? Think about Craig, Lou, Connie—and maybe we can get Sonny into it, too."

Caroline is the next oldest of Donnie's children. At twenty-nine, she is stunning. A former Homecoming and Prom Queen, a natural beauty with no ego baggage, she'd landed a spot with the 'Kathy From Modeling Agency' and is busy doing spots for TV and popular designers.

Caroline and Jason are products of Donnie's youth, and a failed first marriage that started out fine, but somewhere down the road had suffered the post-Vietnam War and late-seventies calamities. Geraldo and Anton are Nita's boys, adopted by Donnie after marriage to her, and as much a part of the family as Donnie's children. Both Jason and Caroline treat the boys like real brothers. Geraldo and Anton make both Donnie and Anita proud, as they grow to manhood. Together, all the children, along with Nita, make for a symbiotic family, sharing Donnie's ambition and love of family.

"Okay, I'll talk to them. But for now, I've got so much to do." Donnie quickly focuses back on his paperwork.

"Dad, you look stressed out. You know, this investment banking firm you're using is the same one doing our refi and stock deal at Cravitz. Although they're big, they have a notorious reputation for exploitation."

"Son, I don't need to hear that now. I've got enough going on. Besides, all these investment firms have a rep. It's part of the game, but I've heard good things too. Tell your sister and the boys I appreciate the gesture and I'll get back to them. And Jason, on the way out, please tell Lenore to get in here. I need her for something."

Jason knows that his father is hard pressed and especially stressed, when hearing him issue an SOS for Lenore, the Controller. He grins and shakes his head as he leaves Donnie's office, but not before looking back at his father, who quickly turns back to the papers strewn across his desk.

★ ★ ★

As the day goes on, Lenore and Donnie struggle to make sense of the mounting fee demands from Triangel, frustrated with the overbearing costs.

Donnie calls Jim Fredericks, his longtime counsel and friend. "Jim, these fees seem ridiculous. The debentures given by Triangel are supposed to be secured by the stock, but the stock isn't trading because Triangel's accounting firm won't finalize the audit for the acquisitions. I can't pay these huge fees and still do acquisitions and keep them, which is what Triangel wants me to do. The acquisitions are sound, but this damn accounting firm they've recommended is getting hung up in compliance nonsense—which they should have thought about before pushing me to grow this company."

"Look, Donnie, I told you as a friend and as your counsel to think twice about this. After that, I told you that Triangel had a reputation for being hawkish, but sloppy in their IPOs and reverse mergers. You seem to like this guy, Goelner, but I've told you stories about him and I don't think you've been listening."

"I do listen, Jim, but what can I do? I'm in up to my ears." Donnie pats his shoulder.

Fredericks is one of the best tax and corporate attorneys in the business. Through the years, he and Donnie have grown together with the company, developing a trusting friendship, as well. Fredericks has an appetite for fun and hijinks. The two have often relished flirting with practical jokes that sometimes crossed the line with their wives—like the time they'd hired strippers for Andersen's birthday party. The festivities had turned into a complete fiasco, replete with loud and drunken enthusiasts indulging in all sorts of noisy sexual activities, brawling and breaking furniture, all ultimately brought to a finale by the local police. The latter, all former Marines and military types, had been satisfied to disperse all the parties involved and pretend it had never happened. But, beyond the fun and friendship, Fredericks is on the ball when it comes to business.

"Donnie, I think you need to speak to Goelner and do something about this quicksand of debentures he's pulling you into, because if you don't start trading soon, these fees could put your company in jeopardy. You don't want a hostile takeover."

DeAngelo is quick to take Fredericks' advice, so he calls Goelner, who seems strangely unconcerned. Donnie tells him of the impending payroll, plus payments on companies he's purchased, along with mounting professional fees for Sarbanes Oxley compliance—part of the public regulation process imposed by the Federal government and the SEC. Then, there are the unreasonable late fees on the debentures. But all Goelner has to give is patronizing good will and the offer of more debentures to stave off the lions. Donnie is uncomfortable, because he sees the inevitable catastrophe that will consume his business and everyone involved. Goelner ends the call abruptly, leaving Donnie in turmoil and desperation.

Monday morning is Goelner's meet-and-greet for staff—staff being Ridgefield and Caputo. Top on the list is Brickman's Bistros delayed listing, along with its mounting debenture penalties and late fees. Goelner seems unconcerned, but tables the issue as a priority.

"Ridgefield, I had a not so nice conversation with DeAngelo about his debenture penalties and his lack of funds for payroll, acquisition payments, and professional fees."

"Yeah, Wesley, he's getting fucked on all sides. His PCAOB accountants—you know, our friends Rossman and Spearson—are jerking him around with requests for approved audits on his last acquisition. But, it's borderline whether or not he needs one—because the purchase falls into the category where he may not need it – but, they're busting his balls. And you're really giving the guy a fucking on those fees! I know you figured if he traded, there'd be enough to pay it, and he'd be public, but he can't trade until he gets through this audit."

Goelner leans back in his oversized executive chair and bites on the end of a pen. "I could push Rossman to wrap up this audit, because they're fucking around with bullshit, even though, you know, I'm not supposed to—and you know, I do follow the rules." He smiles, tongue in cheek, knowing that Rossman and Spearson have been his brainchild for DeAngelo, and that they love making Goelner happy, even at the risk of breaking the rules.

"Look, he's made a clean acquisition. It's not huge, the year of compliance requirements hasn't even started yet, but I'm not sure if I should get involved." Goelner pauses, as Ridgefield seems perplexed.

"But, if he doesn't get listed, nobody makes money." Caputo, who rarely speaks at the Monday meet and greets, puts in his two cents.

But, Goelner is quick to answer. "Listen, my loyal little minion of doubt. If I've told you once, I've told you a thousand times—I always get paid! This is not different. If he collapses and defaults, I get the company, all the assets, plus that monstrosity of a building that I hear may have some serious value."

Ridgefield leans forward. "What do you mean?"

Goelner pauses and spins back and forth, smiling at Ridgefield and Caputo. "I was at a high end venture capital meeting Friday. I heard from CMTI Developers that they have their sights on doing a huge business center and gentrification expansion in Hoboken. Guess what's right in the middle of the business center?"

A moment of expectation turns into a minute of speculation, as Goelner waits for somebody to answer.

Ridgefield lifts his head and mutters, "DeAngelo's building?"

"Yes, Ben, and guess what? If this is for real, his building will be worth more than a few million. It will be worth lots of millions, because it's right in the middle. DeAngelo doesn't know yet, because they're arranging proprietary rights on the plans and assuming he'll be an easy acquisition. They don't want to play their hand too early, but if we move fast enough, they'll be dealing with the new owners. And if you move your ass and work with DeAngelo's COO, Atchinson, we may also have a viable, growing company with a still manageable public entity that we own."

"Wow, that's heavy, but I have to move fast on the default." Ridgefield looks at Caputo, knowing it will be a joint venture.

"He's already in default and he knows it. We just accelerate the process and in the meantime, you make friends with Atchinson and set him up as our man who will benefit by getting control. Once we have things working well, we'll either keep him or dump him, too. Also, keep on top of this revival project in Hoboken, and keep me informed of the players and developments. I'm owed a few favors and I'm going to make sure I call them in."

"One more thing," Goelner says, turning to Caputo. "You go see your friend at Rossman and Spearson, and get the message passed to Rossman to stay the course, that DeAngelo damn well needs those audits done, that the delays are only fair, and that if he must be delisted, he'll be delisted. After all, rules are rules." Goelner laughs and speeds them on their way, but not before telling them to handle another errand.

"Oh guys? Do me a favor, get me another box of those Presidential Cuban Cohibas and some bottles of Crystal? I'm gonna visit my friend Marlena, at Fleur de Nuit. I feel a windfall coming on."

CHAPTER 11
KEEPING ENEMIES CLOSE

It's a not-so-busy Monday afternoon at the well-hidden luxurious Fleur de Nuit escort palace in downtown New York. Fleur de Nuit boasts an elite clientele of rich Manhattan execs who can take long lunches for $500 an hour and up, with the elite ladies of that establishment.

One of the elite ladies is Marlena, the in-house madam, who, at twenty-five, has the worldly experience and business acumen of a woman twice her age. But, with the face and figure of a Victoria's Secret model, she outshines all the others, even the youngest in the stable. Marlena is an anomaly in many ways: angelic face, devilish smile, soft feminine appearance – along with an agile hard side that challenges the most passionate man. Personal warmth and a straightforward honest way keeps her in demand, but at the same time, she reveals a savage side and can be mendacious if her business is challenged. At $1,000 an hour, she keeps herself reserved solely for the elite of Wall Street, and on this festive day, her visitor is Wesley Goelner, a regular, who makes no bones about booking time as he sees fit.

Marlena is the daughter of a Colombian peasant woman. The woman, whose only asset was the same beauty that

Marlena inherited, had experienced enough extreme poverty to send her seeking a reprieve somewhere, some way, somehow. She'd found relief by putting herself in the care of a small drug kingpin who had provided an oasis from the turmoil and poverty of farm life in the villages of Armenia.

Once Marlena was old enough to want more for herself, she used her assets to buy her way into the big city of New York, where she had always dreamed of living and where she envisioned her future. By eighteen, she had a long waiting list of suitors who'd gladly dished out $500 an hour for the pleasure of her company. By twenty-two, she'd acquired her degree with a double major: one in business from NYU, the other from smitten chief executives who tutored her privately about life. Now, at twenty-five, she runs the most elite brothel in New York with a clientele of CEOs, politicians, and underworld figures who make sure she is well-protected. But, still, she keeps her $1000 an hour clients for the fun of dragging them along and keeping on top of her craft.

Goelner, a frequent visitor, tips her well, so Marlena makes it a point to give him VIP treatment and on-demand service. Marlena is always indulgent with Goelner, but at the same time, she keeps a savage side that challenges him, which he admires, rendering him prey to her manipulation. Goelner's mood is always celebratory. Marlena keeps him high on sex and cocaine, the purest and best, as only Goelner can appreciate. Marlena herself rarely indulges—pretending to participate but secretly passing—allowing her client to enjoy while keeping her own head clear. Marlena's only drugs are her family and business. Today is no different. Goelner is quick to shovel the white powder into his nose and grope his vision of beauty. Marlena finds him amusing, overly confident, selfish, and indifferent. Being the showman that she's made herself into, she gives him what he wants.

"You seem especially happy today, Wesley. Usually, you start off with some Johnnie Blue, then graduate to the White Knight."

"Oh, Marlena, my lovely thoroughbred, life is good and I can't lose! I think the gods of fame and success have marked me as their idol!" He laughs and pulls her close.

"Really? And do these gods know you as well as I do?" She gives him a devilish look, dropping her eyes to his crotch.

"No one knows me like you do, Marlena. I'm a lion at my work but you are the lioness with me, and I love how you scratch." He kisses her forcefully and she pulls back for a moment, then poses her question.

"So, are we spending some time together? Or are you rushing off again, like you usually do?"

Goelner smiles and pulls out a large stack of bills, slips them into her cupped hands and tells her to buy some new shoes.

"Looks like I can buy a lot of shoes with this—at least two or three hours' worth!"

They both laugh and as she turns to the side and raises the volume on the stereo, he rips down her top and buries his head in her breasts. Within minutes, they are coupled and pounding to the loud music of Metallica. Minutes seem like hours to Goelner, who lays exhausted on the lavish couch while Marlena pours him his Johnnie Blue. Just then, his cell phone rings.

"Dammit! I forgot to shut this fucker off!" He goes to shut it, but seeing DeAngelo's number and unable to resist, answers.

"Yeah, Donnie, what's up?"

DeAngelo implores him to back off on the fees and use his influence with the accountants to move his audit through, so they can trade. He tells Goelner they have provided everything required, and the audit should have been completed. At this point, the fees are extreme and burdensome, and he can't keep the company going if they demand payments.

"Look, Donnie," he begins, launching into his well-rehearsed lie, "I told you I have no influence over the PCAOB accountants. They're SEC regulated and the fees are the fees. Look, I'll send Ridgefield over and maybe you guys can talk it out, but I'm busy now and gotta go."

Goelner is quick to finish the call and turn back to Marlena, who seems curious.

"So, you're moving in for another kill?" She gives him a predator smile.

"Yeah, another sucker—who thinks I have a heart! Look, these guys want to play with the big boys and they never give a shit about the horns you can get with the bulls." He lifts his phone back to his ears and motions her to wait. "Give me a second, honey, I want to make a call."

Goelner dials Ridgefield and makes it short. "Ben, get over to DeAngelo's place and give him some bullshit about the fees—say that we'll find a way to try and help him. Then, hook up with Atchinson, like I told you, and get him ready to take over. I want to make sure we have that building and his company before DeAngelo gets too smart. He's a nice guy, but out of his league." He pauses for a moment, listening to Ridgefield before answering him.

"Never mind what I'm doing! Get your ass over there!" He shuts off the phone, throws it across the mattress, and then pushes Marlena onto the bed. She looks up at him, quizzically.

"So, no sympathy for the nice guy?" She puts on a forced smile.

"Fuck him! You know, if you play with the bull, you get the horns!" He laughs again and pretends to act like a bull, putting his fingers to the side of his head and pushing his face close to hers.

She smiles back and retorts, "But, sometimes, the bull can get the *estoque*."

"Oh yeah, what's that?" he chuckles.

She pauses, then whispers, "The sword of the matador."

★ ★ ★

Ridgefield arrives at the Brickman's Bistros building shortly after calling DeAngelo to inform him he is on his way. DeAngelo is quick to have him sit down for a talk.

"Ben, we can't go on like this! Your fees are insane and now you're demanding payment! Are you nuts? I haven't got it! And your accounting firm—"

Before he can finish, Ridgefield interrupts to remind him that they have no say over the accounting firm.

"Don't give me that crap, Ben! You guys recommended them! They've done almost 90 percent of your deals and you know damn well you have them in your back pocket—SEC or no SEC. Just like these so-called SEC compliant attorneys who bill me like Fort Knox. They see I'm not trading, their fees get higher and higher and they never get anywhere for me. These guys do ninety percent of your deals, as well."

Ridgefield begins to disagree again, but they end in a stalemate, as Ridgefield promises to do his best. Once outside the building, Ridgefield calls Atchinson and tells him to meet him at a nearby café where they can talk.

Atchinson is quick to arrive. The two men shake hands, order a drink and look around the room for possible acquaintances. Once they realize there is no threat, Ridgefield starts the conversation.

"Look Mitch, our friend Donnie is in trouble through no fault of ours. I assume you want to see the company continue and preserve the business for the employees?"

"Sure, you know I do," he answers anxiously, motivated solely by his own ambition and not by the interests of the employees.

"Who signs your corporate checks?" he asks Atchinson.

"Only DeAngelo, he's particular about that. But I have a stamp with his name that we use in emergencies, or if he's unavailable." He chuckles and fumbles with his pen.

"Okay, so start taking control. Make him feel like there's room to make this work. Perhaps, tell him to take some time off and let the employees see more of you in a commanding position. Then, just as a precaution, save and copy your emails to him and keep us on top of them. Make sure all the files and records are preserved, and have him pay employees and vendors. But you can whisper in his ear that taxes and other things can wait for now, that they will all be paid once he's refinanced or listed. In the meantime, and most importantly, show leadership to the employees and start to take control—if you know what I mean." Ridgefield winks and grins.

"Not a problem. We're in agreement. You know, Donnie is a nice guy, but he did this to himself."

Before he can finish, Ridgefield cuts him off, knowing the cloth Atchinson is made of.

"Yeah, yeah, that's right. He did it to himself. And you can do the right thing. We have an understanding, right?"

"Yes, do you want any updates from me?" He begins to ramble and talk about his experience and how much he knows, but Ridgefield doesn't care, all they want is a stooge and Atchinson fits the brand.

"No, I'll let you know what I want and when I want it. Just do what I tell you. Soon, we will make a move to officially put you in charge."

He stares intently at Atchinson, who nods in the affirmative.

Ridgefield quickly downs the rest of his drink, pats Atchinson on the shoulder, and takes off through a side door, leaving him to finish his drink alone.

CHAPTER 12
CASHING OUT

"I'm sorry, Donnie. I can't stay and watch you fall apart. I know what's coming! You know, I've been down this road before and I just can't do it again." Lenore Reynolds stands erect, holding back her emotions and avoiding Donnie's eyes.

"I understand, Lenore. No one could expect more. There's a tough ride ahead and I don't expect to drag anyone along." DeAngelo stands up to face Lenore and accept her retreat graciously.

Before he can extend his arms to embrace her, she speaks again. "Someone will have to continue as chief financial officer and sign off on your reports and numbers." Her eyes soften and glaze over with a few tears.

"I intend to take that over, as well. I wouldn't expect anyone to jump into a burning building on my behalf. I will try to make this work and perhaps—"

Before he can finish, she interrupts him. "Watch out for Atchinson. I don't trust him."

"Lenore, Mitch has a hard side, but he also cares and he will do the right things. He's already—"

Once again, she interrupts him, whispering in his ear, as

she lunges forward to hug him. "Watch him, Donnie, he's out for Mitch and you might just be in the way."

Before he can respond, she holds him closer, then pulls away abruptly and makes her way to the door. Coincidentally, as she leaves, Atchinson brushes past. They exchange glances for a second, then she rushes off.

"What was that about?"

"Lenore resigned and I'm taking over as CFO."

"You're better off, Donnie. She's an old maid with a negative attitude."

"Give it a break, Mitch. She took good care of us and she cared." DeAngelo's eyes narrow as he speaks firmly, while pondering Lenore's advice.

"Yeah, well, I know you liked the old broad and that's okay, but we need to get down to business. We are short for payroll this week, vendors are way past terms, our compliance professionals won't do anything unless they get paid and—"

"So, what do you expect me to do? You don't think I've been dealing with this? In fact, I haven't slept the past few days, and I don't know what else to do! We're dried up, and we owe payments on our acquisitions, as well. I have foreclosure notices on my house after trying to finance some of this insanity. And now taxes are due."

"I know, but hold off on the small vendors for now. Get the big vendors to extend terms. You know how they like you. In fact, you put many of these guys on the map in the last twenty years. They owe you."

"You think I want them to take a bullet for me? Mitch, we're in quicksand and I don't like it. You loved the idea of this going public and now it's a disaster!"

"Listen, Donnie. Let me handle more things. You know I'm a good operator. You can focus on raising money, putting off vendors, and solving some of this shit with Triangel. You're trying to do too much and you're gonna break down. Then where will we all be?"

"Mitch, look at all this shit on my desk—penalty payments, overdue bills with final notices, compliance fees, foreclosure notices, SEC alerts and inquiries, payroll I can't meet and more! Add to that doctor bills and surgeries for Lou that he needs—or that poor guy will explode! And this is just what's here! Everything at home is going bad—tuition bills I haven't paid, a mortgage that's in foreclosure, credit cards maxed to over $200,000, even utility bills that are on shut off notice. Mitch, it's just too much and keeps getting worse!"

Atchinson puts on a face of concern that seems spurious. He takes hold of DeAngelo's shoulder and mutters, "Look, leave it to me for now. You go home to that beautiful wife, fix some things there, get some sleep, and I'll talk to some of the vendors, compliance people, and operators we owe. I have some ideas with payroll and acquisition payments—they can wait, as well as many others. For now, you focus on your home and maybe getting Triangel to do something."

While feeling uncomfortable about Atchinson taking more responsibility, especially after hearing Lenore's remarks, Donnie reluctantly accepts and heads out the door.

"Okay for now, but I want to handle some things at home and then I'll take over and work on all this stuff. Just see what you can do for now and when I get back, I'll relieve you."

Donnie pauses for a moment, then gives Atchinson a long, hard, questioning look.

"Donnie, go! It's no big deal! I can handle it." Atchinson smiles to reassure DeAngelo, all the while gloating over his victory.

★ ★ ★

The DeAngelo home has always been a work in progress. Donnie goes out of his way to build a little castle in suburbia for his beloved family. He loves seeing the kids enjoy the pool and recreation room and Nita takes pride in the décor. They host parties and gatherings to celebrate their friends and colleagues.

But today is not a joyous day at the DeAngelo residence. Donnie's only daughter, Caroline, is about to give birth, but he can't break free from the chains of the company to spend time with her in California, where she lives. His oldest son, Jason, has just acquired an important position in the international division of an import company, but Dad is not in a celebratory mood. Nita's two boys are in college , working towards a better life than the one they knew in Colombia, but Donnie may not have their tuition money.

A somber-faced Nita is near the entrance of their home when Donnie enters. She pauses before speaking, studying the worn look about her husband's face. "Honey, I know you've had a tough day, but we have more problems."

He looks to the side and asks her for the news.

"The sheriff left this for you. And the boys have a problem at school—they won't let them finish if they don't get paid. And we have more shut off notices for the utilities." She gives her warrior husband a forced smile before handing him a credit card. "And this doesn't work anymore. I tried to use it to pay some things and—they say it no work."

"Nita, can you say something nice, first?"

Her eyes are sympathetic and loving as she embraces him, whispering "*Ti adoro mi rey*, I love you my king."

As they embrace, a knock at the door shakes them apart. It's Connie Ryan, Tommy Ryan's widow. Noticeably upset, she takes Donnie's arm. "Donnie, I tried to reach you, but you didn't answer your phone. It's about Lou. They rushed him to the hospital. He's had another seizure! I want to rush over there and I thought you might want to come along."

"Of course. Nita, Honey, stay here, let me go with Connie."

"I don't stay here, I go with you. I'm also worried about Lou."

The hospital is a short distance from the office and Donnie makes it there in half the time without stopping. Connie, Nita, and he glide past everyone, asking for Lou Williams at the admitting desk. Quickly, they are taken to a hallway bed where Lou is laying sideways, his face buried in a pillow. The big man almost dwarfs the hospital gurney and his large hands grip the sidebars. Donnie sees him grimace in pain.

"Lou, Lou, what's going on, big guy?"

Lou forces himself to appear calm, for his close friend's sake. He glances around, sees Connie and Nita, and forces a smile in greeting. "Donnie, it's these fucking headaches! Oh! I'm sorry, ladies!"

"Never mind courtesies, Lou. When did this happen?"

"Last night. I wrestled with it all night, because I didn't want to be a pain in the ass. This morning, I just couldn't walk and passed out. Then, I guess I lost some of the feeling in my hands. After that, I jerked around a little until Reid, our maintenance guy, came by and told me he was calling an ambulance and here I am."

"Well, what have the doctors told you?"

Lou's face continues to contort from the pain in his head. "Donnie, they just give me the same crap. The Veteran's Administration says I just need painkillers and they've put me off for months. Donnie, there's something going on in my head. I went to another doctor—not the VA doctor—the one you paid for. He said I may have a tumor, judging from the tests, and that I may need some very delicate surgery. But Donnie, you've already spent so much on my tests, other doctors, and helping me out. I don't want to bother you with this, anymore."

"Listen, you big jarhead, we're brothers! Brothers don't abandon each other!"

"Yeah, but Donnie, you've done too much already. And even here, they say I have no insurance. So I told them to check with the VA and they say that won't be enough—"

"Never mind, I'll deal with them." Donnie quickly glances over to Nita, who drops her gaze to the floor. He turns back to Lou and lovingly holds his head. "Listen, you just try and relax. Once you get out of here, I'll meet with your doctors and we'll see about that surgery and what we can do to fix you."

"Aww, Doc, you done enough! I'll be okay—it comes and goes. How's the Triangel thing going? We gonna be okay and get rich?" He smiles, forcing back the pain in his head.

Donnie avoids the answer and yells for a doctor. A young resident comes quickly.

"Listen, this man is in pain—can't you give him something?"

"We can't until his tests come back and we know what we're dealing with. He already takes something for his headaches and we don't want a cocktail explosion, if you know what I mean. Also, they need to see you at the desk."

"Lou, I'll be right back, let me see what they want."

DeAngelo makes his way to the desk where they tell him they are concerned about providing care because the VA is unclear about handling this bill and whether or not Lou qualifies for any reimbursement. DeAngelo tells them he will be responsible and hands them the last remaining credit card that he hasn't yet tried. Luckily, it goes through and he returns to Lou.

"Listen, Big Lou, you're the man and you will be okay! Soon they will give you something, and when you get out of here, we'll see about fixing this thing in that big head of yours." He gently taps Lou on the forehead.

"You know Donnie, that damn Napalm they would dump on us over and over again, was just too much. I never had problems until we got hit with that. Same when they tried all that tear gas shit outside LZ Ross and Baldy that spread like locusts till we couldn't breathe. When they assigned me as an explosive specialist, I couldn't deal with the loud bursts that made my head split. Now the doctors talk about Agent Orange and cerebral tumors. I don't know what's going on!"

"Relax, Lou, first things first. Get some painkillers and then let me deal with the doctors. I promise you we'll figure something out. I'll keep watch over what's going on here, but I got some things to do back home and at the office now. I will check in on you, soon. Okay, big guy?"

"Thanks, Donnie." Lou flashes a warm smile for the man he calls his brother. They shake hands, then Connie and Nita embrace Lou, wishing him well.

★ ★ ★

Once back home, Donnie and Nita resume their discussion in the kitchen.

"*Mi amor*, what are we going to do?" She pauses. "I know everything."

Absent of answers, Donnie pauses, looks at his distraught wife and says, "I'll handle it, Honey. Don't worry anymore."

He takes both her hands in his and kisses her on the forehead. He speaks to her gently. "Nita, I've got to go to the study and do some things. Can you give me some time alone and hold any calls, unless it's about Lou?"

"Okay, are you all right?"

"Yes, I'll be fine." He takes a handful of some papers he notices on the kitchen table and turns to go to his study.

DeAngelo's study is off the grand room, the main entertainment room of the large home where so many happier moments had been shared. His study is more like a library, with a collection of hundreds of books amassed over the years, with DeAngelo being an avid reader of literature and philosophy. He collapses in the big armchair behind his desk and sees more of the overdue notices and bills right in front of him. For a few moments, he rummages through them. He finds the bills from Lou's doctor; the one Donnie had hired to help with Lou's problem. The reports show that Lou needs more tests and, most likely, a costly and delicate surgery. He finds mortgage payments from Connie Ryan's home that he promised to pay after she got sick and lost her employment. Then there are his own foreclosure notices and a mountain of additional bills, all screaming for payment.

He tosses them aside and leans back, deep in thought. His lips clench as he stands up and heads toward a portrait of his beloved grandfather, kept for years. He'd adored the old man more than anyone and remembers spending time with him as a young boy, on a trip with his mother to Messina, Sicily.

Behind the portrait is a wall safe that had once stored emergency money, important documents, his KBAR and 45 pistol that he'd smuggled home from Vietnam. Now, the only thing inside are papers and documents and his Marine weapons. DeAngelo rummages through the papers to find life insurance policies from New York Life. He'd increased them over the years, as protection for Nita, the kids and his friends, in the event something should happen to him. He takes them in hand and stumbles to his desk. Once seated, he stares at the cover page and the amount of coverage: THREE MILLION DOLLARS. He smiles at the irony of it all, mumbling to himself, "I'm worth more dead, than alive."

The words echo in his head as he stares at the photo of his grandfather, thinking about a solution to his problems. He quickly flips through the pages, reading about how the money would pass free of taxes or any other debts, directly to his beneficiaries. Searching for a suicide clause, he finds the section marked: INCONTESTABLE CLAUSE. He quickly takes his pen and circles the words: "The incontestable clause in its simplest form provides that this policy is incontestable after two years from date of issue, except for non-payment of premium." He goes online and finds that he'd paid the annual premium ten months before today's date, so no payment is due. He looks at the calendar and sees July 30, then looks at the policy and sees the start date as January, two years earlier. He begins to mumble to himself. "It could work. Nita could keep the house. Lou could have his surgery and have a place to stay with Craig. The kids could finish school. Connie would be okay in her home. There should be enough to solve everything."

He circles the date of premium payment on a receipt attached to the folder and leans back into his chair, as if relieved to find a way out. His momentary euphoria turns to melancholy, as he flashes back to his moments of joy with his family, Nita, and his friends. He would have to leave all that, but in the end, they would be spared the troubles ahead. His mind feels clear and rested for a few moments, pondering this.

He looks to his library for a book he'd once read, entitled

Everybody Dies, by Mathew Scudder, a book that graphically turns a man's world of good things into a dark place, underlining the question of God, life, and the alleys of existence which hold danger in every crevice. Finding it, he lays the book on his desk next to his papers, and then reaches in a drawer for his vintage scotch, kept for special occasions. He pours a good amount, throwing it down without hesitation. He doubles down, does it again, and begins to read Scudder's novel. Before too long, he falls asleep from the spirits of his drink and the exhaustion of his grief.

What seems like a few seconds turn into hours, until Donnie is awakened by Nita, asking him if he is okay. Visibly startled, he jumps upand tells her he is fine. She sees pain and disparity in his face, along with an overwhelming sadness.

"*Mi amor*, it's late! You should go to bed. Tomorrow is another day." She caresses his face and pushes him toward the door, but not before he flips over his papers to cover the book and insurance policies. Nita notices his gestures, but ignores them, ushering him toward their bedroom so he can continue to catch much-needed sleep. As he walks toward the bedroom, she sees that his steps drag, with no essence of purpose.

Morning comes and though the sun is shining, the bedroom drapes are drawn tightly and the room is filled with darkness. Donnie awakens from a deep sleep, knowing the nightmare has not passed and another day of it begins. He turns to Nita—who is sitting up, her eyes moist, her lips trembling, with the look of someone who has not slept, staring into emptiness. The sheet is pulled up tight beneath her chin and she is withdrawn.

Donnie, always attentive to her, asks what is wrong.

"If you want to do it, let's do it together today. I'm not living without you!"

In an instant, he knows she'd gone back to his study. He knows his Nita, a strong Colombian woman who knows death, whose words are not for show. He knows her too well, knows she would sacrifice her own life, rather than be without him. She turns to him with tears in her eyes, speaking not a word, but telling him she is dead serious, that she would give everything to be with him, always. In that moment of conviction, formed of pure love and devotion, he realizes what he'd been contemplating wasn't an option, that it would be a selfish indulgence, leaving no solution to the problem. It hits him that his promise to save a wonderful endangered woman and her children would be for nothing, if he was to take his own life. In that moment, he knows he will fight. He knows there has to be another way to do it. The warrior in him emerges and the survivor in him is restored. Empowered by his wife's courage, love, and her ultimate sacrifice for him, he knows he is also empowered to win.

Holding her close, his words to her are clear and stern. "No, sweetheart! That will not happen. I won't let it happen to you or me! I've already forgotten that idea. We will make it work somehow, together, and we will get through this!"

They hug, never wanting to let go. They sob together and kiss endlessly until, looking at each other, nodding in the affirmative, they make a silent pact: they'll live, come what may.

CHAPTER 13
BROKEN DREAMS

DeAngelo, driven by the previous night's anguished episode with Nita, moves forward with determination to face a new day, in spite of the storms that have befallen him. The office presents a somber atmosphere, as the remaining staff echo a humble good morning to Donnie. Once in his office, he stares at the ominous mounds of paper with red ink piled upon his desk. He calls for Atchinson, who is slow to respond, but eventually makes his entrance.

"Yeah, Donnie?" He grins, acting incredulous of any problems.

"Mitch, what is all this crap? There are payroll notices and tons of other things that you said you were handling."

"Donnie, I can only do so much! There's not enough money in the accounts so I have to lay them on your desk."

"Mitch, I already drained my own personal bank account to meet payroll, and we even sold Nita's jewelry to keep this ship afloat. Did we hear from Goelner or the bank?"

"Oh, yeah, it's on your desk."

DeAngelo rummages through the reams of paper and finds an envelope with the markings of Triangel. He quickly tears it open to find a notice of default and immediate appropriation of assets. He rebounds, shaking the papers and barking at Atchinson. "Are they crazy? They're trying to foreclose on this business, instead of working this out so we can trade again!"

Before he can continue, Atchinson points to another envelope on the desk. Bewildered, DeAngelo grapples with the document and finds formal notice from the SEC for continuing the delisting of their stock and further inquiries.

"This is bullshit, Mitch! We have a good company and have been profitable for twenty years, but we're being run over by Triangel with their fees, bullshit audits and delays. They promised this wouldn't happen! I may be crazy, but I feel like they're working against us, and they want us to fail."

"Well, we have foreclosure notices on the building, as well, so Triangel wants to protect their interest and take over everything—so they can preserve assets for recovery."

"No kidding, Mitch. You're brilliant! Like I don't know that! But, I'm not giving what I—and the rest of us—worked so hard to build."

"Donnie, it gets worse. Andersen and Lou have been sent notices of eviction. They just don't know it, yet."

"They can't do that! There's no way they can move against me this fast."

"Apparently, they can. You're a public company now, Donnie, and they have the power and interests of the shareholders. By the way, Ridgefield and Caputo are on their way here, so maybe you can speak to them about it."

Atchinson implies deceit in his remark, as he looks around the room with no purpose. His eyes are wide and beg questioning.

"Oh, really? And what's their plan? "

"Not sure, Donnie, better they go over their ideas."

"What are you hiding from me, Mitch?" he demands. Mitch blanches, even as his intercom buzzes to life and he's told Ridgefield and Caputo are in the reception area. Donnie glares at Atchinson, before he leaves to bring them in. He returns to his office, wary of the visit and the outcome. Ridgefield and Caputo are serious in demeanor and quickly move to start the process by opening the conversation. They all take seats and Ridgefield opens the dialogue.

"Donnie, as you know, we're faced with the task of protecting the shareholders and the assets of the company. Considering the position you're in, and our position as secured creditors, we think it's in the best interest of the company that we appoint Mitch as acting CEO. Since we have two of the three seats on the board, we feel this is the way to go. You can still be involved, but under Atchinson's direction."

Stunned, DeAngelo turns to Atchinson, who appears confident and defiant.

"Mitch, did you agree to this?"

"Donnie, it's in the best interest of the company! Besides, you see the toll it's taken on you and the employees. At least now I can move more freely and get things done."

DeAngelo jumps from his seat and bellows out his response. "Move more freely? Get things done? That's all I've been doing! No way, I'm not letting this happen!"

Before he can continue his outburst, Ridgefield interrupts him. "Donnie, you don't have a choice! It's already happened. The papers are drawn up and he takes over, as of today. I suggest you work with him on any issues, and if you don't, you can be taken out of the picture entirely."

DeAngelo is silent. He looks around the room at each individual, then tells them, "Well, we'll see about that! I've put everything I have into this including all my personal assets."

Ridgefield interrupts again. "No one told you to do that! You did it yourself to try and make it work—and it didn't work. Sorry Donnie."

The silence in the room lingers, as Donnie gazes at Atchinson, who is now his adversary and a traitor to Donnie's trust and generosity.

"Well, I guess this meeting is over. So, I'd like you all to leave me alone for now."

Ridgefield stands and moves closer to DeAngelo, while Caputo lags slightly behind him.

"Donnie, don't make this difficult. It can get much uglier."

The two men stare at each other and Donnie responds in a low but hardened tone. "Get out! Now!"

Ridgefield smiles and tells his protégé, Caputo, that it's time they leave. Before he exits, he turns to Atchinson. "Mitch, meet me in your office."

Everyone leaves and Donnie sinks into his chair. He reaches into the lower drawer of his desk and extracts a glass and bottle of scotch. He slams both on the desk and begins to pour until the scotch overflows onto his desk. He ignores the spillage and raises the glass to his mouth, but stops for a moment, with a look of disgust. He gently places the glass back on the desk and speaks to himself. "No, I must keep it together. God, give me some strength and wisdom!"

Reluctantly, he grabs his phone and calls Connie Ryan, Andersen and Lou, one at a time, and asks them to meet him at his office.

CHAPTER 14
SHINE A LIGHT

It takes little time for Andersen and Lou to get to Donnie's office, since they live in the building. Andersen moves quickly with his wheelchair to the conference table in DeAngelo's office. He pokes at the chair next to him and motions for Big Lou to grab it. Big Lou displays a look of suffering, grimacing while trying to find a seat to park his big torso.

"Lou, are you all right?" Donnie is visibly concerned.

"It's these damn headaches, Donnie! I swear, I feel like my head is going to pop open!"

Andersen, always the watchful brother, looks intently at Lou. "What's with those fuckin' VA doctors? You've been trying to get some help now, for almost two years."

Lou rubs his temples and closes his eyes, as he answers. "Craig, the VA doesn't give a shit, man! Donnie's been paying these private doctors to do tests and help me and they gave me these pills for this damn pain. I think they're Triptans, or something like that, but the docs say the tests show a tumor and they keep talking about some surgery to remove the shit from my head. This damn pain comes and goes, but right now, it's coming. You know, I figure once we get our money from this new deal that Donnie's got going, I can get it done. All the Napalm, Tear Gas, Agent Orange, and explosives just wrecked my brain! I always knew that shit would fuck us up, but they kept spraying, and using it, and not giving a damn about us. And they don't, now. But, Donnie's got some plans and he'll get it right."

Andersen holds up an envelope and shakes it while speaking. "Speaking of Napalm and Agent Orange, Donnie, did you see this bullshit?"

"What, Craig?" DeAngelo listens, but watches Lou.

"This notice says we no longer have our apartment here and we're evicted. Is this a mistake, or what?"

Lou jumps in. "Evicted? How come I didn't get it?"

Andersen responds, "You got it. I'm holding it. I just didn't let you see it. You got enough to deal with, suffering from those headaches."

The men all look at each other. Then, Donnie speaks up. "Triangel and Goelner want to take over the company because we are not trading."

Andersen squints and barks, "Are you kidding? This company is gold and keeps growing! Besides, they are the ones making this happen."

"Tell me about it! The problem is, our audits are not conclusive because of some acquisitions, and the money Triangel gives us incurs enormous fees we can't pay."

Andersen spins his wheelchair around like a *dreidel* and continues to banter. "Let me get this straight. They pick the auditors and attorneys. They tell us to borrow money to grow. Then they can't get the audit finished and they shove these fuckin' fees down our throats. Fuck 'em! Call Jim, our attorney, and sue the bastards!"

Lou, riddled with pain, seems oblivious to the conversation, but Donnie answers Andersen. "We can't, Craig. We're broke! I'm broke. They stopped funding us weeks ago, and the SEC delisted us and started an inquiry. I've put everything I have into just meeting payroll for the employees—they don't need to suffer because of our dilemma. And I've sold everything I own to pay some of these bills. My house is in foreclosure and Triangel is a secured creditor, first in line to take everything we have, including kicking you and Lou out, so they can get rent."

Lou joins back in, putting aside his focus on the headache. "Donnie, where am I gonna go and what am I gonna do about this surgery? I was counting on something being done! I gave you all my money when we started this thing and I've been helping my mother with what little I have left."

Andersen looks at Lou, then returns his attention to Donnie and speaks. "Donnie, I'm in the same boat—I put whatever I had into this thing and what little I get, I drink and gamble away. That don't make me a good person, but I have my own demons. This doesn't sound right! You built a great business. We gave you a little bit of money, but with that little bit, you built Brickman's Bistros and a huge coffee business, and you always made good by us, taking care of Lou, me, and Connie. We never thought anything like this would happen—it don't make sense! How can they take it over?"

"They can, and they are. Look, Goelner might have an angle with these auditors and his lawyers to make a quick hit on us. He's built up huge fees on money he loaned us, telling us we would never have to pay it, because once we begin trading, they exchange the debentures for our stock and we just keep getting funds to grow. But the auditors he's given me are dragging their feet on completing the audit and always finding something stupid to delay posting it. So, the SEC isn't allowing trading, and if this continues, as it has, it becomes further complicated because the SEC starts poking at it and asking questions."

"This sounds like bullshit to me!" Andersen tosses the envelopes he is holding across the room.

"There's more," DeAngelo begins. "They've appointed Atchinson CEO."

Andersen yells back. "That scumbag! I never liked him, but I stayed out of your way because you run the show! We all knew that one day he would fuck you! I'll take care of him. Just have him work late, tonight."

"Craig, give it a break." Lou looks down in sadness, and then back at Donnie. "It's not your fault, man! These guys on Wall Street are motherfuckers and they always got an angle to win. We gotta figure something out."

Before Donnie can answer, Andersen jumps in. "Listen, Donnie. Do you remember Major Hendriks? He was the Jag Officer for the 7th Marines. He handled some of my shit and we became good friends. I even did him a big favor a couple of times, which is between me and him."

"Yeah, I remember him. Nice guy. He liked you."

Andersen continues. "Yeah, well, Major Hendriks, being the JAG Officer, needed me to fix some things a while back and we've stayed friends. Wanna guess where's he's at now?"

"I have no idea, Craig. What are you getting at?"

"Donnie, he's one of the senior lead counsels at the SEC and he calls the shots. I think I may have to pay him a visit." Andersen smiles, confident that the end is not near.

"Hold on, Craig. Let's not make this bigger than it is. Wait until I get to Goelner and try to work this out."

Andersen continues. "You're running out of time, Donnie! I need to get to Major Hendriks and stop these assholes now."

"Look, Craig, that's a good idea, but let me get to Goelner

first, today or tomorrow. If he doesn't budge, I'll lay out what we will do. I'd still like to see us make this work somehow—there's too much riding on it."

As DeAngelo speaks, he looks over at Lou, who seems distressed, but intent on following the discourse between Andersen and Donnie. Lou hesitates for a moment, but then adds his thoughts. "Craig, let Donnie do what he has to do. He's always been pretty good at looking after us and building this company. I trust him."

Andersen nods and winks. "Okay, Donnie, you talk to Mr. Goelner and if he can't see his way to make us good, then I will make sure Major Hendriks and the SEC put Triangel Brothers Assets, Inc, and Goelner on notice."

Donnie begins to answer as the door opens, and Connie Ryan slowly enters the room. She seems distraught, holding envelopes as did Andersen, asking what's going on. DeAngelo asks her to take a seat and as she does, she asks him about the bills she is holding.

"Donnie, I have these bills—the mortgage is behind—I thought you were taking care of them?"

"Connie, we have a serious problem, and I don't have the funds for anything right now."

She is anxious and nervous as she answers. "But, you know I put everything I had from Tommy's death benefit into this company, and I'm still paying Sonny's tuition loans and my own medical bills. I don't have the money for this! What's going on?" She looks over at Andersen and Big Lou with curious eyes, searching for an answer.

Andersen looks at her sympathetically, then at Lou, and tells her, "Let Donnie explain. It's not pretty, but we have a plan."

DeAngelo remains silent. He looks around the room, at his three closest friends. He focuses on Lou for a few seconds, seeing his fear of a life riddled with pain and, perhaps, death. He sees Andersen hopelessly alone, without legs, committed to a wheelchair for the rest of his life. Finally, he sees the despondent widow of his longtime friend and Marine brother, killed in battle after saving the lives of the three men in the room. The burden of their broken dreams is too much to bear, but he takes a deep breath and begins to repeat the explanation he has given to Andersen and Lou.

CHAPTER 15
FOREWARNING

"Mr. Goelner, please?"
    "Who is calling?"
"Donnie DeAngelo."
"Please hold, Mr. DeAngelo."

DeAngelo turns over an hourglass on his desk and watches as the sand falls slowly to the empty bottom. It is a five-minute timer and all the grains of sand pass through, as he waits for Goelner to join him on the telephone. He contemplates briefly, how Goelner always responded immediately when they were in the early development period of their enterprise. He begins to turn over the hourglass once again, and at the same moment, hears the bold salutation of Goelner.

"DeAngelo! How can I help you?"

There is a brief silence, as Donnie shakes his head.

"By stopping the nonsense—get me audited and funded and let's move forward."

"You're asking for something I can't do, Donnie! I don't control the auditors and you already owe me millions."

"I owe you nothing! The debenture money we actually received is in the company, which is only a few hundred thousand dollars anyway, and the millions you mention are created out of your fees and penalties."

DeAngelo listens as he overhears Goelner barking commands to an employee while displaying a lack of respect for Donnie, on the other end of the phone call. Goelner returns to the conversation. "Look Donnie, I gotta run! There's nothing I can do. Is there anything else you want to tell me?"

"Yes, I'd like to meet with you to resolve this thing."

"There's nothing to resolve and I'm very busy. Is that it?"

"No, not entirely. So here's the deal—if we don't meet, we go to the SEC and blow this whole thing up."

The silence is heavy between them and lasts for a few seconds.

"Blow up what? You're in default! You can't get listed and we are in a take-over to protect our position and the shareholders." This time, Goelner speaks more cautiously.

"Well, let's just say if I were you, I would find a little time."

Goelner takes a moment to reflect upon the possibilities, then answers. "Be here tomorrow morning at 8:00 a.m. and we'll talk."

★ ★ ★

Morning comes none too soon for DeAngelo. At 7:45 a.m., he is patiently seated in the reception area of the opulent Triangel Headquarters. At 7:55 a.m., Goelner storms past DeAngelo and asks him to wait a few minutes. Once inside his office, he calls for Ridgefield, who as of yet, has not come in. Goelner tells his secretary, Marlene, to hold calls and to summon DeAngelo to enter. DeAngelo is sharply dressed in a grey tailored suit and lacks the demeanor of a defeated man. Instead, he walks in boldly, makes eye contact with Goelner, and takes a seat.

"So, DeAngelo, what is it you want to discuss, that we haven't already beat to death?"

"I need you to have the auditors play fair. We are clean and the acquisitions we made are clean. Also, I need you to withdraw your hostile takeover and your exorbitant fees, and install me as CEO so I can remove your lackey, Atchinson." DeAngelo is firm and deliberate in his demands. He never breaks eye contact.

Goelner smiles nervously, as if to hold back complete laughter. "Is that it?"

"Yes."

"Well, forget it! You just wasted your time and mine. Nothing's changing! You screwed up, DeAngelo, and now we're going to protect ourselves."

"I didn't screw up, you did! And if you don't respect my requests, we will go to the SEC and inform them of the compromised position you put us in with the auditors and compliance attorneys, and your relationship with both. We will show the intent of the debentures and the oppressive fees and penalties, plus the situation you placed us in to extract those fees. And there's more, Mr. Triangel!"

Goelner lifts a lower lip as if to absorb the forewarnings, then retorts, "What makes you think they will listen?"

At this moment, with contempt and confidence, DeAngelo responds, "Let's just say we have the right listener and the right spokesman, and I have no doubt there will be an outcome that you will not enjoy."

"Oh, really? Listen, I can't be bothered by idle threats! You have nothing and I have to finish my business, so let's call this a day, okay?"

"Listen, Goelner, I've done everything I can to keep my

guy, Craig, from pouncing on you with a very close military friend in the legal management of the SEC—and I'm not talking about a clerk! Now, I've asked him to hold off so we can work something out, but if you insist on this reckless race to garner the assets of Brickman's Bistros and everyone involved, then I have no choice but to let him do it. I want to make this work for both of us. I can't understand why you seem hell bent on taking us over! It won't help your stock price or create market appeal on the public offering. At least, if you back off we can make it work for both us, " he said this knowing in his mind there was a time that he would have handled a weasel like Goelner differently. He or his wise guy friends would have paid a different visit that would make a lasting impression. Instead he chooses to work in the system, a system that he hoped has integrity but is failing him.

Goelner ruminates greedily on DeAngelo's building which could be worth hundreds of millions, and the upside of the renewed IPO of Brickman's Bistros with ownership by Triangel. At the same time, he wonders about the possibilities of a debacle with the SEC on his association with SEC compliant auditors and attorneys, as well as his framework for debentures and fees.

"Okay, DeAngelo, I will think about it and meet with my executive team and I'll get back to you."

"Don't take too much time, Goelner. I can't promise I can hold back Andersen."

Goelner stands to end the meeting and extends his arm for a handshake. DeAngelo ignores the gesture and leaves.

CHAPTER 16
QUI FACIUNT INIQUITATEM—
THE EVILDOERS

"Where's Ben?" Goelner barks at Melanie, his secretary. She jumps, startled, and then quickly recovers, laying down some documents in front of him.

"He's in the conference room with those new IT people you wanted him to hire," she says, avoiding his eyes. Goelner has a temper that flares only when he is compromised, which doesn't happen often, but when it does, Melanie knows enough to make herself scarce.

"Well, get his ass in here, now!"

The meeting with DeAngelo has left Goelner with a growing uneasiness. As the uneasiness bubbles over into intolerable tension, he finds himself reaching for the Johnnie Walker bottle he keeps close at hand. Downing two fingers' worth, he returns the bottle to its cabinet with its multiple alcoholic companions.

Only a few minutes pass before Ben Ridgefield comes through the door.

"Sit down Ben, and just listen. I just met with our friend,

Donnie DeAngelo, and he's getting to be a pain in the ass!" Goelner finishes the last two fingers of his Scotch, rises, and pours himself another without asking Ridgefield to join him.

"He's got nothing, Wesley!" Ben says, eyeing the booze. "And besides, he's finished. Why do you let the guy aggravate you?"

Goelner starts to pace. "Because his *amigo*, Andersen, has an SEC pawn in his pocket. Some guy who runs their legal is another war hero asshole like Andersen, who was with Andersen in the war. You know what I'm saying? They're asshole buddies or Marine brothers, and DeAngelo says that Andersen is going to turn this whole thing upside down—put us under the microscope if I don't fund him, you know, liquidate our interest. I don't need this shit! We got too much going on! That building can mean hundreds of millions to us, and I need my reserve equity program to remain intact. If these SEC lawyers start looking into this shit, they're liable to charge us with something and we'll lose everything!" Goelner takes another gulp of scotch and makes it back to his over-sized leather chair. He plops himself down, leans back, and glares at Ridgefield—as if this whole mess is his fault.

Ridgefield meets Goelner's glare. After a period, he clears his throat and looks out the window. "Yeah, he knows Hendriks," he admits. "They were Marines together in Vietnam, and I hear that Andersen actually saved the guy's ass in a firefight or something. They meet up every now and then. Hendriks has a soft spot for Andersen, but I don't think—"

"You don't think! Or understand!" Goelner cuts in frantically, slamming down his glass. "Otherwise, you would have told me all this!" He sits there, breathing heavily for a moment, then suddenly becomes calm. His eyes travel up to the ceiling as he says coolly, "You know Andersen's a cripple, no legs and all. In fact, from what I understand, he's almost a street wino hanging around that bar by their building. He can be a sad, mean machine from what I'm told; and he has a big mouth. One day, he's going to piss someone off and get hurt, and that would really devastate his good buddy, DeAngelo. And then there's poor Big Lou and his sick, fucked-up head. If something happens to him or to any of DeAngelo's friends, he wouldn't care about this deal! I think he would forget all about causing trouble and so would Andersen. Wouldn't it be a cruel twist of fate if that happens? I mean, what are the chances of something like that happening so soon?" His last words are softened and hang in the silence of the office, as if dangling by a whisper-thin thread.

"Well, I think fate is full of surprises," says Ben, "and I feel the need to deal with some of these surprises right now." He stands up and looks down at Goelner, who appears unaffected by his remark, still staring at the ceiling.

After a moment, he turns to gaze at the New York City skyline and mutters, "Do whatever you feel you should do."

Ridgefield knows where to go for doers of dirty work. He knows that Tony Caputo, his assistant, keeps a stable of security people who live up to the reputation of wanna-be wiseguys. Two such wannabes are brothers, Joe and Larry Sica, who dabble in the street art and work for a Cantino auto dealer, named Ricky Mancuso. Caputo makes sure Mancuso gets all the auto sales business from the company, and in return, Mancuso loans out some of his part timers for "security work" to Ridgefield.

That afternoon, Caputo meets the Sica brothers at Dino and Harry's, a nice little stop near the place in Hoboken. The joint is crowded as always, and especially so on Friday afternoons. The Wall Street yuppies mingle with the locals in a kind of *Cheers* atmosphere. The music and noise of the crowd drowns out most conversations, and Ridgefield wants nothing better.

As he spots Joe and Larry entering the crowded bar, Caputo scribbles on a napkin and folds it twice. The brothers are in a good mood and not affected by Caputo's brusqueness. They sense a payday coming. Caputo has little taste for the dirty work that goes with his six-figure salary, but as a trusted soldier, he never fails to deliver. After ordering a round of drinks, he gets straight to the point.

"Listen, I got something for you that puts five grand in your pockets within the week. I need you to arrange a disability policy for a friend." He pauses, waiting for their response.

"How much disability coverage will he need?" asks Joe, the older brother and hothead, who likes to be in charge. Larry always lets his big brother take over, even though he is usually a little more level headed than him.

"We need good coverage. He's already a cripple, so it's an easy one. We'd like to make sure he remembers us as doing this favor for him, but we don't need any life insurance right now. Just the disability." Caputo smirks and looks over their shoulders.

"Where and when?" Joe asks.

"There's a bar next to an office-apartment building. Here, take this." Caputo slides the napkin across the bar to Joe. "You can read, right?" He is serious.

Joe nods.

"Don't open it now. Do it tomorrow night. He's known to close the place. His name is Andersen and he's in a wheelchair. You can't miss him. Remember, it's a disability plan he needs, nothing more. Call me after."

Caputo leaves abruptly. The Sica brothers stay for happy hour.

✶ ✶ ✶

Saturday night at Stefanos finds it filled with the usual crowd of college fraternity heroes and a few muscle heads from the docks. Stefanos doesn't advertise five-star service or epicurean delights, but the waitresses are busty and attractive, and the beer is home-brewed. Everyone is welcome and everyone fits in, no matter what they wear or don't wear. The bar and restaurant are owned by Billy Stefano, who inherited the landmark from his father, a former longshoreman. The elder Stefano had retired to his booking practice, which fit in well with his little bar. As the real estate market in Hoboken turned a corner and gentrified, Billy Stefano found himself sitting on a valuable piece of property. Not looking to lose his father's legacy, he'd kept the business alive and tended to sidestep eager real estate agents.

Billy and Andersen are good friends. Billy admires Andersen for his military service and all that he'd endured. After Andersen's wife took flight, Billy began to let Andersen park his wheelchair in his bar, never asking him to pay a tab, although Andersen is known to throw money at the bar when in a paying mood. In Andersen, Billy sees a man burned inside and out, but still fighting to remain relevant.

Before his deployment, Sonny would join the two of them for a long night of who had the better story: Billy about his father's bookie business; Sonny about his Seal training; or Andersen, always about his friends—Donnie and his business, Big Lou and his football days, and Tommy Ryan, the ace pilot who made everyone feel important and died too young. Andersen isn't one for war stories, being more apt to celebrate the comedy and the fuckups. He is loud and sarcastic, but everyone gives him a pass. They know his heart is big, his courage unyielding, and his load, heavy.

Andersen adores Tommy Ryan's son and treats him like his own. The feeling is mutual, as Sonny sees in Craig Andersen the father he never knew and the man he always wants to be, brave and loyal to his friends. As far as Sonny could ever remember, Uncle Craig—the name he calls Andersen—has been good to his mother, and his mother has been good to Uncle Craig. The two share a bond in their love for Tommy, Sonny's father, and the son Tommy has left behind. Tommy Ryan died a hero and Andersen wants to make sure no one forgets that.

That night time drags, so does Andersen. Sonny isn't there to lift his spirits, nor are there happy friends to help detour his sorrows. Only Billy is present, keeping the beer flowing as the hours draw toward closing time.

"Hey, Billy, when are you gonna sell this place and cash in on the big time?" Andersen asks.

Billy just laughs. "Yeah, and where would you be, you and your friends? Where you gonna go?"

"To hell, where we all go!"

As Billy clears away the last glasses, he can hear Andersen feeling the beer and desperation as he hums and sings the Marine Corps Anthem, 'From the halls of Montezuma.' He turns to Billy and yells, "I'm gonna teach those motherfuckers a lesson and get my friends out of this shit!" With that, he bellows his Marine cry, "OOOOH RAH!"

Without much more to say after that, he heads for the door. Fingering the control stick on the electric wheelchair that Donnie insisted he have, he whizzes past Billy and tells him to remember that without friends, life isn't worth living.

"Yeah, yeah, you're right," Billy says. "You be careful. It's late and it's dark out there."

Andersen's apartment is in the building next door and the wheelchair ramp Billy Stefano had installed makes it easy for Andersen to motor out of the bar and up the entry to his apartment. Between the buildings is the alley leading to Donnie's office building. Once inside the building, an elevator would take him right up to his apartment.

It is chilly and once outside, Andersen pauses for a moment, staring up at the building his friends and he had purchased all those years before. Now, he thinks, we're facing losing everything.

It is, in essence, all they have and it means more than a building or business; it is something that says they had *made it.* He looks at the stars and feels the chill, as he zips up Tommy Ryan's old flight jacket. He takes a deep breath and measures the sidewalk as he motors to the alley beside the building.

Then he hears the footsteps. He pauses for a moment. They stop. But when he continues, they start up again. Andersen has always been cavalier about danger.

He yells out, "If you're looking for money, I ain't got shit, so piss off!" He continues to move forward and is just a few feet from the side door of the building that would take him to the elevator and his apartment, when a tall figure wearing gloves, steps in front of him.

"What the fuck do you want?" Andersen looks up, and then feels the presence of another person behind him. He turns around and sees another large man standing erect, not speaking.

"Listen, if you two are looking for a payday, I hate to disappoint you. So fuck off!"

The man standing before him speaks clearly. "Listen Andersen, you and your friends better forget about causing trouble with the SEC or you won't live too long—if you call what you're doing—living." He looks down at Andersen and laughs.

Andersen feels a mixture of anger and apprehension, knowing exactly what is going to happen next. He slowly reaches down for his .45 caliber pistol, kept concealed in the fold of the seat, but before he can finger the trigger and point it, the man behind him, also wearing gloves, grabs Craig's arm and yells: "Don't think about it, old man!" He yanks the .45 from Andersen and holds it up for his brother to see.

"Now listen old man, you're behaving poorly!" With that, Joe, standing in front of Andersen, throws a hard punch straight at his nose. He hits Andersen so hard that the bone cracks and blood shoots out, staining the attacker's clothing.

As Andersen's wheelchair rolls backward, he is pushed forward by Larry, standing behind him. Joe hits him again, with even greater force. Blood splatters everywhere.

As the blood rolls down and into Andersen's mouth, he senses the fate awaiting him. He decides he will not go out any way but on top. He spits a heavy shower of blood into the big tyrant's face, and huskily calls out, "Am I supposed to be scared? You hit like a pussy!"

The big man, infuriated, afraid and confused by Andersen's show of fearlessness, spots Andersen's leg stumps, which are dangling at the edge of the wheelchair. He musters all his strength and kicks at one of them. Andersen screams in agony and reaches for it, but in the same instant, the other man begins to tip the wheelchair. He throws Andersen out, but not before Andersen grabs Joe's leg and hits him savagely in the balls.

Joe wails as Andersen, then able to cling to the thug by his clothing, pulls him to the ground, where he can more easily reach his head.

Through the blood and mucous gathering in his throat, he gurgles, "Now you're my size, asshole!" He then pummels the brute tirelessly, while screaming at the top of his lungs: "OOOHRAH!"

Larry, taken aback by this astonishing turn of events, wildly grabs the pistol and slams it repeatedly against Andersen's head, until he hears his brother sputter, "Stop it, you'll kill him!"

As Joe drags himself erect, seeing the outline of Andersen lying in a pool of blood, his head bashed in by the beating and his wheelchair lying next to him, he feels a dark, ominous feeling. He begins to back away, holding his face with one hand, shoving his brother with the other. Rapidly his pace increases. "Let's get out of here!" he hisses.

His younger brother is fixated on the results achieved by his actions and tells Joe, "Take his wallet and wedding band."

CHAPTER 17
A FINAL FAREWELL

At 6 a.m., Reid Jackson, first shift maintenance worker at DeAngelo's Brickman's Bistros building, pulls his pick-up truck into the back lot. Reid's morning routine never varies. He picks up his morning coffee, donuts, and scratch-off lottery tickets and sits in his company pickup truck, eating and hoping for a big payday. The big payday never comes, but the donuts have left their mark, and Reid's once-athletic frame has gone fat and soft.

Reid is gazing absent-mindedly out the window, thinking about his high school glory days and what could have been if he hadn't blown out his knee, when he notices something unusual on the ground, near the dumpster. It's a little before sunrise and the light is scarce. Reid gets out of his truck and grabs his flashlight. He advances towards what looks like a pile of clothes in a heap, but soon realizes it's a human body, and nearby, an abandoned wheel chair. He trains his flashlight on the form and sees the bloody, beaten, lifeless body of Andersen.

"My God!" he says aloud. "What kind of animal would beat a man in a wheel chair?" He looks further and sees Andersen's Vietnam Vet cap lying near him, bloodstained and trampled.

"A handicapped vet," he mutters to himself. "Animals!"

Reid immediately reaches for his cell phone and dials 911 to report what he has found. "Hoboken Police, Dispatcher Johnson speaking, what is your emergency?" the voice at the other end of the phone says.

"I'm a maintenance worker at Brickman's Bistros. I just arrived at work and found a dead body—a beaten, handicapped war veteran. Horrible," he says.

"Stay at the scene," the dispatcher replies. "A cruiser is on the way."

Reid hits end and then dials his boss. After two rings, Reid hears a voice at the other end of the phone: "DeAngelo here."

"Boss," Reid says, "I'm out back at the office, and I found a dead body in the back near the dumpsters. I called the police and they are on the way. Maybe you should come here, too?" Reid says.

"I'm inside," DeAngelo says. He'd spent another night in his office, falling asleep on his couch after working until 3 a.m. "I'll come out. Any idea who he is?" he asks.

"Don't know him, Sir," Reid replies. "But I do know that he is, or rather was, a handicapped Vietnam Vet."

A cold chill runs down DeAngelo's spine. It takes him a moment to regain his composure. "Does he have a football-shaped scar on his right cheek?" DeAngelo asks.

Reid shines his flashlight on the deceased and looks at his cheek. "Yes," he says. "You think you know this guy, boss?"

There is silence at the other end of the phone, as his boss clicks off.

DeAngelo and the police arrive at the same time, finding Reid standing over the body as the sun starts to come up and illuminate the gory scene. The whole time Donnie is making the run down three flights of stairs and across the parking lot, he is praying that the body isn't going to be that of his old friend, Andersen, but to no avail. Donnie gets a sick feeling in the pit of his stomach as he runs toward his old friend. He is almost there, when a burly police sergeant stops him, keeping him a few feet away from Andersen.

Donnie struggles with the cop. "Let me go!" he screams.

"It's a crime scene," the cop replies. "You gotta stay back!"

Donnie breaks free of the sergeant's grip and runs to his dead friend. Tears fill his eyes as he looks at his broken, battered pal. He kneels beside Andersen.

Two cops grab Donnie. The younger detective, Marcus, says, "You really got to get back and away from the victim. You're contaminating the crime scene."

"The victim," Donnie says, "was like a brother to me. His name is, or rather was, Craig."

"You still gotta get back," he repeats.

The two detectives nearly drag Donnie away from the lifeless Andersen, but not before Donnie notices a subtle, yet compelling detail. Andersen had drawn what looks like a triangle in blood with the forefinger of his left hand. He must have done it as he was dying. It is uneven and the tip of the triangle is where Andersen's finger rests. It is subtle, but Donnie sees it.

It brings back memories of the messages Andersen had left Donnie when they were on recon in Vietnam. Andersen typically took point and left messages for Donnie in the dirt, which Donnie would read and then stomp out. It had been a thing with them, a silent and secret form of communication that had kept Donnie out of harm's way more than once.

Andersen's messages are never words, always pictures. Over the years, they had agreed to certain symbols with meaning only to the two of them—indications of an upcoming booby trap or enemy personnel. Memories rush back to Donnie, as the detectives drag him back.

There is no triangle in the code, but he is sure the bloody drawing is a final message from Andersen. His mind races, trying to interpret the message, but then it hits him all at once. The triangle is similar to the name Triangel of Triangel Brothers. Could Andersen be telling him that the person or persons who caused his death are from Triangel?

A wave of anger washes over Donnie. Clearly, the battle between Ben, Wesley, and him rages on, but up until now, it's been a battle fought mostly by lawyers, in an arena where Donnie is not particularly skilful, and with limited resources. That said, as angry as Donnie had become throughout the process, he'd kept his cool and dealt with Triangel like a gentleman, going through the system and conforming to society's rules.

Sadly, the system is hopelessly broken, favoring the adversary with the biggest checkbook. There is no justice, just endless motions and document requests designed to spend hardworking businessmen, like Donnie, into submission. Triangel realizes that it's only a matter of time and money before Donnie won't be able to pay his lawyers anymore, and he will lose by default.

He learns a bitter lesson. The system he'd risked his life to protect is not there for him. The harsh reality of Haves vs. Have-Nots is drilled home each time another twenty-page legal document arrives, along with an associated legal bill to respond to. Still and all, he refuses to color outside the lines.

Although he has grown to loathe Ben and Wesley, his opinion up until now has been that, while they are selfish, arrogant, and evil men, they are white-collar criminals. They use and pervert the system to feed their greed, but it seems that it's all about money—making it, or stealing it. The casualties and collateral damage they leave in their path are monetary losses, and while painful, monetary losses are not the be all and end all, of life.

This is different—possibly a whole new and much more elevated level of loathsome behavior. If it turns out to be true that Triangel Brothers is behind the death of his friend, everything will change. The battle will escalate and enter a realm, buried by design, where Donnie is far more skilled than Ben and Wesley.

It had seemed, as the legal battle wages between Donnie and Triangel, that Triangel always has the upper hand. It's their world, after all, and they know the rules. But, Donnie hopes, at some point, they'll make the kind of mistake that his lawyers can use to turn the tables and exact justice.

As time goes on though, it appears more and more unlikely that will happen. It isn't about right and wrong, as he'd naively thought—it's about gamesmanship, influence and money. The honest, hardworking and under-capitalized American doesn't have a chance against a well-funded and corrupt adversary, certainly not within this system.

If the symbol drawn by the dying Andersen means what it suggests, according to Donnie's growing suspicions, then Triangel has made a mistake—not what Donnie hopes for, a legal misstep, but the worst kind of mistake Triangel can possibly make. Now the battle will rage in unfamiliar territory, in an arena where the perps of Triangel will be as helpless and compromised, as Donnie has been these last few years. Filled with conflicting emotions—the agony of the loss of his friend, tempered with the thought of what's to come, Donnie dares to imagine bringing Triangel to justice—not society's version of justice—but the biblical kind, far more satisfying. An eye for an eye!

CHAPTER 18
DEVIN'S INQUISITION

Donnie sits on the loading dock and watches the activity surrounding the crime scene. Dazed from the realization of what has happened and probably half in shock, he watches as Detective Marcus strings incident tape from telephone pole to telephone pole, and then back to the building, setting up the investigative perimeter. More police cars arrive on the scene. Homicide detectives, the CSI crew, and the coroner's office make appearances.

Reid Jackson comes and sits beside Donnie, putting a tentative hand on his shoulder. "You all right, boss?" he asks. "Can I get you something—cup of coffee, water?"

"Thanks, I'm fine." Donnie replies, lying to Reid, as well as to himself. "I'm fine. Head into the office, there's nothing more for you to do, here. Thanks for calling me."

Reid stands up. "Okay, boss," he says. "I'll be inside, if you need me."

Reid walks off, leaving Donnie to survey the increasingly busy scene. The various law enforcement officials pour into the area, each going about his or her appointed tasks. "This is just routine business for these people," Donnie thinks. He guesses you'd have to harden yourself to the violence that surrounds this job, or you wouldn't be able to function. It reminds him of the similar mental discipline he'd utilized back in I Corps, in Da Nang, Vietnam, in order to keep sane and alive. He tries to tap into that mind state and separate his logical mind from his feelings, as he watches the activity surrounding his now-deceased friend. It doesn't work. Perhaps he has lost that ability due to age, or perhaps, this is so personal a violation, that separating himself from it is impossible. In his dazed state, it's impossible to tell, and he decides to stop thinking about it before his head explodes.

The crime scene is like a ballet. Each participant is either acting alone or in concert with others to create the tapestry that is a homicide investigation. Each individual seems to be autonomous for a while, until a pattern of hierarchy begins to emerge, and then a team leader becomes apparent. The flurry of activity continues—photographs, measurements, chalk out-lines, bagging samples, etc. The investigators look like ants moving around, clearly in patterns, occasionally bumping into each other. It looks a lot like the ant farm he'd had as a kid. For a brief moment, memories of happier times wash over him.

As he watches the activity, he notices that Detective Marcus takes command. He stands near his unmarked car while the various crime scene investigators appear to be reporting to him. They exchange a few words or hand him a piece of paper, then walk back towards the body.

After getting a handle on the crime scene, Detective Marcus thinks it's time to report to his boss, Captain Emilio Rodriguez, a twenty-five-year veteran of HPD and the go-to officer for major crimes. Rodriguez comes from a family of cops and his younger brother – by two years – Julio, is an NYPD captain, as well. Both captains had been having breakfast with a longtime associate and advisor to law enforcement agencies, Carey Devin, when they heard chatter on the radio about a crime scene investigation, just before receiving a call from Detective Marcus.

"Boss, I think you might want to come down here," Marcus says, interrupting what the elder Rodriquez had hoped would be a relaxing meal with the extremely attractive, and hauntingly sexy, Devin.

Rodriguez considers not responding to Marcus's request—Carey looks so good in her tight, just a little bit too short grey skirt, white silk blouse, and black patent leather spike heeled pumps at the end of her tanned, toned legs.

She looks better than most women half her age and she knows it. Her looks are deceiving. A casual observer would see a confident, sexy woman and for most men, their thoughts would stop there. There's a lot more to Carey, however—she's bright, clever and as deadly as any military operative he'd ever come in contact with. Her reputation always proceeds her, but only for those few privy to that information.

The conversation has just the right amount of flirtatious dialogue to intrigue the normally-composed Rodriguez, but sadly, his sense of duty overrides his pleasure center.

"There's a homicide nearby," Rodriguez says to Devin. "As much as it pains me to interrupt our rare and always pleasurable time together, I have to go." He pauses. "Want to come along?" he asks her.

"You are such a romantic!" Carey says. "Breakfast by the river and a trip to a homicide crime scene! You and your brother are remarkable lotharios. I don't know how I'll manage to maintain my composure. You both really know how to put a girl in the mood. Or, am I being a bit presumptuous?" she says, with a sparkle in her eye that isn't lost on Rodriguez.

"Not presumptuous at all," Rodriguez says, "more like intuitive—what you're known for, I understand."

"That and other things," she says, winking at him.

"All that considered, want to come along?" he asks.

"Sure," Devin replies. "Let's go."

The Rodriguez brothers and Devin arrive at the scene and find Detective Marcus standing by his cruiser while the younger Rodriquez chats with someone from the coroner's office.

"What do we have, sergeant?" Rodriguez asks.

Marcus looks up, sees the captain and then spots Devin. "Looks like some sick fucks decided to mug a cripple. I doubt we need the NSA here," he says sarcastically, looking over at Devin.

"Now, sergeant," Devin says. "Where did you come up with the NSA? I'm just a behavioral consultant, a working stiff just like you."

"I'm sure," Marcus says, and then glances back at the captain. "Nothing much here, Cap. Victim is missing his wallet, keys, and it looks like a ring was forcibly pulled from his ring finger. I think it's pretty clear what went on. A man in a wheel chair seems like easy pickings to the street trash roaming this neighborhood at night. It looks like the old guy put up quite a fight. According to the ME, not all the blood you see on the ground is his. Good for him."

"Do we know who the victim is?" Rodriguez asks.

Before Marcus can answer, Devin says, "I know him."

Both the captain and the sergeant look at Devin with surprise.

"Who is he, and how do you know him?" Rodriguez asks.

"His name is, or rather was, Craig Andersen," Devin says. "He's a war hero, a Vietnam vet, and somewhat of a legend."

"How would you know this guy?" Marcus asks.

"We crossed paths many years ago," Devin says, "when I was doing some 'consulting' in Afghanistan."

"Afghanistan?" Rodriguez asks, "Consulting? You're an interesting woman!"

"Interesting?" Marcus says. "That's one way to describe her."

"Okay, enough of this small talk," Rodriguez says. "It looks like a simple enough case, tragic and appalling, but simple. Do what you have to do and let's get back to the precinct. We have the governor coming tonight, and we need to establish our security protocol. Let the junior guys clean this up. It doesn't need our expertise."

"You think this is a simple robbery?" Devin asks.

"Yeah," the captain and sergeant reply, almost in unison. "Don't you?"

"I'm not so sure," Devin says.

"Of course you're not sure," Marcus says. "You crime busters live in a different world, where everything is suspicious."

"First of all, I'm an ex-spook—if I ever was one at all," Devin says. "Second of all, there are things that don't feel right. I'd like to get a closer look at the crime scene."

"You're wasting your valuable and expensive time," Rodriguez says. "But, feel free."

"Thanks, captain," Devin replies. "Sorry our 'date' took such a wrong turn."

"I'll make it up to you," Rodriguez says.

"Funny, that's what your brother always says," Devin says with a smile, as she turns and walks towards the crime scene and in the direction of Donnie. Carey approaches the body and is cautioned to stay back by one of the CSI investigators.

"It's all right, Vinnie," Marcus yells, "she's sort of one of us."

"I don't want her contaminating the crime scene," Vinnie

shouts back.

"She won't," Marcus retorts. "She's like a ghost. She doesn't even leave footprints, I'm told."

"What's that supposed to mean?" Vinnie yells back.

"Just let her do as she pleases! She won't contaminate anything—will you, Devin?"

"You have my word," Devin answers. Carey circles Andersen's body, stopping to look and even taking a few pictures with her phone. When she finishes, she walks over to both Rodriguez brothers. "What does this look like to you?" she asks him.

"Seems pretty clear," the overworked homicide detective says. "Robbery gone bad – tragic, but unfortunately, not uncommon. You don't agree?" he asks.

"It doesn't feel like that to me," Devin says.

"Don't make this more complicated than it is," the senior Rodriguez says. "I know that you knew the guy, and I understand your interest, but we've got this."

"I'm sure you think you do," Devin continues, "but I'm not sure. Did you know that Donnie DeAngelo and Craig served together in Nam?" she asks.

"No," Rodriguez replies, "how do you know?"

"They have matching tatoos," She smiles confidently. "And how would you know that?" Julio asks. With another fleeting smile she tells him: "Trust me, I know."

"Did you notice the symbol Craig seems to have written in blood?"

"Yes."

"It's nothing."

"You think it was just the twitching of a dying man?" Cary says.

"Yes," Rodriguez replies.

"Well, I don't," Devin says. "I'll tell you what I think. I think something very different than a robbery occurred here. I think the perpetrators made it look like a robbery to make your overworked HPD close the case, quickly. There are no finger-prints anywhere. It's 75 degrees and I doubt common street thugs were wearing gloves. Something just doesn't feel right."

"I think you're reading too much into this," Rodriguez says. "I know you think my team isn't the sharpest, but they're better than you give them credit for."

"Craig was a great guy and I have history with him. This is no way for him to go out—or maybe it is—considering the fight he obviously put up. In any event, I owe it to him to not let this get written off by an overworked police department."

"Look all you want," Rodriguez says. "I know that telling you otherwise would be a waste of breath, but you're not going to find anything."

"I appreciate your viewpoint, Captain, and I will look into this just a little bit to satisfy my own curiosity."

"Fine," Rodriguez says, "just don't impede my investigation."

"Never," Devin says, "I would never impede. Your team won't even know I'm involved. I'm quite adept at being invis-ible. Isn't that true, Julio?" She spins around and flashes a big smile to the younger brother, Captain Julio Rodgriguez, stand-ing next to her and facing his brother.

"So I've heard," he answers and grins.

CHAPTER 19
"TIME TO DELIVER"

DeAngelo, visibly shaken by the spectacle of Andersen's remains, leans against the wall of his building. The police shuffle about, marking the crime scene while pushing away spectators. He glares at the assemblage of characters moving about the murder scene—as if in slow motion, with no sound. His wounded heart pounds with anxiety as he grapples with mourning, anger, and sorrow.

"Craig, you dumb jarhead, why did you have to try so hard? Why didn't you just let it go?" Tears fill DeAngelo's eyes as he stares upward, looking for an answer. He turns away from the scene and peers into the street at the morning traffic streaming by—imagining all those drivers in their cars, oblivious to the recent catastrophe.

"Mr. DeAngelo, may I ask you a few questions?" Suddenly, DeAngelo senses the presence of a stranger holding up a police shield to get his attention.

"Mr. DeAngelo, I'm Carey Devin. I work with the Hoboken Police Department and other agencies as well. I'm sorry for your loss. I believe he was your friend?"

DeAngelo studies the woman in front of him. Poised and

unemotional, she shows some sincere warmth in her eyes. Devin is far from threatening in appearance – attractive, fair complexion, well-dressed in business attire, with a subtle and deliberate voice. For a moment, she reminds DeAngelo of his daughter, but a little older, in her mid-thirties with short brunette hair and a dimpled chin.

"What do you want to know?" he asks, looking past her.

"Who would do this?" she answers, wasting no time.

DeAngelo pauses. He knows his answer, but wrestles with his response, mulling over how to handle this. "I don't know," he answers with displeasure. "Everybody loved him."

"Do you think it was a robbery?"

"I told you, I don't know," DeAngelo answers softly.

"Mr. DeAngelo, I saw you studying what might be an inscription of a triangle in his blood. Did that mean anything to you?" She speaks gently, with compassion.

"No," he answers quickly and looks away.

"Nothing? It would seem to me that he was trying to say something, don't you think? Perhaps a clue or something we can go on?"

"Look, I told you, I don't know anything. Now I need to tell his friends and my wife. Can I leave?" He is speaking quickly and she stares at him, studying his response for a few moments.

"Sure. Here's my card, Mr. DeAngelo. If you think of anything, please call me. I'm truly sorry about what's happened here." She holds out her calling card and he reluctantly accepts it.

DeAngelo turns and walks away. Police Officer Carey Devin watches him with empathy and curiosity as he walks to his building. She looks back to the scene of the murder, then turns back to see that DeAngelo has disappeared. She taps her pen to her cheek knowing there's more to DeAngelo and his story. She grins. She'll find out what it is.

Once inside the building, DeAngelo notices everyone bustling about with stories, but they grow wide-eyed and quiet as he struggles to move past them and avoid questions. He makes it into his office, closes the door and locks it. He gazes at the photos of Andersen, Big Lou, Tommy Ryan and himself on the wall where he has enshrined memories of better days. Tears run down his cheeks as he slams his fist into the large mahogany desk that Andersen gave him when he went public. He grabs a bottle of whiskey to pour a drink and stares at it, before he throws it across the room. Andersen had been the heart and soul of the group. He'd made them all try harder and appreciate what they accomplished because he had so little and only needed their friendship. He was tough and sarcastic, but loving and loyal.

DeAngelo takes a deep breath, pulls out his cell phone and calls Big Lou.

"Lou, it's Donnie. Something bad has happened. Please get over here and call Connie, and get her down here right away. Look, I can't talk now, just come down here with Connie and meet me in my office."

DeAngelo calls Nita and tells her to do the same. She pushes for answers, but he barely has the breath to speak.

They all arrive at the same time. Big Lou and Connie enter first, with Nita joining them, moments later, in his office. DeAngelo asks them to take a seat and remain quiet for a few moments. They are all nervous and inquisitive.

"What's going on? There are police all over." Nita cannot hold back. There is absolute silence in the room.

Then, DeAngelo speaks, holding back his emotions in a stern attempt to control his words. "Craig is dead."

"What?" They all stand and come closer.

"HE WAS MURDERED LAST NIGHT, IN THE ALLEY OUTSIDE OUR BUILDING!" He utters the declaration loudly, with anger, not looking at them, but directly at the wall behind them.

"HOW? WHO?" It is like an echo in his head as they all ask the questions at the same moment. He is not about to give answers, he only wants to share his sadness with the people who love him.

Big Lou comes closer and stands next to him. DeAngelo motions Lou to come even closer. He leans into DeAngelo, who whispers to him, "Please take them outside into the conference room. Just tell them I will explain more to them once I handle a few things. Give them coffee or something, and then come back in here right away. I need to talk to you."

Lou always listens to DeAngelo, his friend since school and in combat. He knows DeAngelo always looks out for him. He trusts him with his life—whatever is going to happen, Lou will always be there for him.

"Please go with Lou. We're all upset. I need a few moments." DeAngelo motions them to follow Lou.

Once Lou leaves DeAngelo's office with Connie and Nita, DeAngelo sits erect on the couch in front of his desk, waiting for Lou's return. His appearance transforms from grief to cold hard indignation. His eyes become narrowed, his breaths deep and slow. This man is a new man – no longer the complacent get-along Donnie.

Lou returns in minutes. He sits next to DeAngelo, quietly studying his close friend who always showed composure and calm, but who now appears transformed into a predator with a mission.

"What goes, Donnie?"

Steely and implacable, DeAngelo looks deep into Lou's eyes. Remaining silent, his appearance grows even more grave and resolute. He turns to look, once again, at the picture of his friends on the wall, and then shifts his glance towards the window and back to Lou. Lou's eyes are glazed from tears, his own pain obvious, waiting to hear what his dearest friend will tell him.

DeAngelo puts his hand on Lou's shoulder, then speaks. "The gloves are off, Lou. We're gonna take out the enemy."

CHAPTER 20
"THE FRIENDS OF ILL REPUTE"

"DOC! DOC! I can't take the pain! Please do something! Help me! Doc!"

DeAngelo, stilled by the voices in his head, hears the cries that echo from years past. He'd been a Marine's Corpsman then and every scream of men suffering in combat called him to their side. The first few times, he'd been hesitant and nervous—his own life hanging by a thread, one skillful bullet or hidden mine and he'd have become just another casualty. But, in time, with the cries growing more frequent, worrying about preserving his own life began to feel meaningless. These were cries of fallen brothers—suffering young heroes fighting for a cause, a country, or their own survival. It didn't matter to him about the reasons why, only that they were there, brave young men reaching past their fears to conquer an enemy who was everywhere—and nowhere. This was an enemy unfettered by the broiling heat, the incessant mosquitoes, the filth and muck of the rice paddies and the stink of death. This was an enemy that would never die, never diminish and always return. There were too many young boys who became men, and then boys again in his arms, as they begged him not to let them die. And all too often, he'd found himself gently closing the eyelids of so many nestled next to him, as their screams turned to placid silence. Each time, it was his failure that he nurtured inside but pushed him to run faster when he heard them yell his moniker, "DOC!"

DeAngelo gazes at one of his favorite photos. In it, Andersen had his arm around Donnie, both were laughing and Andersen still had his legs. For a moment, he puts aside the spectacle of Andersen's murder.

He remembers how Andersen had come to his aid when he'd been pinned down in a firefight just north of Hill 270. DeAngelo had been everywhere during that battle, running from one wounded Marine to another, when suddenly he was encased by crossfire and surrounded by an enemy closing a circle around him. He'd felt a bullet hit him in the leg, and then another one entering the same area, and his side had gone numb. There'd been nothing he could do. He'd returned fire with an M2 Carbine which he had taken from a fallen North Vietnamese officer, preferring the ease and weightlessness of the rifle over the usual M-16 and its semi-automatic action over a quick scatter of ammo. But this was no match for the AK47s that pounded him from all sides. He'd felt helpless, choking on the dirt beneath him as the bullets whizzed past his ears.

He remembers Andersen's voice as clearly in the present moment as on that terrible day back then, yelling to him to "Stay down!" Somehow, Andersen had made his way to him. It had seemed impossible for anyone to come to his aid, surrounded as he was by wounded and dead Marines and fire everywhere. But, somehow, Andersen had crawled and made his way to DeAngelo.

Andersen had been an expert sniper with a talent for finding his target, even in the thick of the bush during an attack.

He never lost his cool and always took his time. One by one, he'd picked off some of the enemy. He'd hurled a few fragmentation grenades into the source of the remaining fire, before he yanked DeAngelo onto his back as he squirmed his way back to the gulley where they could drop away from fire. Once there, Andersen had treated DeAngelo's leg, and then went back to returning fire.

"I thought I was supposed to do that," DeAngelo had muttered the words as Andersen lay on the ground just in front of him, giving fire to the enemy, but seemingly protecting DeAngelo's body at the same time.

"Yeah, right, you dumb fuck! Don't you know when to stay the fuck away from a suicide party?" Andersen had shouted, while giving fire. Then, he'd turned to DeAngelo and smiled, knowing his friend would be okay.

"Listen, they radioed out and got some hueys coming in with those kick ass guns. They're gonna dump some artillery over there, which should scare the shit out of these gooks and they'll drop back. We told them we need some med choppers and with luck, you'll be on one soon, you lucky son of a bitch." Andersen had smiled at DeAngelo and winked.

DeAngelo had been lucky, the medevac really did come. His friend had saved his life, as DeAngelo had done for Andersen, once before. They'd been brothers in combat and in life, but now, only one brother lived.

DeAngelo feels the pain of missing Andersen much more than the pain of the bullet he'd taken that day. This pain would not go away, nor would it heal.

As the thoughts of Andersen fade, DeAngelo sees Big Lou staring at him, wondering if he is all right. They had all been friends for a long time and Big Lou leaves Donnie to his memories and sorrow. Once DeAngelo acknowledges Lou's gaze,

Lou speaks.

"So what are we gonna do?"

DeAngelo remains silent for a moment. Then he looks straight into Lou's eyes.

"Nothing, for now. But, I promise you, you will be the first one to know what's next. In the meantime, I need to contact an old friend for some information." DeAngelo is no longer the pleasant businessman, his voice has become deep and stern. He remains silent again for a few seconds while staring at Lou, then speaks. "*Optima vindictae nota.* Have you ever heard that, Lou?"

Lou is still visibly upset from the loss of his friend but, like DeAngelo, he knows they have to find justice for him. He shakes his head saying no, waiting for Donnie's explanation.

"It's Latin. It means, 'the best revenge is well planned.'" He puts his hand on the big man's shoulder and walks him to the door, opens it and gives Lou his instructions.

"I want you to find Sonny and tell him I want to see him as soon as possible. I'm sure his mother will be looking for him and he'll know. Tell him not to do anything and to see me. You know Sonny, he's no pushover and he has a mean streak when someone calls it out. But, he's not to do anything. You tell him Uncle Donnie must speak with him first. In the meanwhile, you just remain close, Lou. I need you for something very important. But I want to reach an old friend first. And don't worry. We will do what's right for Craig. You'll have your chance, big guy. For now, make sure Connie is all right and make sure she gets home okay. Tell her there's an investigation and we'll know more later, but for now, to wait at home. Then tell Nita to come in here. I need to talk to her."

He pulls Lou close and hugs him. Lou looks at Donnie still holding back tears, and nodding in affirmation and support, turns to leave.

In seconds, Nita is through the door and, though still visibly shaken by the tragedy, she is concerned for Donnie.

"Honey, are you okay?" She places both hands on his face, forcing him to look at her.

"Yeah, I'll be fine." She is taken aback, noticing a different Donnie. He is cold, focused and engaged, as if prepared for battle. This is a Donnie she doesn't know, a Donnie who could kill his enemy to save his Marine brother. This is a man she'd never met, but one who'd existed in the jungles of Vietnam, a long time ago.

"Nita, you remember Alicia, Frankie Cavallo's wife?"

"Well, not really." Nita still had contact with Alicia, but knows Donnie had frowned upon her seeing or speaking with Alicia, ever since the FBI had gotten on his case for his former relationship with Cavallo.

"C'mon, don't give me that. I know you still speak with her. I heard you talking in Spanish with her just the other night. I have bigger fish to fry, but I don't want the FBI or that agent Tobias on my ass. So, if you talk to her, especially in Spanish, maybe meet her for coffee or something, and tell her I need a favor from Frankie, nothing special or big, just some information. Okay?" He smiles for a second, to relax her fears. Reluctantly, she turns away and leaves his office.

CHAPTER 21
DEVIN'S QUEST

Carey Devin is sitting on the back porch of her mountain retreat, enjoying a morning cup of coffee and thinking about
Craig's beating-turned-homicide. She is processing an assort-
ment of thoughts and feelings – for openers, sadness over the
death of Craig, her dear friend and mentor, and discomfort
with the open-shut robbery theory the police are going on.

She wants to conduct her own private investigation into
the matter and wondering if she should share this concern with
her friend, Rodriguez, or "go this one alone," as Craig had often advised her to do. "You never know who you can trust,"
he would tell her, "but you can always trust yourself." She is
leaning towards taking Craig's sage advice once again, thinking
that she owes it to him. After all, she would be dead, if not for
his remarkable, selfless actions in Afghanistan, while working
for a private contractor. But that was Craig, always one to put
himself in harm's way to protect those he loved.

She flashes back to a moment in the trading square, a calm,
sunny day in an ordinary marketplace that wasn't supposed to
turn into a war zone. She'd been casually admiring a scarf displayed by one of the street vendors. She and Craig had been

working a covert mission together, but had taken a mental health day to clear their heads and act like human beings again, not cold-blooded killers, at least for a little while.

Cary, a young operative, working with and learning from Craig and others, was following more of an apprentice learning curve, than a curriculum-based training regimen. Sure, the Army had provided its share of mental and physical training, but that only partially prepared a person for the real—or surreal – world, as Craig called it.

This day, her guard had been down—she'd been just another young woman looking at fabric. Craig, a few feet away, had been deciding on a snack, while watching her out of the corner of his eye. Suddenly, before Carey could react, Craig had rolled his wheelchair in front of her, just in time to take a round in the shoulder—a round meant for Devin! The force of the gunshot had knocked Craig and his chair over, but before the gunman, a fourteen-year-old boy, could get off another shot, Craig had produced a 9mm revolver—seemingly from nowhere—and killed the gun boy with two remarkably accurate bullets to the head.

Carey remembers being so shocked and frozen with fear that she'd stood there and watched what was happening in disbelief. Sure, she'd been trained for this, but the reality had been so much different from the training. Carey will never shake the embarrassing memory of standing there as the scene unfolded, like she was watching a movie, rather than starring in it. Somehow, Craig had managed to right his combat wheelchair—constructed to resemble a rolling mountain bike—get back on it and roll to a position just in front of Carey.

"Back into that alcove!" Craig had yelled – an order Carey had followed, moving in shock. Craig had told her to get down. He'd guarded her until the arrival of ambulances and a few of their more seasoned team members. Apparently, in addition to saving her life, the wounded Craig had also radioed in for assistance.

When help arrived, Craig had turned to Carey and said, "Pretty sad, Devin, to be saved by a cripple. You'd better toughen up if you want to survive out here." And then, he'd promptly passed out from blood loss. It was a memory that would be etched into her mind forever.

Carey had never questioned why Andersen was there in the first place, or what his assignment had been. She'd only known he'd been hired by Dickson and Gray, the armament company contracted to reinforce all the trucks and armored vehicles exposed to missiles aimed at tearing out their underbellies. Andersen had supposedly been there as a support consultant to the young mechanics and engineers. But why would an old Vietnam vet, a double amputee in a wheelchair, be of any value to Dickson and Gray?

Later, she would find out through her own Army Intelligence, that Dickson and Gray was really owned by billionaire patriot Ben Wadsworth, an old Marine commander of Andersen's, son and heir to the Wadsworth fortune. Futhermore, as unofficial army intelligence friends whispered in her ear, Wadsworth had wanted the cowardly Taliban assassins of innocent GIs taken out by a covert unsuspecting expert—none other than former Marine Corps sniper, Sergeant Craig Andersen, Wadsworth's good friend. The respect and affection Wadsworth felt for Andersen was enormous. When several bodies of Taliban insurgents showed up with a few holes in them, no one could understand why—no one except Andersen and Wadsworth. There'd been a story making the rounds that Wadsworth, or Dickson and Gray, had paid handsomely for the short time Andersen had spent in country.

Now, with all the pieces of the puzzle falling into place, Devin realizes Andersen must have used some, or all of the money, to help Donnie DeAngelo start Brickman's Bistros. Andersen, always the friend and never self-serving, had possessed a code of honor, loyalty and patriotism to country and combat brothers, which exceeded his own personal interests.

Carey had taken Craig's words to heart, making a mighty effort to toughen up. Reflecting back on her career accomplishments—a PhD in Criminology, a PhD in Behavioral Psychology, two tours in the Middle East as a Behavioral Specialist for the Army, many off-the-record and unofficial engagements for various branches of the government—she realizes her core motivation had always been to make Craig, her training officer, proud. That she'd succeeded in this had been confirmed during the rare moments when he'd allowed himself to communicate emotion. Carey cherishes those memories, which always serve to inspire her.

Leaving the clandestine service of the government for what she'd hoped would be simpler times, a sort of semi-retirement, she'd offered her services to law enforcement agencies. Her uncanny talent for finding the proverbial path through the trees on complex cases—usually involving clever and particularly skilful sociopaths – had rendered her a valuable, and very welcome addition to personnel in these places.

As such, she'd worked for HPD and Captain Rodriguez, in particular, most notably helping to apprehend the duct tape killer, a twisted psychopath who'd posed as a professor at the engineering school. DTK, as he came to be called, had kidnapped and raped three coeds before being captured. He would attack at night, raping them, and then duct taping their naked bodies to trees, to be found by passing students in the morning. Carey, posing as a student, had lured him in and slit his throat before he'd had a chance to chloroform her like the others.

She remembers Rodriguez's face, when arriving on the scene, he'd found her standing over the dead DTK. "Did you have to kill him?" he'd asked.

"Someone had to," she'd replied, as calmly as someone ordering a latte at Starbucks.

Devin decides to conduct her own quiet investigation into the murder. She does some digging to find out Andersen's home address. She is surprised at how nice the apartment building is and wonders how Craig, who'd never earned much and spent what he earned "living each day as it's my last," as he used to say, could afford to live there.

She finds out the building is owned by Donnie DeAngelo and she decides to meet him, to see if he can shed any light on the crime against Craig. Devin shows up at DeAngelo's building, which is beautiful and opulent. Marble floors lead the way to elevators constructed from polished walnut wood and beautiful bronze hardware. The elegant doors flank a well-landscaped courtyard, which features, at its center, a huge, glistening fountain.

Italian music plays quietly in the lobby, as Devin checks the electronic building registry for the location of the Brickman's Bistros' corporate office. Finding it, she takes the elevator to the third floor and exits there, facing two large glass doors labeled in gold leaf with the words "Brickman's Bistros." Entering, she approaches a mahogany reception desk. There, a young and pretty receptionist with a headset on, turns away from her computer, flashes Devin a charming smile and says, "Welcome to Brickman's Bistros. I'm Jennifer. How can I help you today?"

"I'd like to see Donnie DeAngelo," Devin says.

"Do you have an appointment with Mr. DeAngelo?" Jennifer asks, cheerfully.

"Sorry, I don't," Devin replies. "Please give him this card and ask him if he can spare a few moments for me?" Devin continues, handing her card to Jennifer. It reads "Carey Devin—Criminology Consultant." On the back, she has written "Regarding Craig Andersen," in perfect script.

"Mr. DeAngelo is very busy and doesn't usually see anyone without an appointment. But I'll try," she says, walking off through a door into what looks like back corporate offices. In a few moments, Jennifer returns. "Mr. DeAngelo says that he will be happy to see you," she says, with the same warm smile displayed since Carey's arrival. "Follow me." Jennifer leads Devin through some doors, down a long hallway, and into a bright, corner office with windows on two sides that look out at the fountain-graced courtyard.

Donnie comes out from behind his desk, puts out his hand and says, "Ms. Devin, glad to see you again."

Carey takes his hand and they exchange a firm, warm handshake. Donnie is clearly a charming man—well-groomed and coiffed, sporting a stylish haircut, an expensive, tailored suit, expensive but tasteful jewelry—appearing every bit the vision of a successful CEO.

"How can I help you?" Donnie asks.

"I am looking into the sad and untimely death of Craig Andersen," she says.

"Is this an official police investigation?" Donnie asks. "Because I've already been interviewed by a Detective Flores and a Captain Rodriguez."

"Not official," Devin says. "Craig was a friend. I'm looking into this on my own time."

"Understood," Donnie says. "What would you like to know?"

"I see that Craig lives—or rather, lived—in an apartment

owned by you. Was he an employee?"

"No," Donnie says. "He was a dear friend. We served together in Vietnam, back in the 70s. Craig saved my life, more than once." The words resonate heavily with Devin. "Giving Craig the apartment was my way of saying thanks."

"Do you have any thoughts on what happened, other than the surprise and grief that I imagine you are feeling?" she asks.

She notices that Donnie thinks carefully about his response. "The police describe it as a robbery gone bad. I guess they are probably right. Craig wasn't the kind to give up without a fight. Sadly, it seems that he fought his final battle. I'm sad that it was in the streets behind a dumpster, but Rodriguez told me Craig must have put up quite a fight and injured at least one of his attackers."

"Yes," Devin says. "That's what I heard."

"I don't have any thoughts beyond what the police think." Donnie's demeanor darkens and his voice takes on a hard edge. "I think Craig was the victim of a senseless robbery perpetrated by cowards who prey on the weak and handicapped—the worst kind of scum. They underestimated Craig's resolve and sadly, it got him killed. But at least he died fighting. He would have wanted to go out that way. I hope the police find the lowlifes who did this and crucify them." Donnie takes a moment to compose himself before continuing. "What are your thoughts, Ms. Devin?" he asks.

"I feel the same as you." Devin lies, as Donnie has. "I think the police are on the right track, a robbery gone bad. I just want to make sure they get the trash that did this."

"Me too," Donnie says. "Would you be kind enough to keep me posted on your progress, if any—unofficially?" he asks.

"Sure," Devin says. "Thanks for your time and honesty. Can I call you if I think of other questions?"

"Absolutely, any time," Donnie says.

She shakes his hand warmly and starts to leave, but turns back. "Do you think I could have a look around Craig's apartment?" she asks Donnie.

"It's okay with me," Donnie says. "The building manager's name is Carl. I'll let him know that you might come by and tell him to grant you access."

"Thanks," Devin says, leaving.

Both she and Donnie feel that the other is hiding something, but it's clear that there will not be any more information sharing at this juncture.

Devin heads back to her home office. She decides to put this aside for a while and do some work for paying clients. She opens a state police file she's working on, involving the brutal murder of three seemingly unrelated businessmen, who were all killed in exactly the same fashion. But she cannot concentrate.

She closes the file and decides to head over to Craig's building, snoop around, and see what his neighbors might know. She gets in her sensible car, the blue Volvo, and heads over to Craig's old apartment. She only drives her Corvette when not conducting business. She parks in a visitor's spot, enters the nicely appointed marble lobby and looks for the building manager's office. She cannot help but notice that Donnie seems to have a penchant for opulent marble entranceways—not a bad thing.

She finds the manager's office and knocks on the door. Carl answers. He's a nice looking guy, in his early thirties. He has the build of a Marine and she glimpses the outline of a USMC tattoo through his white tee-shirt sleeve.

"Ms. Devin, I presume," Carl says, before Devin can introduce herself.

"Yes."

"Mr. DeAngelo said you'd be by," Carl says.

"How did you know it was me?"

"Mr. DeAngelo described you—quite well, I might add."

"I hope that's a good thing?" Devin asks, with a sexy twinkle in her eye.

"Indeed it is, ma'am," Carl replies. "How can I be of service?"

"First of all, you can stop calling me 'ma'am.' I'm Devin." Still smiling, she asks him, "Can you show me Craig's room?"

"Sure ma—I mean, Devin."

Devin follows Carl down the hall to Craig's old room.

"Craig was somewhat of a legend around here," Carl says. "The other tenants loved him. Many of them either knew him, or knew of him."

"Are most of the tenants here retired military personnel?" Devin asks.

"All of us, Devin. Mr. DeAngelo bought this place to take care of some of his old friends who didn't do as well as he did, financially."

"Really?" Devin says. "Mr. DeAngelo is quite a guy."

"Yes, he is, Devin."

They get to the door of Craig's apartment. Carl unlocks it, while asking if he should stay.

"Not necessary," Devin says. "Thanks for letting me in. One question, before you go. Anyone in this building have a beef with Craig?"

"Not a chance," Carl replies. "We're all family here. If any of us had been around when this attack occurred, the police wouldn't have needed to send detectives—just the coroner."

"Understood," Devin says. "Thanks for your help. I hope we see each other again."

"Probably at the funeral," Carl says. "Just close the door when you leave. It will lock itself."

He walks off, leaving Devin alone in the apartment. She feels uncomfortable, walking around Craig's apartment. She feels as if she is invading his space. She isn't even sure what she is looking for, but feels the need to look around and see if something catches her attention.

The apartment is nicely furnished and rather neat. She walks through the kitchen. There are no dishes in the sink, but items in the refrigerator need attention—there would be some science projects here, if it isn't emptied soon.

The bathroom is also neat, with many shelves filled with medical supplies Craig used for his various health conditions. She makes a mental note to have someone donate them to the Veteran's Administration. That's what Craig would have wanted, she's sure.

Nothing unusual in the neat bedroom, not even a book on the nightstand.

The last room is a small office. There is a basket on the desk with unpaid bills and a manila folder labeled "Triangel." Devin picks it up and opens it—an inch thick, crammed with papers. She begins to look through them, when something catches her eye. There's a post-it note on what looks like a transcription of texts between Craig, and Ben Ridgefield from Triangel. On the post-it, Craig had scrawled, "They're getting pissed." in red. Interesting she thinks. Devin looks around some more and then leaves the apartment, taking the Triangel folder with her. On the way out, she passes Carl in the hall.

"All done," she says. "What is going to happen to Craig's stuff?" she asks.

"Mr. DeAngelo says he's got that covered. Do you need anything else?" he asks.

"No. Thanks for your help, Carl. See you around."

She leaves the apartment. Carl never questions the folder

she is carrying and she doesn't offer any explanations. Devin returns home, pours the fourth cup of coffee of the day, slips off her shoes and sits on her couch, preparing to peruse the Triangel folder, She ponders on the depth of this pit and the animals preying on each other.

CHAPTER 22
WELCOME HOME

Donnie is watching late night TV in his basement man cave, while his wife, Nita, sleeps upstairs. Donnie doesn't sleep much these days. He goes to bed with Nita and holds her until she falls asleep. He lays there for a while, listening to her breathe and wondering how he is going to put their life back together again. He cuddles next to her, trying to sleep, but jolts of anxiety-driven adrenaline keep him wide-eyed and awake. He slips out of bed, careful not to wake his wife, and heads downstairs, hoping to fall asleep in front of the TV. This goes on almost every night, a new and exhausting routine.

He is drifting off to sleep, his eyes half closed, when he feels the presence of someone behind him. His first thought is that it's Nita, coming down to check on him as she sometimes does But the footsteps are much heavier and when that knowledge resonates, his military training kicks in and he is instantly awake. He spins around as he stands, ready for a fight, but is surprised to see Sonny standing there, dirty, badly in need of a shave, and carrying his duffle bag.

"Sonny!" Donnie exclaims, opening his arms.

Sonny drops his duffle and gives Donnie a big hug. "Sorry

if I scared you," he says. "You know, you gave me a key. I was going to crash down here and surprise you in the morning."

Donnie lets go of Sonny and stands there looking at him, shocked. "It's great to see you, Sonny, and you know you're welcome here anytime, but I don't remember ever giving you a key."

Sonny grins and shrugs his shoulders, as if no answer is required.

Donnie knows the answer and changes the topic. "So how's Afghanistan? Any Taliban left?" He relaxes, feeling the good energy of Sonny, then continues, "I guess you got Lou's message?"

"Yeah, and I was slated to be back next month, but my team leader got me a special leave. I'm a short-timer, anyway." Sonny stares intently at Donnie. "Uncle Lou knows my team's commanding officer and made sure I got the message. How did this happen?"

For the next hour, Donnie tells Sonny what he knows. He explains what has happened with Goelner and Triangel, how he believes one of Goelner's henchmen had sent someone to scare Craig away from looking into their less than righteous activities. He tells Sonny about Ridgefield, confiding his belief that Ridgefield takes care of the rough stuff when that kind of persuasion is needed.

"Are the police involved?" Sonny asks.

"They are," Donnie says. "There's a detective named Rodriguez from Homicide, who is heading up the investigation. He seems to be a solid guy."

"So you're content to leave this with the police?" Sonny asks.

"Don't know, I'm working on it." Donnie dismisses the question, looking Sonny up and down.

Sonny paces, while Donnie looks him over and then, with jaw clenched, Donnie speaks. "Guys like Goelner and

Ridgefield, they have fancy lawyers and strong political connections way above Rodriguez's pay grade. My guess is that even if the police connect the dots, Goelner and Ridgefield skate with a slap on the wrist and some low level grunts take the fall—maybe in exchange for a payday. That's what bothers me, Sonny. I've always been a 'by the book' kind of guy. Went to Nam. Served my country. Tried to protect the same 'system,' which seems to be failing me now."

Sonny puts a hand on his shoulder and stares intently at Donnie. "Maybe the system won't fail you this time, at least where Uncle Craig is concerned."

"What's that treacherous mind up to?" Donnie smiles, knowing Sonny, and continues, "I was naïve about the system. It is broken and corrupt."

He turns away from Sonny and rambles on a bit. He explains what is happening to his business as a result of the corrupt Triangel situation. He explains how plugged in Triangel seems to be, legally, and how the system he'd fought to protect isn't there to protect him. "Now Craig is dead and I don't think the guys responsible will ever really be punished by the system. I'm starting to think that maybe I need to go outside of the system to make this right. That's where you come in—to some extent."

For a few moments, the men stand silently facing each other. Then Sonny's eyes narrow into a squint and he forces a grin. "As far as Uncle Craig's untimely and senseless death is concerned, the system won't fail you."

"I know, Sonny. I have a plan and I need you. I'll take care of Goelner and Triangel. I need you to take care of the two stooges, Ridgefield and Caputo. Meet with Lou, so the two of you can work it out. He has some information from my friend, Frankie Cavallo, and that's all you need. But, this is a big chance you're taking—and you could go down."

Sonny's smile widens as he leans in closer to Donnie. "You forget who I am and what I do for a living. I remove 'bad' people and leave no trace. I'm good at what I do. Some say I'm the best! I will get whoever killed Uncle Craig and take that person out. They'll never see me coming and no one will ever know I was there."

Donnie is silent for a while. Eventually, he speaks. "Maybe it's time for a lot of things to be put right, but you run everything by me first and we synchronize—just like on a mission. Only this mission is for us, not anyone else. You understand?"

Sonny nods. "You've always been like a second father to me, Uncle Donnie. Uncle Craig loved and admired you, and I know you felt the same about him. I saw the way you looked after him. If you need or want my help to bring justice to this situation, I'll stand with you. First, let me do what I need to do, and then we can turn our attention to Triangel for whatever you have planned. I gotta do something for Uncle Craig—it's eating at me like a disease. I know what has to be done."

Donnie looks around, fearing Nita might enter. Once he's sure they are alone, he continues, "I need you for the next couple of days. I have something all worked out and you, Lou, and I will be on the same page. You have to trust me and you will have your revenge."

Sonny nods and answers, "Okay if I crash here for a few days?"

Donnie smiles, nods, and holds his hands up. "You know, you don't need to ask. The guest room is made up and ready for you—always."

"Thanks, Uncle Donnie."

"I'm going to grab a shower and go to sleep. I suggest you do the same. I guess we have a lot of work ahead of us."

The two men embrace and Sonny heads off to the guest

room, thinking along the way what a beautiful house this is and what a shame it would be if Donnie lost it. He doesn't know if he can prevent that, but he knows for sure that if it happens, the people responsible will not live to savor their malicious victory. He thinks about how many lives Donnie has touched, how many people who'd served with him became beneficiaries of his kindness and generosity. Perhaps, Sonny thinks, he should call some of these people and alert them to Donnie's struggle. Forget perhaps—he resolves he will do that, for sure.

His thoughts turn back to his beloved Uncle Craig. Years of clandestine service to his country's dark side has made Sonny a lethal force when fueled purely by orders from above. He wonders what kind of a force he will be when fueled by emotion and a lust for revenge. It frightens him a little, but he embraces his feelings.

After a quick shower, Sonny heads off to bed for some much needed sleep. Eyes closed, he focuses on the support and love Uncle Craig provided throughout his military career and after that, when he worked as a government contractor. Sonny recalls the comfort Uncle Craig's letters brought to him, the sage advice his uncle shared at critical junctures in his life. The man or men, responsible for Uncle Craig's death will pay dearly for what they did! He will think this through and make the punishment fit the crime. This is his last thought, as sleep overwhelms him.

Donnie decides to go back upstairs and try to rest, although his mind is racing from the conversation with Sonny. He puts a note on Nita's nightstand, in case she wakes before him. He wants to let her know Sonny is downstairs, so she won't be startled upon finding him. Watching her sleep, he experiences emotions he hasn't felt in years—those long forgotten feelings of resolve that surface in certain men, after identifying the correct path leading towards a just end.

His mind is back where it was when he was a young Marine, full of passion and purpose, anxious to fight the good fight. In those days, he'd felt that an undefined force referred to as the enemy was endangering his country and he was willing to do whatever was necessary to eliminate that danger. Now, years later, an enemy in a clear form—Triangel—is endangering *his family*. If he'd been a force to be reckoned with in the jungles of Vietnam, now he is far more formidable. This is an attack on his blood! A vicious and devastating response is indicated and justified.

He knows what he has to do. He feels better than he has in years. In the morning, he will begin to execute his plan with focus, intensity, motivation, and a honed skill-set ready, at last, for use. For the first time in many months, the road ahead seems clear. Thoughts rush through his head, concluding in a satisfying decision, a feeling of well-being and finally, a deep and much needed sleep washes over him.

CHAPTER 23
CANDID CAMERA

Two days pass since the meeting with Sonny and Donnie at Donnie's home. It's a dismal dark night at Buddy's Cabins in West Orange, NJ. Sonny slips inside cabin 14, unheard, just as Ben grabs Irina's long, thick blonde hair and slams his cock into her from behind. Irina's wrists are tied to the headboard. She is naked, except for her black patent leather high-heeled pumps. Her body is toned, tanned and oh, so sexy. It's clear—from the look of pure ecstasy on Irina's face—that this isn't an assault, but adrenaline filled sexual role-play.

Both Ben and Irina glisten with sweat, as he pounds her again and again. "Take that, you Russian whore!" Ben hollers. "What would Victor think if he saw you now?"

Sonny starts the video camera. Both the sounds and images are captured with great clarity.

When he has enough, Sonny shuts the door loudly, startling both Ben and Irina. Ben whirls around, his cock disengaging from Irina. "What the fuck?" he yells, as he sees a smiling Sonny shooting the escapade like a porn director.

Ben lunges at Sonny, scrambling off the bed and grabbing for the camera. At 6' 3" and 250 pounds, with an overabundance of body hair, Ben resembles an angry bear coming toward Sonny. In his early football days, Ben was a formidable opponent, but the years of alcohol and overeating haven't been kind to him. He's fat and out of shape.

Sonny is twenty years younger than Ben and fresh from combat training. His six foot, 180-pound body is all muscle, and it performs like a well-oiled machine. To him, Ben is moving in slow motion. As he reaches for the camera, Sonny hits him with a sharp and powerful jab that breaks his nose and unleashes a torrent of blood from both nostrils.

Ben grabs his smashed nose and grimaces at the pain. The blood flowing onto his hands enrages him, and he lunges at Sonny again. This time, Sonny side-steps and then sweeps Ben's ankles. Ben falls hard to the floor.

In an instant, Sonny is on him, securing his hands behind his back with nylon ties. Ben struggles like a beached whale, but Sonny puts a knee to the man's neck and quiets him.

"Do you know who I am?" Sonny asks.

The stunned Ben mumbles a weak, "No."

"I am Tommy Ryan's son."

Ben's head starts to clear, as he realizes with whom he's dealing.

"Remember when my mom came to your office and asked nicely for the return of the money she gave Donnie that you scammed from Donnie?" Sonny asks. "Do you recall what you did? You brought in your attorney, formerly with the SEC, and told her that we were out of our league. You both dismissed my mother with contempt and disprecpect and no one treats my mother that way!"

Sonny flashes back to the letter he received from his mother. His mother sounded more dejected than he'd thought possible. "Mom," he had told her, "I can't let this son of a bitch take your death benefit from Dad. I know how to deal with men like this. He won't be so smug with a few broken ribs and a crushed finger or two! Lawyers aren't the only way to settle disputes."

His mother had forbidden it, though. "That's not how we do things," she'd said. "Your uncles and I made a mistake and now we're paying for it. We got a little greedy. I wanted a better life for you. I should have left well enough alone."

"That doesn't give this piece of dirt the right to swindle you!"

"I know, but I don't want you to handle this your way. I'll figure out something and be okay. Your uncles and I will get by."

Sonny had abided by his mother's wishes. He'd always looked up to his uncles and to her. She was the wife of a decorated Vietnam War vet who had died, but who'd been awarded a Silver Star, a Purple Heart and many other medals. God only knew the kind of tragedy and suffering she bore, and yet, remained a peaceful and loving mother. Sonny didn't quite understand her altruism, but he admired her and stood down, as he'd been asked to do.

Things had changed a little, months later, after his mother's minor breakdown, brought on, Sonny would always believe, by the stress of what Triangel had done to her. Dragging herself through each day, she'd said to Sonny, "Son, things are different now. We'll have to struggle a little harder to get by." Those were the words she'd spoken to him, as she lost the death benefits bequeathed by her husband. Sonny pushed the thoughts back down and returned to reality.

"At this moment, Ben, I believe I can say the same thing to you that you once said to my mother and me: 'You are way out of your league.' So I suggest that you lie there and listen to what I have to say. I don't need to hurt you more than I have already, but I will enjoy making you suffer, if you continue to fight me."

Sonny turns and glances at Irina, stilled tied to the headboard, but watching and listening. After a few moments of silence and being stared at she finally speaks: "Does someone want to untie me?"

Both Ben and Sonny ignore her.

"What do you want?" Ben growls.

"It's quite simple," Sonny replies. "I wish to trade you this video camera for the money you stole from my parents. I'm guessing you wouldn't want its contents seen by your lovely wife, or by Irina's husband, Victor."

Both Ben and Irina are silent.

Sonny places nylon ties on Ben's ankles and then releases the pressure on his neck. "Don't do anything stupid, Ben," Sonny says. "Just lie there and listen."

Sonny unties her while nursing a smile, and then covers her with a sheet.

Sonny takes a laptop from his backpack and sets it up. Once it acquires an internet connection, he produces a paper with a bank routing number and account number. "I'm going to untie your hands, Ben. All you need to do is wire the money you scammed to my mom's account. I'll leave quietly, and you can have the camera."

"How am I going to explain the wire to my partners?" Ben asks.

"Return of investment capital. I know they'll be shocked at the idea of your having an attack of conscience! But it happens, even to scum like you. Do we have a deal?"

Ben hesitates.

"Give him the money, you idiot," Irina says. "You need to make this go away, for both our sakes."

"Okay, untie me and let's get this done."

Sonny frees Ben's hands and gives him the laptop. Ben types for a while . "It's done, you prick! Now fully untie me and give us the camera."

"Just a moment," Sonny says. "I need to check that the transfer was made. I don't trust you further than I can throw you, and that isn't very far."

Ben glares. "At another time and place, this would end very differently."

"I'm sure that's true," Sonny replies. "But we're here and now. And believe me, you don't want to see me again."

Sonny takes the laptop and confirms that the transfer has been made. As promised, he cuts Ben free and hands him the video camera.

Ben places the camera on the floor, puts on his shoes and stomps on it repeatedly, until it's destroyed. When he's done, Ben looks at Sonny.

"I know what you're thinking," Sonny says. "Maybe I can take him, now that I'm not caught by surprise. Would you like to give it a try?"

Ben and Irina remain where they are.

"Good decision. As you were." Sonny laughs, as he backs toward the door.

"Wait!" Irina says. "How do we know that you aren't going to tell anyone about this?"

"First of all, unlike your lover, Ben, here, I'm a man of honor and my word is good. Second, I wouldn't tell Ben's wife because I imagine she's a sweet woman who's already suffering for making the mistake of marrying this scumbag. I don't need to add more misery to her life. As far as your husband is concerned, Victor is a very dangerous man. I wouldn't make the mistake of telling him something like this without ironclad proof—which I no longer have."

"You know my husband?" Irina asks.

"I do," Sonny says.

"My husband is a pig and an idiot!" Irina shouts.

"I think you would be better off keeping those thoughts to yourself." Sonny backs the rest of the way to the door and opens it, about to leave.

"How did you find us?" Ben blurts out.

"Oh, your boss, Goelner, filled me in," Sonny lies. "Apparently he's a little upset with you, since you tried to throw him under the bus with the FBI."

"I never spoke to the FBI about Wesley!"

"Really?" Sonny says. "I thought you had. Perhaps you can catch him before his deposition tomorrow."

Sonny leaves, closing the door behind him. He slips into the woods, retraces his steps, gets into his Land Rover, and starts the engine.

Sony drives the nine miles back to his hotel room, removes his jacket, and unhooks the button cam and mike from his shirt. He starts up his laptop and plugs one end of the cable into the spy cam and the other into his computer. The spy cam software fires up and he watches the footage he'd taped earlier. It's better than the footage on the camera he'd surrendered—because it includes Irina calling Victor "a pig and an idiot." He emails a copy of the video to himself, just to be on the safe side.

Sonny puts the laptop into his backpack, and walks to his local restaurant to celebrate the successful first part of his mission with dinner and a cold beer. Tomorrow, he'll visit his mom and give her the good news. That will be a moment to savor!

Tough as he is, Sonny's parents mean the world to him. He is sad that his dad isn't here to witness this, but it fills him with pride—knowing he can give his mom her security back and fulfill his dad's last dying wish. Sonny credits his mother and uncles for their unconditional love and support, enabling him to become the man he is. Now, he's returning the favor, and it pleases him greatly.

After he visits his mom, he'll take a trip to Brooklyn to his old neighborhood, now nicknamed Little Odessa. He has a lunch date with his old friend, Victor Zalenko.

CHAPTER 24
CAUTIONARY TALE

After Sonny leaves, Ben and Irina sit on the bed staring at each other. It's awkward—both of them are naked, but missing the sexual tension they'd enjoyed before Sonny's visit shattered their fantasy world.

Irina finally breaks the silence. "We've got a big problem," she says, getting up, shedding the sheet she had wrapped herself in when Sonny burst in, and starting to dress. "If this son-of-a-bitch, Sonny, is lying to us and decides to talk to Victor and Victor believes him—we're dead."

Ben also begins to dress. "I don't think Sonny will have the balls to approach your husband. And even if he does, there's no evidence. I just bought the evidence! It cost me $100,000 dollars, remember? It was only ten minutes ago! Also, Sonny gave us his word that it ended with my returning the money and, to people like Sonny, giving your word means something."

"Unlike when you give your word," Irina says.

Ridgefield ignores her. "Anyway, if Sonny breaks his word and tells Victor without any evidence to back up his story, chances are Victor will throw him out after a beating – or perhaps, kill him. He is, as you've described him, a vicious and possessive man."

"What if Sonny made a copy of the tape?" Irina asks.

"Don't be an idiot!" Ridgefield says. "I destroyed the tape and the camera. There can't be any copies. I'm even going to throw the remains of the camera in the furnace at work, just to be sure nothing can ever be retrieved from it."

"I'm just not so sure it's over," Irina says. "Sonny's a soldier, and he has a mission. He's nothing like you and your pal, Goelner—with your country club phony sense of toughness. He doesn't hide behind lawyers and courts. He'll do whatever he feels is necessary to avenge what you did to his mother! Our getting hurt along the way will be of no concern to him. You stole from his mother, for Christ's sake! You might as well have walked into a lion's den and kicked one of the mother's cubs! When you screw with enough people, sooner or later, you're bound to encounter someone like Sonny."

Irina is almost dressed. She sits back on the edge of the bed and pulls on her nylons. "This isn't one of your scams for simple folks with a dream, who you can scare off with your lawyers and fancy talk when things go bad. You can't bully a man like Sonny! We'd better pray that getting his mother's money back satisfies his thirst for revenge against you and Wesley."

Ben is almost dressed, too. He stands in front of a mirror, adjusting his tie. "Thanks for the advice, Irina. But, I deal with hotheads like Sonny all day long. Investors who lose their money are belligerent at first, but they calm down—once my lawyers, you have so little faith in get involved, or in rare cases like this, where we make them whole. When marks realize I can spend them into submission, they go away. If that doesn't work for some reason, we write them a check. Either way, they go away."

"If you believe that about Sonny, then you are as naive as a schoolboy," Irina says. "Let me tell you a story."

"I've got to go. You can tell me later." Ben finishes with his tie and heads for the door.

"Get back here and pay attention! This might save your sorry life!"

Ben stops and sits on the chair near the door. "Fine. Let's get this over with."

"You weren't completely wrong about me, tonight." Irina begins brushing her long blond hair in front of the mirror. "I was a whore of sorts in Russia. I worked at a massage parlor that offered 'full service.' Victor was one of my clients. Back then, he was a low-level street tough, acting as a collector for a moneylender. He was taken with me, which wasn't unusual— men often confused my enthusiasm for money with affection. Somehow, it was different between Victor and me, though. Eventually, we fell in love – or, what passes for love between two people as fucked up in the head as Victor and I.

"I was living in an apartment provided by my pimp, Yuri. He was a businessman, similar to you. He was smart enough to know that he if stayed below a certain size, he wouldn't be bothered by the gangsters who controlled prostitution in our village. He was rough with us girls, but not vicious like the men who controlled the streets. Still, all the years of bullying us girls probably made him overestimate his toughness. She pauses and reflects. Ben remains quiet.

"Victor and I went to Yuri to tell him I'd be leaving the massage parlor. Victor offered to pay off Yuri and take over payments on the company apartment I'd lived in for years, so I wouldn't have to find a new home. Yuri told Victor I had twenty-four hours to leave, or I'd be locked out and my belongings thrown to the curb. That would've meant street urchins would steal all my things.

"Victor asked Yuri to not make the mistake of doing that to me—and to *him*. Yuri laughed and told Victor he had people who would teach him a lesson. He ordered us to clean out the apartment immediately, and be thankful he didn't take what little I had.

"Yuri ended by looking at Victor and me, spitting on the ground, and telling Victor, 'You and that trash better get the fuck out of here before I have you both beaten.'

"Victor's face, as we left, was terribly cold. I could feel the violence he was keeping contained with every ounce of his being.

"Victor and I moved my things, with the help of some of his thug friends, and they placed me in an apartment located in a more desirable part of the village.

"The next day, Yuri was beaten half to death by some unidentified masked street toughs.

"An hour later, Yuri's massage parlor was burned to the ground.

"The local police made a show of questioning Victor. But Victor was drinking in a local pub at the time of the beating and while the parlor burned. There were many witnesses.

"That is the kind of man Victor is—and Sonny is the same. Fix this, or you will end up like Yuri."

Ben starts to answer. Before he utters a word, however, Irina continues, "Save yourself or not, I'm out of here.

Irina goes to the door and walks out, leaving Ben still sitting in the chair.

A cold chill runs up his spine. He tries to draw upon his bravado to calm himself, but deep inside, he senses Irina is right.

CHAPTER 25
THE VACATION

DeAngelo stares intently at the mounds of bills, foreclosure notices, and medical reports about Big Lou's cerebral tumor. Lou's professional bills are mounting up and his options for surgery are becoming limited, if Donnie doesn't find the money to cover it all. He takes the calls from Connie Ryan, while wondering what will become of them all. Connie is behind on her own bills and facing bankruptcy from the collapse of the business. Nita's boys are away at school and their bills for insurance, tuition and other necessities are marked past due. His eyes moisten as he crumples the funeral charges for Andersen's final service, stamped 'payment due.'

DeAngelo throws the papers everywhere and glares across the study walls filled with the mementoes and awards both he and the company acquired over the years. He focuses on a worn black-and-white photo of himself, holding a 45-caliber pistol and an M2 Carbine, while standing watch over a perimeter crossing into his base camp. He remembers his determination as an eighteen-year-old to not only protect his Marine brothers while on watch, but to eliminate any enemy that would attempt to invade their home. While he gazes at the image, he becomes even more intent on protecting his family, friends and the honor of their lifelong struggle to achieve something that would make all their lives better. They had fought in a different way for honor and independence back then, but this time, like that time, it was for keeps.

His mind rummages through the bloodied crime scene of Andersen's murder and Nita's screams of pain when her brother had been killed. He flashes back to the moment of Lou's agony when his headaches had become unbearable and then to the disgrace he'd suffered when vendors he'd known for years implored him for payment that he could not afford to give them. He swallows a lump of humility, remembering the moment when he and Nita lay side by side in bed—she knowing the disparity of everything, and Donnie intending to commit suicide for the insurance money, until she'd told him that if he did anything crazy like that, they'd have to go together.

Instantly, he jumps to his feet and with teeth clenched, bellows, "NO!" He hadn't realized it had reached the point where Nita would not want to live without him. He feels embarrassed and ashamed.

His thoughts return to a complacent, confident and blithe Goelner, mocking the genuine trust that Donnie and his friends had given him. His bitterness turns to smirking as he calls for Nita.

Nita runs into Donnie's study, concerned about why he's summoning her. Her eyes are wide and curious.

"*Mi amor, que?*"

"It's time for a vacation!" He smiles, while Nita looks simply astonished.

"You and I deserve a vacation! Get your things! I'm calling the airlines and booking us a flight to Colombia. We still have some credit left on our credit cards!" He smiles like a man with a mission.

"Are you *loco*? With all that is going on?" She is bewildered, but seems compliant.

"Yes, *loco como un lobo*, crazy like a wolf!"

Nita smiles. "You mean, fox!"

"No, *mi amor*, I mean wolf." DeAngelo hugs her and pats her butt, telling her to go pack and to just trust him. She leaves with a questioning glance, but returns his smile.

The welcoming sun and warmth of tropical Colombia brings some peace to the hearts of both Nita and Donnie. He remembers his frequent trips to the land of coffee, emeralds and other commodities, and most of all, his many romantic enjoyable moments with Nita. They are greeted by Don Vito, his people, and Nita's brothers—Juan and Miguel. The hugs and smiles are endless, as the friends and family are pleased that their American family returns to visit. Donnie's visits have been few and far between since the marriage, because of work and commitments, but the endearments are alive and fresh. Vito's bodyguards are quick to take Donnie and Nita's luggage. This leaves the family and friends to share salutations.

Don Vito had developed a bond of friendship with Donnie over the years. The common link between them had always been the love of Nita's family, their strength in business, and the relationships with people for whom they both cared. Vito had viewed Anita's mother as his own, since his deceased mother was Colombian, but his Sicilian father had given him the brand of businessman and protector of family. They could see in each other similar qualities and talents, although their businesses were uniquely different. At his core, Donnie was a motivator and strategist, with a keen sense of business and honesty, and Vito the same, but with a ruthless old-world hand on the vices men wanted most—women and gambling. Vito owned that part of the business in Cali and parts of New York, but he'd steered clear of drugs, disliking them. That area of business was left to the cartel bosses and the other Colombian and Sicilian families.

At one point, Don Vito had trusted Donnie's business savvy so much that he'd offered him management of all his interests in New York. While understanding that Vito's culture had a place since time began, Donnie had made it clear that he was walking a straight line and wanted the same for his family. Vito, for his part, had always appreciated Donnie's honesty and continued their friendship and common bond in Anita's family, which made them both extended family. They'd both mourned the death of Nita's brother, Domingo, and had made certain to protect the rest of the family.

After weeks and months of darkness and desperation, Nita shows some signs of life at finding her family alive and well. Donnie can no longer throw lavish parties at the best restaurants as he once did, but Vito, knowing the situation, offers his resort, La Princessa, for a family feast.

This is the same resort, with private underground tunnels, that had once hosted the world's leading cartel leaders. Standing atop a hill overlooking all of Cali, it's miles away from the threats of Colombian and Narco police. Throughout the years, Vito had shown loyalty and hospitality to all the cartel kingpins, but he'd disliked their business. He often complains to Donnie that they sell death and misery to too many families, and for that, he smiles on the outside, but hates himself on the inside. These are "friends" forced upon him, but they like him and would do anything for him. In turn, he is left alone to run his prostitution and gambling. About these things, Vito knows that men will always want and need women, and as if forced by nature, they'll gamble, whether in business, sports or social life. While Vito is an enforcer not to be underestimated, he has a warm Sicilian-Colombian side that nevertheless, remains selective in its application.

Vito has an unsightly scar engraved across his left cheek, bearing the signature of his profession. As he'd once told Donnie, "You see this beautiful crevice across my face? It's a sign of what I learned in my first business lesson: *Lucha por lo que es tuyo o no merece que lo mantenga*, fight for what is yours or you never deserve to keep it." Those words would echo in Donnie's brain.

The two men laugh, drink Colombian Crystal, and exchange stories throughout the night. Vito offers big Cuban rolled cigars to Donnie, who passes on smoking, but knowing Vito's love of both cigarettes and cigars, hands him a beautiful gold lighter with the inscription, "TO MY GOOD FRIEND AND SICILIAN BROTHER VITO, FROM DONNIE."

Vito holds the shimmering gold lighter in his hand and reads the inscription. He looks deep into Donnie's eyes and mutters, "We are brothers from another place and you will always be my friend." They hug each other and Vito lights his cigarette after urging Donnie to celebrate with a freshly rolled cigar. Smiling, Donnie accepts, and the two look out over the spectacular view of Cali. Donnie comments on how beautiful the lights from Cali sparkle beneath the hills of La Princessa.

Nita joins the two men and whispers in Donnie's ear that she wants to go home. She is worn out from the trip and nostalgic for her brother, Domingo. Vito offers Donnie his Presidential Suite and though Donnie begins to decline, Nita jumps to accept. Just before leaving the party, Donnie turns to Vito.

"Vito, I need a favor." Donnie's demeanor is solemn and credulous.

"Anything." Vito's response is immediate and firm. He smiles and nods affirmatively.

Donnie smiles back and puts his hand on Vito's shoulder. "We can talk tomorrow. I will come to see you. *Gracias mi hermano*."

⋆ ⋆ ⋆

Once inside the lavish suite, Nita and Donnie are taken aback by the amenities—a manmade flowing waterfall, a wall-to-wall and floor-to-ceiling window overlooking all of Cali, and a bed the size of Texas. These are surroundings they don't need, as both flashback to the first time they made love in a simple Colombian farmhouse where Nita had once lived.

Nita had grown up amidst the guerillas and violence that besieged Colombia. She'd longed for an escape for herself and her children, but she'd wanted a man she knew she could love—someone strong, but warm, and capable of loving her boys. She'd taken Donnie to the farmhouse on one of his visits. It had been vacant, but clean and available to her through a friend, and there, they'd made passionate love for the first time. She'd known then that she was his. She'd taken a knife from her bag after making love and brandished it in front of Donnie, who was not sure what was going to happen. Then, in a moment of romantic animus, she'd sliced at the ends of her long black hair to cut a piece for him. She'd placed the lock of hair in his hand, then closed his fingers around it.

"Take this piece of me to never forget this place and what

we have shared," she'd told him. "I know you will go back to your home, but remember I will always be here, waiting for you. Whenever you need me, I will be here for you." He'd never forgotten her words and he'd kept the lock of her hair.

As they gaze at the lights of Cali through the large window, their thoughts return to a simpler time and they began to kiss and fondle each other. Donnie realizes that through all the adversity, calamity and misfortune, he'd lost sight of Nita's beauty and passion. Nita is fifteen years younger than Donnie, but at forty-one, she shows little sign of aging and hadn't changed much since they first met.

Together, they make an attractive couple. Her long, soft, ebony black hair is pinned up in the front, but when he removes the pin, it falls over the side of her face with the same allure of the young woman he remembers. Her feline eyes are engaging and full of desire. Nita has a few small facial lines, but her beauty is radiant and her fire, contagious. Nita has always been a passionate woman who loves power.

Donnie puts aside the tragedies of the last few months and is hard with desire. He removes her clothes in seconds, exposing a flawless body. Nita is blessed with skin composed of the essence and color of youth. Her tiny waist is a pedestal for her ample breasts and beneath that, hips curving like the timbre of a spoon. Without hesitation, he kisses her again and again and, as they engage furiously, she tears away at his clothes until they are both naked. After months of frustration and disappointment, Donnie is overwhelmed with desire, the Donnie he used to be. Fondling her body, he lifts her onto the satin-covered bed, and then buries his head between her legs as she squirms and yelps with ecstasy and fulfillment.

There is a sea of fire between them as they each scramble to consume the other. Donnie pulls at her long beautiful hair and as he mounts her, whispers "tu eres mio" in her ear and begins an endless pounding from all positions. She loves it, bellowing back in the tone of a growling panther, as he mixes his x-rated expletives of desire with words of love. They carry on for hours until exhausted, they collapse, listening to the gentle splashing of the waterfall near the bed.

Colombia is a welcome reprieve from the betrayals and disasters at home. Donnie knows that Atchinson was never his friend or loyal colleague. He knows that Atchinson has collaborated with Goelner to secure a hostile takeover. He feels foolish for trusting all of them, but especially Atchinson, to whom he'd offered friendship and commitment. He'd elevated him to Chief Operating Officer and helped him solve his personal problems. Atchinson had a gambling problem and augmented "vigs" to street guys, but Donnie made all that go away. Atchinson's actions revealed anything but gratitude. But that had been yesterday. Tomorrow is another day he has to face and be strong. He knows now that with Nita, he will do whatever he has to do.

Monday morning at Brickman's Bistros resembles visiting day at the local funeral home. Sad faces and silence are all that remain throughout the offices and once-friendly lobby. Each employee stares at Donnie as he enters, wondering when he will collapse from all the hardship. Donnie is cordial and forces a grin, greeting each employee. As he approaches his office, one of the secretaries tells him Mr. Atchinson wants to see him. Donnie replies, "He can wait."

Once inside his office, he heads for the phone on his desk

like a man on a mission. But, before he can begin, he is interrupted again by a secretary who tells him Jenay Tobias from the FBI, has just arrived and wants to see him.

"What could she want now?" he thinks to himself, then tells the secretary to bring her in.

Donnie quickly organizes his desk to tone down the disarray. He tells his assistant to hold all calls. Tobias is quick to enter, and with a big smile extends her arm for a handshake.

"So you're back! How was Colombia? Can I take a seat?"

"Yes, of course. How did you know I was in Colombia? Never mind, I suppose you know a lot of things."

Tobias doesn't answer, she just continues to smile and look around the office.

"I understand there are a few changes here." She brings her focus back to Donnie and changes her grin to a more serious expression.

"A few things I will have to accept." Donnie clasps his hands on the desk, leaning forward to show a forced interest in her visit.

"More than a few, as I understand. I'm curious—why would an almost broken man make a casual trip to Colombia? I mean, there's enough to keep you busy here." She looks into Donnie's eyes as if sympathetic, but still on a witch hunt.

"My wife needed a break, we both did. Her family has suffered a lot lately and she needed to be there for them."

"Oh, I see." Her answer is terse. "Did you know your friend, Frankie Cavallo, has been convicted and will face lots of prison time?"

"No, I'm sorry, I didn't follow any of that."

"And did you know that several of his colleagues and associates," she continues, clearing her throat in a sarcastic gesture, "face being convicted, as well?"

"I guess that comes with the territory." Donnie serves little meat for her appetite.

She smiles and turns away, looking at the montage of awards and war photos.

"But, it seems that you are clean—for now! You have a brilliant war record and on the surface, you would have made a fine FBI agent yourself, but I don't know, I still have my reservations. Anyway, I just stopped by to tell you that if anything comes up, I would welcome your input. Do you get what I mean, Mr. DeAngelo?"

"Oh, please call me Donnie, we are friends by now." He smiles, coaxing her to lighten up. She does, flirtatiously extending her arm again to finish the conversation.

"Friends might be a stretch, but you certainly have a curious charm to you." With a guileless grin, she blinks her eyes, revealing a modest attraction to Donnie. She turns and wishes him good luck.

CHAPTER 26
SONNY'S SIN

Sonny sets about his plan to drive a wedge of suspicion between Ridgefield and Caputo. It is elegant in its simplicity. Sonny calls upon one of his mercenary buddies, Ed Summers, an electronics expert, specializing in clandestine surveillance. He has a small audio and video equipment repair shop down on Main Street, creatively called Ed's Appliance Repair. The shop, which does do some actual consumer repairs, is a front for Ed's real business, supplying surveillance equipment to—shall we say—non-authorized agencies and individuals.

Sonny heads down to Ed's and enters around lunchtime, carrying two street vendor meatball sandwiches and two cold Coronas. Ed looks up as Sonny enters, thanks to the cowbell attached to the front door.

"Look what the cat dragged in," Ed says to Sonny.

"I need a favor," Sonny says, "and I brought lunch."

"And a healthy lunch, to boot," Ed says, "all the major food groups—grease, cholesterol and bacteria. Perfect!"

Ed changes the open sign on the front door to closed and Sonny follows him into the back room.

After they gorge on the delicious street food, Ed asks,

"Okay, what do you need?"

Sonny explains that he wants to set up a phony record of communication between a few people who never actually communicated.

"And I thought you were going to bring me a difficult problem, in order to earn this high-class meal," Ed says. "This will be easy! I can set up what will look like genuine back and forth communication. I'll need the email addresses of the intended victims, as much other information as you can give me about them, and info about the intended nature of their fictitious dialogues."

Sonny hands Ed a sealed envelope. It has Caputo's, Ridgefield's and Irina's email addresses next to their names, plus pictures of each, some surveillance photos showing license plates, the address of Triangel, and a few other odds and ends.

"Always prepared," Ed says. "Saved us both, many times."

Sonny replies, "Indeed."

Ed agrees. "Brief me with what needs to happen."

Sonny briefs Ed on exactly who Irina, Ridgefield, and Caputo are. Sonny explains that he wants Ridgefield to think that Caputo and Irina are having a romantic relationship behind Ridgefield's back and, in addition, he wants Caputo to think that Ridgefield is threatened by the screwed-up beating to death of Andersen, and is contemplating dealing with Caputo in a most unpleasant way.

Sonny also explains about Irina and her relationship with Victor. "You remember Victor?" Sonny asks.

"Yes, not a man to be trifled with, as I recall."

"Exactly right."

"Okay," Ed says. "I've got the picture. You have any naked pictures of Irina?" he asks.

"No, why? Do you need some?"

"Not really, but they would be fun to look at," Ed says.

"Funny."

"Maybe I'll find some, when I start to snoop around. Any other details?"

"Yes, about the guy, Ridgefield, who Irina is actually having a relationship with. I want him to think that Irina and Caputo are laughing about how they are carrying on behind his back."

"So, it's not just about conveying information—you want to create anger and fear?"

"Exactly."

"Done. Fear and anger are my specialties! Give me a week," Ed says.

Sonny rises, shakes Ed's hand, gives him a quick bro hug, and leaves.

Late that night, Ed gets to work, first spoofing the email addresses of Irina, Ridgefield and Caputo. This allows him to send outgoing emails from those addresses, which will appear to be genuine. Although people naively think that email is private and relatively hard to spy on, they are wrong. Unless there are sophisticated protocols and encryptions, email is easy to hijack, especially for a man of Ed's talents.

Next, Ed fires up an application that he's developed to send bogus texts from and to various phones. Again, the sense of security that most users have about their supposedly private communications, like texts, is misunderstood. Electronic communications of any kind are far from secure when basic, unprotected equipment is used.

Now that the phony communication network is set up, it's time to start the process. Clearly, the communications have to be staged over a period of days to appear real, so Ed creates a task list and spreadsheet to track when and what he will send out – kind of a road map heading towards chaos. Usually, doing this work is tedious when working toward a financial end, but in this case, it's being performed to help a close friend exact revenge, a friend who has saved his life more than once. Ed is very motivated to get this done to perfection!

Task One: Fabricate a romantic, or at least, a sexual relationship, between Caputo and Irina and leak it to Ridgefield. This is easy, Ed thinks. He has been monitoring the emails of all three parties and has learned that Ridgefield is going out of town on a business trip for Triangel to meet a new prospect—or pigeon, as Goelner's email to Ridgefield sarcastically characterizes the new client. Ed also learns that Ridgefield shares the information about his trip with Irina, telling her he will be away for a few days and that he will miss her.

Ed then sends a text that looks like it is originating from Irina's phone to Ridgefield. The text says, "Tony – Ben's going away – I'm rid of that pig for at least a week – we won't have to sneak around – dinner and me for dessert on Wednesday?" Elegant in its simplicity, Ed thinks. Press the wrong key on your smart phone and the wrong person gets your text. It happens all the time. That's why Ed never stores numbers in his phone.

Ridgefield gets that text and is furious. That son of a bitch, he thinks and Irina—oh my God! He thinks about confronting one or both of them, but decides not to act in haste. He is pissed mostly at Irina, but he is also afraid of her since, after all, she is Victor Zalenko's girl and he has already dodged a bullet there. He heads out of town, with the taste of bile in his mouth.

Task Two: Fabricate a dialogue between Ridgefield and an unknown, but scary individual, and leak it to Caputo. Ed creates an alias email and names it simply: TJ.

He sends an email from TJ to Ridgefield, which simply says, "I'm ready to deal with the problem when you are – agreed upon terms.”

Ed sends an email back from what appears to be Ridgefield’s email to TC, Caputo’s email, saying, “I’ll meet you next week and we’ll tie up some loose ends.”

Caputo opens the email and is confused at first, but soon surmises that Ridgefield sent it to TC, his email, by mistake—and he is chilled by the message. Tony thinks Ridgefield will stop at nothing to protect Triangel and Tony knows that Ridgefield can be a dangerous man. Ridgefield has mentioned his discomfort about this law enforcement consultant, Devin, who keeps showing up and asking questions. Tony is scared and not sure what to do. Is he a loose end?

Ben is glad that he is away. It gives him time to think. He feels like things are spinning out of control and he doesn’t know whom to trust. The police are sniffing around Triangel, still investigating the killing of Andersen. His trusted henchman, Caputo, is screwing his girl, Irina, and who knows what they are scheming? Irina knows an awful lot, information he now wishes he hadn’t divulged to her during testosterone-fueled pillow talk. He doesn’t feel comfortable, anywhere.

“Are the police tapping the Triangel phones?” his paranoid mind asks him. “Are the police planning to implicate him in Andersen’s murder?” They will, if they squeeze Caputo. He finds himself falling into a sea of paranoia, from which there seems to be no escape. He begins to drown himself in scotch, hoping for clarity and numbness, but only getting sleepless nights and raw nerves.

While the paranoia and distrust builds between Ridgefield and Caputo, the police are actually planning to close the Andersen case, as a mugging gone bad. They are extremely overworked and not taking the 30,000-foot view, that perhaps, they should be. Devin is, however, taking the long view and she is starting to put the pieces together. She is unsure about what to do about the fact that she sees a vastly different picture than her friend, Captain Rodriguez. She continues to gather facts and make notes. She will do nothing for now. She wants to see where all of this is going.

Ed calls Sonny and tells him the tasks he asked for are completed. Ed describes what he's done and says that he will continue to monitor the emails and texts of Irina, Caputo and Ridgefield, if Sonny wants him to. Sonny does and promises a year's supply of greasy vendor food when this is over.

"Where is this leading?" Ed asks Sonny. "If you don't want to answer, it's fine. It's none of my business, anyway."

"No harm in asking," Sonny says. "Do me a favor? Please keep records of the texts and emails in a way that I can retrieve them, if I want to. I may want to share some of them with our old friend, Victor, at some point."

"I understand," Ed says. "Remind me not to fuck with you, or your friends and family!"

"Yes," Sonny says. "That will always be a mistake. Thanks, Ed," he says, as he leaves. "I won't forget this."

CHAPTER 27
GOELNER'S GREED

Goelner is sitting in his stark, but opulent, glass and chrome office, talking with his best friend of the moment, DeAngelo's former COO, Atchinson. One of the first things Wesley has done upon invading DeAngelo's company, is to turn DeAngelo's tastefully decorated office into an abomination to the eyes, the kind that screams, "I have a lot of money—and no taste!"

In a cruel, but strategic move, Goelner has promoted Atchinson to CEO of what used to be DeAngelo's company. Goelner is gloating out loud to Atchinson about his hostile takeover of Brickman's Bistros and DeAngelo's building.

"I really kicked your old boss's ass," he tells Achinson. "I took it all and he barely put up a fight. It was like taking candy from a baby!"

Achinson just nods. If he'd had any sense of loyalty or honor, he'd be horrified by Wesley's remarks and drop him with a hard right, before resigning. That is not the case.

It turns out that DeAngelo has been completely wrong about Achinson. Donnie had taken him in when no one would hire him, had helped him dry out and get control of his alcoholism, and had provided him with an income and benefits, that essentially set him up for life. Achinson has repaid Donnie's kindness by jumping ship the first time Goelner makes him an attractive offer. He is truly a piece of shit and, probably, a certifiable sociopath. He doesn't feel an ounce of remorse for his actions.

"I think it's time for you to fire DeAngelo and take him off the payroll," Wesley says.

"Done," Achinson says, coldly, feeling nothing.

Oh, boy, good-hearted Donnie has been so wrong about him! He should have listened to his wife when she was telling him about her bad feeling for the guy, years ago. Her intuition has trumped Donnie's misplaced good nature, for sure.

Achinson, in a final display of disloyalty and cold blooded self-serving motivation, texts the bad news to Donnie.

Moments later, a simple, uncharacteristic text comes back from Donnie. "Once from the gutter and back to the gutter you will be." And so ends what has appeared to be, from the outside, a close friendship, but is in actuality, a relationship similar to a host and a parasite.

Goelner tells Achinson that he plans to pull DeAngelo's company out of bankruptcy by taking a loan on the building Donnie used to own, which Goelner has foreclosed on. In a clever move, Goelner waits until Brickman's Bistros is in bankruptcy, and then buys the building from the bankruptcy trustee for a fraction of its value. He will now borrow against the building and infuse the company with money. This will make it look fiscally healthy, so he can relist the company on the pink sheets, poised for trading and growth. His stock public relations company will soon be at work, sending out press releases designed to encourage investor activity.

The corrupt cycle begins again, as he constructs yet another house of cards. Goelner is a blight on society, Robin Hood in reverse. He steals from the poor and gives to the rich. He is just like his dad, who would be proud, if only he had the capacity to be proud of anyone other than himself.

Goelner tells Achinson to begin the process of evicting all of the tenants in the building, including Big Lou Williams.

"Clean house of all the freeloaders and drifters that DeAngelo has allowed to live here for little, or no, rent." Goelner has no idea that Donnie has been repaying a debt of honor to the people he cares for, by housing all who live in the Brickman's Bistros building—but if he had known, he wouldn't have cared. Wesley lives for Wesley. He doesn't realize it, but in the end, his greed will do him in.

Goelner, being a creature motivated by the pursuit of his own pleasure and feeling giddy from his latest victory, feels the need for a decadent celebration. He books a playdate with his favorite hooker, Marlena, from the elite, high end *Fleurs de la Nuit* agency. Goelner holds VIP status at the agency, so they take care of booking the Presidential Suite at the Four Seasons Hotel—Goelner's favorite. When he goes decadent, he goes all the way! He heads out for a night of debauchery, spending money like it is water. It's easy to do, because he knows he can always steal more.

The next day, Donnie shows up at his old building and is stopped by security, the same security people he'd hired, years ago. The two guys at reception, of course, recognize him and since they possess human emotions, unlike Goelner and Achinson, feel awkward stopping their old boss.

"Sorry, Mr. DeAngelo," Ian says. "I feel awful holding you here until someone comes down, but I need my job."

"It's okay, Ian," Donnie says, patting the big man on the back. "I completely understand."

Ian rings Achinson's office and shortly thereafter, Achinson comes down and escorts Donnie to his old office. They ride the elevator in silence. Donnie asks for some file boxes and begins to clean out his office. He tells Achinson that he and Goelner make quite a pair—two snakes in the grass.

"I wouldn't get too comfortable," Donnie says. "You're not the top snake."

"Don't worry about me," Achinson says.

"Worrying about you is the last thing I'll ever do," Donnie says. "I'm just making conversation."

Achinson tells Donnie about the evictions to come, including Lou. "Goelner wants all your friends out by the end of the month."

Donnie laughs to himself.

"You find this funny?" Achinson asks.

"What I find funny is the thought of you and Goelner trying to evict Big Lou. I realize that will never happen. Cowards like you will never show up for a real fight." Donnie finishes packing, takes one last look around and leaves, a tear forming in his eye as the elevator door closes.

A few days later, Achinson is sitting in his new office – Donnie's old one, and he gets a call from security. "Someone to see you," Ian says.

"Who is it?"

"She says her name is Carey Devin."

"Send her up," Achinson says. He knows who she is and wonders what she wants with him.

Carey is ushered in by the receptionist and greeted by

Achinson in the manner that most men greet her—a warm handshake, backed up by a lustful smile.

"Nice to see you again, Ms. Devin," Achinson lies. "How can I help you?"

"I have a few questions, if you don't mind. I'm still trying to make some sense of the brutal, and seemingly senseless Andersen murder."

"Are you working with the police?" Achinson asks. "Because we all gave them statements."

"I'm not working for anyone but myself," Devin says. "Craig was a dear friend and I'm just trying to tie up some loose ends, more for my peace of mind than anything."

"Very well, I understand loyalty," Achinson lies again.

Carey gets nowhere with him, as she questions him about the murder gone bad. "Don't you think it's odd that the perpetrators were also former security personnel at Goelner's company?" she asks.

"No, I think it's just an odd coincidence, as do the police, I might add. Security guards are not the highest level people, you know. Eight dollars an hour and they get to carry a gun! It's a pretty screwed up system."

"Agreed," Cary says. "Thanks for your help. Do you mind providing me access to the residential part of the building? I want to speak to some of Craig's former friends. I know that they live there."

"Not at all."

Achinson guides Devin through the locked door separating the commercial part of the building from the residential section. He swipes his card, the electronic lock clicks and he opens the door for her. She walks through and he says, "Nice to see you again," this time, meaning it—staring at her long legs and tight ass, as she walks away from him.

Carey looks at the resident directory encased in glass on the other side of the locked door Achinson has just ushered her through. She locates Big Lou's apartment number and goes down the hall to find it. Devin notices that the entire residence wing is handicapped-enabled. There are ramps and railings everywhere.

She knocks on Lou's door and Lou answers it, after a fashion. "Yes?" he says, somewhat rudely.

Carey introduces herself and explains that she is looking into the murder of his friend, Andersen.

"The police have already been here," Lou says. "They think it's a robbery gone bad."

"I know," Carey says. "I'm not the police. I'm an old friend of Craig's."

Lou ushers her into his apartment. It is extremely neat with sparse, modest furniture and no clutter anywhere—true military style. Lou shows her to a living room chair and she sits down. He doesn't offer her anything, but sits across from her.

Williams is a hulk of a man, and even though he has prematurely aged from the aftermath of his Agent Orange exposure he is an intimidating presence. Sitting across from her is a stoic, retired Marine, who simply looks tired and slow, but Carey imagines would be neither—if the proper motivation arose.

Lou is guarded, but somewhat open, knowing that he and Devin share the bond of friendship with the now-deceased Andersen. He describes his friendship with Andersen and the kind of guy he'd been. Much of it resonates with Devin and thoughts of Craig rush into her head, especially when Lou describes a time when Craig saved his life by taking out two shooters during an ambush aimed at Lou.

"Craig had a knack for spotting trouble where no one else saw it. He saved my life more than once." Lou said emotionally.

Carey knows this aspect of Craig very well. She ruminates on Craig's experience, as well as her own, in Afghanistan, as Lou describes a man they both loved in different ways, but with similar intensity. Carey is touched by the emotion coming from such a tough, intimidating man, as he talks about his old friend.

"I would have taken a bullet for Craig without hesitation," Lou says. "I only wish that I had been with him on the fateful night."

Devin is impressed by Lou's loyalty and she feels the depth of sorrow and misplaced guilt expressed by Lou. Clearly, he hasn't been responsible for Craig's wellbeing, and he couldn't have been expected to be with him at every moment, but still, regret plagues him.

Williams is getting more comfortable with Devin and he becomes more talkative. He admits, that if it weren't for Donnie, he and Craig would probably be homeless or living in squalor somewhere.

"Donnie is a prince," Lou tells Devin. "He did well after the war and he took all of us in like the Marine family he considers us to be. We were all proud, and it was hard at first, to accept his generosity, but he made us all believe that he would be genuinely offended if we didn't move here, so we did. We take care of this place like it's our home. We do all the maintenance and, with Donnie's generous financial support, we put up all the handicapped aids."

Devin listens intently, as Lou talks about Donnie. She can hear the love, respect, and admiration in his voice. Cautiously, her suspicions of DeAngelo as a suspect, diminish.

Lou goes on to explain how Donnie has helped Tommy Ryan's widow, Connie, put her boy, Sonny through college. Lou explains that Sonny follows in his father's proud soldier tradition. After a few tours in Afghanistan, Sonny has become a skilled government contractor. Devin understands that occupation, only too well.

When Lou is finished, Devin thanks him for his candor and hospitality, says goodbye and leaves. She has gotten more than she came for. She now has an understanding of the deep connection that all of these brothers-in-arms share. She understands their fraternal bond, their love for their fallen brother, and their respect and admiration for Donnie.

She thinks about what she will do if she finds out that Craig's murder hasn't really been a mugging gone bad. She knows what guys like Lou will feel compelled to do, as a matter of honor and brotherhood. She has a lot to think about. There are a lot of unsorted pieces of information floating around in her head—for example, the murderers of Craig, being ex-Triangel employees. She is impressed by what she now knows of Donnie DeAngelo and how the people he has chosen to care for feel about him.

She doesn't know what is about to unfold in the tranquil building she has just left. Achinson certainly hasn't shared the impending eviction proceedings or talked about the termination of Donnie. She has no idea what kind of shit storm is on the horizon when this band of brothers is once again united—against a common enemy.

CHAPTER 28
A DATE WITH DESTINY

Lou Williams is sitting in the dark, his head in his hands, waiting for tea to brew. A smell, putrid to most, fills his apartment—but to Lou, the smell is relief. He has another one of his screaming headaches, which come out of nowhere and range between mildly painful to the upper limits of unbearable. Years of doctors and piles of meds have proven to be without value. In desperation, he'd been driven to seek the counsel of a Chinese healer recommended by his friend, Yin.

How vividly he recalls that day, with his friend leading him through the back alleys of New York's Chinatown into an over-crowded pharmacy stocked with pills, herbs and powders of all shapes, smells and colors. All of these remedies, all labeled in Chinese, fill all available space behind the center counter in this strange drugstore. Presiding over all of it, sits a lone counterman reading a Chinese newspaper. Lou's friend, Yin, speaks to the worker in broken Chinese. A few moments later, a small, kind looking man, who appears to be about a hundred years old, comes out of a back room, pushing aside its beaded doorway curtain, approaching the counter. Yin tells Lou to approach the other side and have a seat. The Chinese healer says a few words to Yin and Yin tells Lou to give the healer his hands. The big man puts his hands on the counter and the old Chinese man reaches across the counter and takes them gently in his. The healer's hands, squeezing and kneading Lou's big mitts, appear tiny, like a child's hands. After he finishes squeezing, kneading, and looking, he gazes at Lou's weathered face. Examining Lou's eyes, he gently lifts first the top and then the bottom lid. After that, for the first time, he speaks—in English.

"Open mouth, tongue out."

Lou complies. The healer examines his tongue and then suddenly, he is done. Taking up a pad and pen, he writes – in Chinese, Lou assumes—what appears to be a shopping list. He hands this list to the counterman who scurries around, assembling packets of powders and herbs. Done, he puts them in front of the old man who proceeds to empty them into a clay pestle, grinding them together with a clay mortar. The healer then pours the contents into a bag, packs the bag in a box next to an ancient looking teapot, probably dating back to the Stone Age, hands it to Lou, and says: "One teaspoon, one quart water, boil four hours, drink hot."

Lou opens his mouth to ask a question, but the old man interrupts him. "One teaspoon, one quart water, boil four hours, drink hot, pain gone." That said, the man gets up and abruptly exits the room through the same beaded curtain hanging in the doorway.

"Let's go," Yin says.

"That's it?" Lou asks.

"That's it." Yin leads Lou out through the alleys, back to the car.

"We didn't pay," Lou says, suddenly remembering.

"No pay necessary," Yin says.

"Why not?" Lou asks.

"Long story," Yin replies. "Old man's grandson was a gang member. You made that stop."

Lou nods, understanding. Yin has proven to be a great friend and an interesting man with an even more interesting past. Lou doesn't question him further.

The timer goes off, bringing Lou back to reality. Relief at last, he thinks. He turns off the stove, takes the teapot with a potholder, pours some of the nasty stuff into a cup, blowing on it until it is tolerable and then, he takes a sip. It's bitter and spicy going down his throat, but after a few swallows, the pain is gone—just as the old man had said. Lou never varies the ritual and the result is always the same. Feeling much better, he decides to go out for a walk.

But, then the phone rings and rings, until he picks it up. Without identifying himself, the caller says to Lou, "Get a pad and pen."

Lou obeys and reports to the caller as such. The caller proceeds to give Lou two names and two locations, all of which Lou writes down.

"First guy, 1 a.m. Second guy, 5 a.m. Got it?"

"Got it," Lou says and the caller disconnects. Lou stuffs the paper into his pocket and goes for a walk.

At 1 a.m. that night, Larry Sica, one of the two thugs who killed Craig Andersen, is leaving his bouncer job at the Ringside Pub in midtown Manhattan. As usual, he has spent the night bragging about his fictitious mob ties and chatting up the young girls. He has created a larger than life persona at the pub and the regulars buy him drinks all night in a pathetic quest to be a tangential part of what they think is the glamorous life of a wiseguy in New York. Larry fuels the fire with his made-up stories and the gin-soaked patrons eat them up.

Feeling like a rock star, he heads for his car, energized but foggy from all the beer and shots. He takes the elevator to the ground floor parking garage and half walks, half staggers to his car. As he searches in his pocket for his keys, he realizes he doesn't have them, must have left them in the bar.

"Shit!" he yells. Turning to walk back to the elevator, he runs into a large man who is dressed all in black, right down to his black leather driving gloves. Being half in the bag and stumbling through a dimly lit garage, he barely notices the guy, even after making physical contact. "Fuck out of my way," he says, annoyed, shoving Big Lou aside.

Lou lets him walk past before silently wrapping his powerful arms around Larry's neck, quietly rendering him unconscious.

"This is for Craig," Lou says. It's the last thing Larry hears before he slips into unconsciousness, his body going limp without making a sound. With a quick twist, Lou breaks his neck, killing him instantly. He allows the now lifeless body to sink to the ground and then sits Larry up against one of the cement columns that support the garage.

Now he punches Larry hard in the jaw, so hard that the jaw breaks. Next, he slams the head against the cement column, fracturing his skull. It's in this position that he will leave the body, but first, he makes sure to get some of Larry's blood on his gloves.

Reaching into Larry's pocket, he takes out the wallet, removes cash and credit cards from it, tosses the wallet on the ground, removes Larry's gold Rolex watch and walks off.

One down, he thinks as he opens the door leading from the garage to the stairs, climbs them to street level and quietly exits the building. He ducks into the alley behind the parking garage and kneels behind a dumpster. He carefully removes his gloves and blood-soaked black boots. He stows them in the garbage bag he'd left behind the dumpster, along with

Larry's credit cards, and changes to his sneakers. He stuffs the cash into his pocket. Folding the garbage bag containing the evidence, he puts it into the duffle bag he'd left behind the dumpster. That done, he heads around the corner to his car and drives home – carefully, so as not to get stopped by the police. Home, he hides the evidence bag in the secret space below his living room area rug, settles into bed and drifts into a coma-like sleep, exhausted, but somewhat satisfied.

Next morning, the building janitor arrives for work and finds Larry's body as he is walking to the elevator. He immediately calls 911. The police dispatcher tells him to stay put, she is sending a patrol car. The horrified janitor stands there and stares at the gory scene until Detective Flanagan and his partner arrive.

Flanagan notices the discarded wallet. Checking it, he notes the absence of money or credit cards, but he learns Larry's identity.

Flanagan calls Julio Rodriguez, the younger brother of Emilio. "Captain? Better come down to the garage, around the corner from the Ringside Pub. Looks like we have another 'Knockout Game gone wild' incident, but this one turned into a homicide." Flanagan gives Captain Rodriguez the exact address.

Meanwhile, Carey Devin is across town, on her way to see a client. When she hears the call on her police scanner, she turns around to head to the building. She arrives shortly after Rodriguez, walking in as the police captain and Flanagan are kneeling by the body. The crime scene crew is just arriving.

"What are you doing here, Devin?" Rodriguez asks.

"Heard the call on my scanner. Just curious, I guess," she replies.

"Sure," Rogriguez says. "Is my brother tagging along?"

"What does it look like?" Devin asks.

"No, but this looks like a 'Knockout Game' incident gone bad," Flanagan says.

"Really?" Devin says.

"Lots of crazies out there, you know," Flanagan says. "Kids think it's cool to sneak up on someone and try to knock him out with one punch and if they knock them out, rob them. They think it shows how powerful they are. I think it's an act of extreme cowardice. In this case, it looks like the victim's jaw got hit so hard that his head slammed into one of the cement piers holding up the garage. It looks like he went unconscious and bled out. I'm sure the ME will confirm that."

"Anything unusual about the victim?"

"Nope. Ex-fighter turned bouncer, worked at the Ringside at night and as a security guard at a company called Triangel, during the day. His wallet was missing cash and credit cards and the tan line on his wrist indicates that he was probably wearing a watch that was stolen. I guess when he went unconscious, the creep who nailed him decided to rob him, as well. Piece of shit, low life."

"Interesting," Devin says. "Ex-boxer gets knocked out by some street thug, probably a kid, with one punch?"

"It can happen," Flanagan says. "You can do a lot of damage with one lucky sucker punch. Poor Larry is just another unfortunate victim of a bad economy in a crowded city."

"Must be," Devin says. "See you, captain! Nothing interesting here." Devin leaves, thinking to herself, "Robbery gone bad? Hardly! This was a hit disguised as a robbery and the guy worked at Triangel. This stinks!"

★ ★ ★

Big Lou wakes up after a restless sleep, but surprisingly, his headache hasn't returned. The miracle tea usually doesn't last *that* long, still, he doesn't overthink it. He is just grateful. He showers and dresses. He's promised his friend, Yin, that he would help him at the youth center Yin had opened on the south side. The two of them are teaching a group of borderline thugs the finer points of boxing and wrestling in an attempt to help them channel their aggressions in a non-destructive way. The city is already overrun with gangs. Anything he can do to help Yin stem the tide is worthwhile, he thinks. He heads off for a day of mentoring and teaching. It will keep his mind off last night's activity and whatever is to come.

Although he knows Larry deserved to die, killing is something he never gets used to. Even in Nam, when he was defending his own life or that of his brothers, he'd never disconnected with the reality of what he was doing. He couldn't completely disengage, like some of his brothers in arms. In some ways, he envied them.

The day passes quickly, the kids are lively and engaged, as Yin and Lou work them out – first, for fitness and then, for combat. Today is a day devoted to wrestling. He leaves the group at 8 p.m., exhausted, chowing down on the pizza and soda he and Yin provided. He wants to get home at a reasonable hour and grab a quick nap. He has more work to do. Yin is happy to clean up and lock up. Lou sets his alarm for 3 a.m. and settles down for some much-needed sleep. He still doesn't have a headache—strange, but wonderful.

At 3 a.m., Lou gets up and dresses in a black outfit similar to the one from the night before, but with different boots and gloves. He'd purchased both pairs of gloves and boots from secondhand shops in the Bowery—partly to make it a little more difficult to trace them to anybody, but also because this secondhand shop is one of the charity outlets owned by Triangel—supposedly set up for the good of the community they serve, but more likely, set up as a tax write-off. Nonetheless, it is convenient for Lou's ultimate plan.

Lou drives to Metro-City Gym, where Joe Sica, the other thug who killed Craig, works. Metro-City is a 24-hour gym, frequented by local wannabe boxers and thugs. It's a no-frills facility, but the right place to go if one wants to toughen up. Joe works there—a poor man's version of a personal trainer. He has no formal training other than beating up on guys weaker than he is and playing some mediocre football in high school.

That said, he is a big strong guy and he can spot a lifter when necessary and maybe even provide some motivation in the same sadistic way his old football coach used to. He is quick with an encouraging, "What's the matter, Nancy boy, can't get the weight up?" or "Two hundred? My grandma can bench that! Let's see you push some man's weight!"

He finishes spotting some young football players doing sets with 225 on the bench. They listen intently between sets to his bragging about the bench press records he supposedly set in high school.

"You kids need to hit these weights a lot harder if you want to play college ball," he tells them. "When I was your age, I was pushing 315 during my cool-down set." It was just talk, but he is a big hulk of a man and his story is believable to an impressionable group of kids. He says goodbye to his fan club, gathers his stuff, and heads out because his overnight shift is over.

Joe takes a side alley shortcut to where his car is parked, the same one he takes every night. Halfway down the alley, he is confronted by a hulk of a man dressed in total black. The man is bigger than Joe—which is saying something—so Joe reaches for the 9mm he carries in his jacket pocket for just such occasions.

He produces his weapon and points it at Lou. "Step aside, big man," he says. "I'm tired and don't want to put two in your chest, but I will—if you're still standing there in five seconds."

Moving faster than Joe could imagine a big guy could, Big Lou steps to the side, away from the barrel of the 9mm, grabs Joe's wrist and twists it backwards until the gun drops and Joe's wrist breaks.

"Shit!" Joe yells, clutching at his painfully broken wrist with his other hand.

In another swift move, Lou steps behind Joe, grabs his head in his powerful hands, and utters "This is for Craig!" With that, he snaps Joe's neck. Joe collapses to the ground.

Lou takes Joe's wallet out, removes the cash and credit cards and throws the wallet on the ground near the body. He takes out a six-inch hunting knife, stabs the now lifeless Joe in the heart, makes sure he gets some of Joe's blood on his gloves, and leaves, taking the knife with him. Lou returns to where his car is parked. He removes a plastic garbage bag from the trunk, into which he places the knife, bloody gloves, and boots. Then, he places the bag in the trunk and drives home. He is exhausted and thoughts and memories are racing through his head but once again, no headache.

Several hours later, a man on his way to work discovers Joe's body as he is cutting through the alley. He calls 911. A patrol car is in the vicinity, responds to the call, and acknowledges that they are enroute to the crime scene.

Both Flanagan and Devin also hear the call and arrive at the scene about the same time.

Flanagan gets out and sees Devin. "You following me?" he asks her.

"Yes," Devin says, sarcastically. "My life is so boring that I need to follow you for excitement."

"Very funny," Flanagan says. They approach the patrol officers who were first on the scene. "What's the story here?" Flanagan asks.

"Robbery gone bad, detective," the patrol officer says.

"A lot of that going around," Devin says.

"It's a rough city, in case you didn't notice," Flanagan says.

"Yes," Devin says, "I know. The victim didn't, perchance, have a Triangel employee ID in his wallet?" she asks.

"He did, but the cash and credit cards are gone," the patrol officer responds. "How did you know?"

Devin just walks away and heads to her car, deep in thought.

CHAPTER 29
ATCHINSON SAYS

Mitch Atchinson enters the conference room of Brickman's Bistros for his scheduled staff meeting. He is confident and anxious to mark his territory in front of a solemn audience of loyal DeAngelo management personnel. Once inside, he directs each vice president, district manager and sales supervisor to take notes and pay attention. He makes it clear there will be changes and new reporting standards. He further implies that there will be no challenging of his authority or mention of DeAngelo's previous style. He also makes it clear that anyone who disagrees with him can leave.

Atchinson is the product of a blue-collar upbringing. His father, a machinist, and his mother, a seamstress, were good disciplinarians and fine people, but Atchinson always harbored resentment for his lot in life. A skinny kid with severe acne and over-active ambitions, he'd detached himself from other schoolmates by finding chemistry and math projects that would make him the teacher's delight and a model student. He'd also been an informant, turning on other schoolmates when they indulged in childhood mischief. He'd earned the title, 'Snitch,' and an occasional beating from the school jock. Upon entering college, he'd found his calling in business and embraced those classmates who had the same ambitions and questionable talents. Always the candidate and never the real player, he'd grown to unseat his superiors in business, first by earning their trust, and then, by finding their weaknesses to push them aside, in order to make his move.

After a rocky road in his previous companies and always relieved due to his questionable management style, he now had his "brass ring"—he was the CEO of a public company and one of the most prominent restaurant and coffee enterprises in the industry. Named as one of the Top 50 Food Companies in America, he had finally arrived—not on his own, but on the back of a friend who trusted him and gave him the keys to the kitchen and a fresh start.

The meeting takes a turn as some of the employees refuse to back down, pushing Atchinson for answers regarding the IPO and Donnie.

The first to speak is Ron Brinkman, Vice President of Operations, who'd started with Donnie almost twenty years before, and who was raised to the position of VP by Donnie, during his years of service. "Mitch, what's going on with Donnie?"

Atchinson seems annoyed by the question, but bites his lip and answers, "Donnie is still here, but in a lesser capacity. We value his service, but clearly, we have to take another direction and our investors prefer to follow my lead."

Brinkman continues, "What does that mean? Are we still going to be public and trade—and what is Donnie's position?"

"Yes, we will repair what's been done incorrectly and move forward. Donnie's position has no title for now—let's just say he's a consultant."

"Well, how do we support our new acquisitions? Plus, I have complaints about payroll and late paydays and other items."

Atchinson smiles, pointing to an agenda he has posted on the presentation board. "We have a new payroll company and we will be funded as needed, but we first need to clean up some things. That will all be handled in time. Let me handle that and as I fix things, I will update you. For now, just do your job, make things happen, and keep me informed of every activity. I want this meeting of our management staff every Monday and I want a morning meeting with my VP's every morning. Is that clear?"

The response is faint and delayed.

Atchinson repeats himself. "Is that clear?"

They all murmur, "Yes."

"Then, the meeting is over."

The rank and file march out, as if drugged. Each one gives Atchinson a questioning stare, as if to say, this isn't going to work. After they leave, Atchinson is told he has a call from Colombia. Confused by the origin of the call, he tells one of the secretaries to ask what it's about. She tells him it's a coffee distributor in Colombia with an interesting offer for the company. He tells her he will take the call.

"Hello, to whom am I speaking?"

"Yes, Mr. Atchinson, this is Juan Carlo Mendoza, of Colombian Cantina. We are a premier coffee distributor in Colombia, with the finest blends of Arabica coffee, at a price I will provide to Brickman's Bistros—that none of your competitors can touch, and which will move you toward a bigger market share."

"Mr. Mendoza, I already buy my coffee through a broker and they negotiate good prices and quality for me, but thank you for your interest."

"Mr. Atchinson, what are you paying now for your finest Arabica blend?"

"That's not for me to tell you."

"Okay, how would you like this deal? If I cut your current cost by fifty percent, with a better quality coffee, and guarantee to keep that price for one year, which will allow you to get larger market share and reduce your costs in your restaurants, would you be interested?"

"I don't know. That sounds inviting, but I don't do deals like this over the phone."

"Fine, then I will meet with you, sir. I'll be in New Jersey and New York this coming week. I will bring you some samples to show you why we are considered an outstanding up-and-coming respected distributor, along with an agreement that will make what you have now look like a joke. All I ask is that you give us exclusive rights to your coffee purchases and allow us to use the Brickman's Bistros name in our marketing. You grow and we grow in market share—and we both win."

The wheels turn in Atchinson's head. He knows if he can immediately cut costs on both his coffee distribution outlets and his restaurants, plus improve profitability in a big way, he will be an instant success. Driven by ego and greed, he agrees to a meeting.

"Okay, Mendoza, be at my office next Monday, at 8 a.m., and we'll see."

"Fine, Mr. Atchinson, you won't be sorry. This is something that will really impact your company and investors."

Atchinson, in his haste, makes his phone call to Goelner, who'd asked him to call after the meeting and give him a report on how it went. He quickly glosses over the meeting and tells Goelner they all understand who's in charge now, and about the improvements that Atchinson will make to advance the company. He informs Goelner that Donnie is relegated to a non-issue, as he'd made it clear to the management. He will provide the new plans for moving the company forward. Goelner is patronizing, but has little use for Atchinson, except in the capacity of transitioning the company to new management.

"That's good, Mitch, keep it up. I knew it would work with you there, as CEO."

"Wesley, I've already begun on working down costs and improving quality. My sources will get me one of the primo Colombian distributors of Arabica Coffee. I believe we can distribute to our outlets and customers at a much lower price and, at the same time, decrease our coffee costs by nearly fifty percent."

"Mitch, if you can do that, we can push like crazy—add locations, and a richer bottom line that would make the stock jump. I like what you're doing! Stay on it and good luck, I gotta go, someone is waiting."

Smiling and leaning back in his chair, Goelner begins to imagine the new Brickman's Bistros rising to the top twenty or even the top ten rankings in the industry media and he, himself, turning into the industry titan he always dreamed he would become. Full of himself, he leaves to play golf and tells his VP of Operations, Brinkman, to cover while he conducts important outside meetings.

The Monday morning meeting with Mendoza is pregnant with possibilities for both parties. The coffee distributor is anxious to make a deal and Atchinson is anxious to be a hero. He moves quickly to learn if the offer can translate into a reality, soon. Mendoza opens the meeting with brochures and reference letters and photos of his plant in Colombia and the farms they own. They brew and taste the coffee that is rich with body and gourmet appeal. Atchinson is anxious to finalize an arrangement and takes the lead as the buyer.

"So, Mr. Mendoza, we have a reputation as having not only a fine coffee in our restaurants, but we distribute to over 100 other restaurants on the East Coast. How can we distinguish between our restaurants and what we distribute?"

"Mr. Atchinson, we can provide two blends—one very high end Arabica blend for your restaurants, and a second blend, just a step below, that you provide to your outlets or customers, which will still give you the edge. Or you can offer the same blend that you have now in your restaurants as your brand name in the other outlets. This would give you market appeal in other areas of distribution, while defining the Brickman's Bistros name. It's up to you."

Atchinson, in his anticipation of a quick start, but needing to appear diligent, refrains somewhat, making Mendoza work for the deal.

Mendoza senses Atchinson's appetite for his proposal and makes him an offer he knows will be difficult to ignore. "Mr. Atchinson, I know you are reluctant to make changes, so here is what I will do for you. I will send you a first shipment sample of our finest blend coffee, large enough for you to see we can supply your needs and that we are consistent in our merchandise. This will give you more than enough to distribute to your restaurants or outlets, and I will give it to you for a price that will be very profitable, which will make you and your investors immediately happy."

Atchinson feels the move toward his ultimate great success coming closer and closer to reality and hastens to find out more. "And what amount and cost will that be?"

"We will ship you 20,000 pounds at one dollar fifty per

pound, plus shipping. That's less than my cost, but it will get us into your bloodline and you will see you have the best. But, I must require a fifty percent deposit—and the balance and shipping charges, on delivery. Do we have a deal?"

Atchinson holds back his excitement at the possibility of covering much of their coffee needs for the first month and making a formidable profit. He feels he needs to act quickly, to show Goelner he's been on the deal for some time. He doesn't worry about the deposit—it's small enough that even if the deal is not real, it's small enough to hide. He shakes Mendoza's hand. "You have a deal, Mr. Mendoza! My secretary will prepare a check for you. Perhaps you and I will grow immeasurably over the next year, but how soon can you have the sample shipment sent to me?"

"I will call my plant immediately and prepare to ship to your warehouse this coming week. Is that good?"

"Perfect! I look forward to trying it! If it's as good as you say everyone will benefit."

Mendoza smiles and shakes his hand enthusiastically. "Oh, don't worry, it's really good! You will be surprised."

CHAPTER 30
HUMPTY DUMPTY HAD A
GREAT FALL

It's last call at the Starlight Lounge in Harrison, the preferred hangout of Tony Caputo and a cast of generally unsavory characters. Tony sits in the back at his table, smoking a big cigar, even though smoking in bars has been outlawed in New Jersey for years. Tony, a big guy, about 6'3" and around 225 pounds, is a little soft around the middle, but still capable of handling himself. Years of boxing in local gyms has given Tony a reputation as a tough guy.

In addition, he behaves like a wiseguy and even though he isn't really a made man, he does some low level jobs for the made guys—collecting money and such. Some of the other Starlight patrons are annoyed that Tony is smoking, but in the Starlight, no one tells Tony what to do. He has painted a larger than life picture of himself to the bartenders and managers— none of whom want to engage a hot head like Tony, with or without his expressed mob connections.

Tony stubs out his cigar in the only ashtray on the bar, left there for his express use, writes his name and number on a fifty dollar bill and leaves it with Casey, the new cute waitress he thinks has been flirting with him all night. In reality, she would probably prefer root canal to an evening with a pig like Tony, but she is good at her job and conveys flirtation, rather than disgust. She is new to the Starlight, having recently relocated from Florida, but is no stranger to dealing with guys like Tony. Tony buys her pretended sexual interest partly because he wants to and partly because his ego makes him think that all the girls want him. His self-image makes Casey's con that much easier.

Tony stumbles out of the bar, perhaps a little drunker than usual, and starts the short walk home. Another reason that he likes the Starlight is that it's walking distance from his apartment.

He may be a thug, but he knows enough not to risk driving drunk and getting pulled over for a DUI. You never know what the officers might find, should they decide to search the vehicle. Tony may be an uneducated thug by academic standards, having barely finished high school, but the college of hard knocks has taught him a few things and he understands the way of the streets.

Tony walks the two blocks to his apartment. It's three o'clock in the morning and the streets are early morning quiet. There is only the sound of the occasional sewer rat foraging for food by the restaurant dumpsters. It's a dark night and for some, it would be eerie walking in the quiet darkness, but Tony feels invulnerable on his home turf.

Tony climbs the front steps to his ground floor apartment and puts his key in the lock. He opens the front door and stumbles inside. He flips the light switch, but the lights don't go on. Before his fuzzy, half-drunk brain has time to process the lack of response from the light switch, Sonny pounces on him from the darkness. Sonny charges at Tony, coming in low and grabbing the bigger man's ankles in a much practiced football tackle. The big man goes down hard.

The intensity of Sonny's attack, combined with the complete surprise to his already fuzzy brain, makes him an easy target. Tony starts to shift into fight mode as he realizes what is happening, but it's too late. Sonny is on him as he lays face down on the floor and before he can react, Sonny is slipping nylon ties around his ankles and tightening them. Tony, now completely alert and awake, starts to thrash violently, so Sonny slams his face into the carpet, kneels on the small of his back and binds his wrists together, behind his back, with another nylon tie. Sonny then gets off of Tony.

Now Tony is alert and enraged. He tries to get to his feet, but Sonny kicks him back down.

Sonny roughly rolls Tony onto his back with his boot, so Tony can see him. Tony glares up at Sonny. "You have no idea who you're fucking with!" Tony screams at Sonny. Sonny grabs Tony by the hair and slams his head against the floor. Tony is stunned and his eyes close briefly as he struggles to stay conscious. Sonny grabs the roll of duct tape that he brought with him and deftly tapes Tony's mouth shut to prevent any further outcries. When Tony finally opens his eyes, he sees the silencer of Sonny's 22-caliber pistol, inches from his face.

Sonny is dressed in surgical scrubs, complete with the sterile booties worn to prevent the tracking of bacteria into clean rooms. He is wearing surgical gloves and Tony has no idea who this crazed madman is.

Fear grips the normally unafraid Tony. He feels at the mercy of a man who he perceives as a crazed intruder. Tony's head starts to clear. He looks at Sonny, but he has no idea who he is or what he wants. Tony's mind goes into bargaining mode, but he can't speak because his mouth is taped. He is helpless and afraid.

Sonny puts a knee on Tony's chest, puts his Glock to Tony's forehead and speaks quietly. "I'm going to take this tape off and you will be silent," he says. "Nod if you understand."

Tony nods.

Sonny roughly rips the duct tape off of Tony's mouth. "How does it feel to be helpless?" Sonny asks Tony.

Tony opens his mouth to answer, but Sonny silences him by putting the muzzle of his silencer into Tony's mouth. "What kind of a piece of shit beats a man in a wheel chair?" Sonny asks.

Now Tony begins to understand what this is about and fear grips him anew. Sonny takes the gun barrel out of Tony's mouth. "It wasn't supposed to go that way," Tony stammers.

"Shut it," Sonny says.

"We were just supposed to scare him," Tony continues, hoping to reason with Sonny.

"Not interested," Sonny says, placing the end of the silencer to Tony's forehead. "The man you beat and killed was my uncle Craig—the finest man I will ever know. You took him from me and left him to die in a back alley like garbage. He was a hero and like a second father to me."

"I'm sorry," Tony says, in what sounds like a dry whisper.

"Too late for misplaced, self-serving regrets," Sonny says. "Actions have consequences. Live by the sword and die by the sword. This is for you, Uncle Craig," Sonny says, as Tony's eyes widen with fear. Sonny puts two rounds into Tony's head, avenging the death of his beloved uncle.

Sonny removes a business card from his pocket. The business card is one of Ridgefield's cards. Sonny takes a pen that he has wiped clean of fingerprints from the duffle bag he brought with him. He forces Tony's dead hand to hold it. He uses the pen to make the dead man scrawl "10K – Craig Andersen" on the back of the business card. Sonny then crumbles the card slightly, dirties it a little with grime from the carpet, walks into the bedroom and places it on Tony's nightstand next to a half-drunk beer and the latest copy of Hustler.

He retrieves his duffle bag and goes into the kitchen and takes a water glass out of his bag. The glass has Ridgefield's fingerprints on it. He'd been keeping it in a Ziploc bag ever since he stole it from the lunchroom in Ridgefield's building, while posing as a busboy. He places the glass on the kitchen table by one of the chairs. He then goes to the cupboard and, as he has imagined, finds an array of mismatched bowls, plates and glasses—exactly what he has expected. He takes out one of Caputo's glasses. He goes back into the living room and places Caputo's dead hand on the glass. He then goes back into the kitchen and places that glass across from the Ridgefield glass. The glasses don't match, but that won't arouse suspicion when the police finally get there, since nothing in Tony's sloppy apartment matches.

Sonny goes to the refrigerator and looks inside for some open beverage. He finds a bottle of screw top wine and removes it. He pours just a trace into each glass and replaces the wine in the refrigerator. The scene is exactly as he has envisioned. It looks like two people, now clearly identifiable by their finger-prints and DNA, sat at the table and shared a drink.

Finally, Sonny goes into the sloppy catchall room that could, perhaps, be called Tony's office. He looks around for something that could identify Caputo. To his surprise, he finds that Tony has business cards—Tony Caputo, odd jobs, with a number on the back. Wow, he thinks, even thugs have busi-ness cards, these days! He takes a card, brings it back into the living room and places the dead man's thumb and forefinger on the card to transfer prints and DNA. Sonny then places the dead man's hand on the pen he used previously and this time, scrawls 'call me' on the back of the card. He does his best to copy Tony's handwriting from the signature on the driver's license he finds in Tony's wallet. Sonny then tosses the pen onto the desk in Tony's office and puts the business card into a Ziploc bag and back into his duffle bag. He then puts Tony's license back into his wallet and puts the wallet back into Tony's back pocket.

Sonny then removes the nylon ties he'd bound Tony with and puts them in his duffle bag. This will be viewed as a surprise murder, Tony knowing his assailant and not needing to be bound, as he wouldn't have seen this coming. Finally, Sonny tightens the light bulbs that he had loosened so that they wouldn't go on when Tony flicked the light switch.

His work done, he checks the alley behind Tony's apartment. There is no one around. Sonny exits the apartment into the dark night through the same bathroom window he'd used for entry. He walks a few blocks and then removes the booties, scrubs and gloves behind an abandoned building. He places the items he removed into his duffle bag and walks the two blocks to the subway.

Fifteen minutes later, Sonny gets off the subway and walks the three blocks to his apartment.

Once inside, Sonny retrieves the flash drive he has been keeping, containing the video of Ridgefield and Irina in bed. He places the flash drive and Caputo's business card – upon which he'd written, "call me" with Caputo's dead hand—into an envelope. On the outside of the envelope, Sonny writes "Victor Zalenko – PERSONAL."

Sonny puts on a jacket, slips the envelope into the inside

pocket and heads back outside. This time, he's headed to Zalenko's night club in Brighton Beach – Club Z. Sonny knows Victor is typically there all night, drinking and enjoying his girls.

Sonny finds Victor's car in the parking lot. Victor drives an old Cadillac, no alarm and most importantly, no GPS. Victor likes to remain under the radar when possible. It is easy for Sonny to use a slim-jim to open the driver's side door on the older Cadillac. Sonny places the envelope on the driver's seat, locks the door and quietly closes it.

Sonny heads back to his apartment. He removes the disposable cell phone he'd bought for this purpose and calls Zalenko. Victor answers and the background noise is loud. Russian music is playing and girls are laughing. "Who is this?" Victor shouts over the din.

"There is a package from Tony in your car," Sonny says, in a muffled voice.

"What?" Victor shouts. "Who the fuck is this?"

"Check your car," Sonny says in his loudest yell-whisper and hangs up. His mission is complete for the night and he is exhausted—exhausted, but at peace. He has avenged his uncle's death. It is cold comfort, but it is the best he could do. These are his last thoughts, as he slips into a coma-like sleep.

CHAPTER 31
THE CRIME SCENE

Sonny is still sleeping the next morning when Tony Caputo's housekeeper, Alana, shows up to clean his apartment. It's 7 a.m. and the sun isn't really up yet, so the apartment is dimly lit. But she knows it well enough to navigate the path to the kitchen where she usually begins her work. Her first task is to start the coffee so it's ready for Meester Caputo—as she calls Tony—when he wakes up.

As she makes a beeline for the kitchen, she trips over Tony's corpse. Her bucket of cleaning supplies goes flying and she lands with a thud on something soft. She collects herself, and as her eyes adjust to the light, she realizes that she is lying on top of Meester Caputo and staring into his lifeless eyes. She screams in horror and continues screaming until Cindi from across the hall comes running to see what is happening. She also screams as she sees the grisly sight and reaches for her cell phone to call 911. She tries to console the almost hysterical Alana as they both wait for the police to arrive.

The uniforms arrive quickly and begin securing the crime scene. The crime scene tape goes up and Alana and the neighbor are escorted to the kitchen for questioning by Detective

Daniel Flores, a young, but up-and-coming five-year veteran of HPD. Flores is about to seat them at the kitchen table when he sees the empty glasses and realizes they may become evidence. He apologizes to Alana and Cindi and directs them to the back bedroom/office and asks them to take a seat on the couch.

Detective Flores begins asking them routine questions: When was the last time you saw Mr. Caputo? What did you see exactly, when you came in this morning? Do you have a key to this apartment? Does anyone else have a key? Did Mr. Caputo have any enemies?

Detective Flores is getting very little valuable information from Alana and less from Cindi. Alana certainly has a key, but knows little of Mr. Caputo's activities or acquaintances and Cindi only knows that he is a big, loud man who frequently smokes stinky cigars in the common areas of the building. Alana can offer little information and is quite shaken. After some brief questioning, one of the uniformed officers offers to drive her home. She accepts.

Detective Flores moves around the apartment, questioning his colleagues and looking around so he can assess the situation effectively. He wants to have something useful to offer Captain Rodriguez when he arrives.

Rodriguez has been somewhat of a mentor to Flores ever since arresting him in a gang sweep many years ago and convincing him that there were better places for a sharp kid than on a slab in the morgue or doing time in a state prison – places Rodriguez thought Flores was headed if he didn't get his head on straight. Rodriguez got to Flores – and got to him at a critical time.

Flores was the child of parents who'd had no business having a kid. His mother had been a drunk and a cheap hooker who frequently brought her Johns home. She would lock young

Daniel in his room and tell him to turn the TV up loud until Mommy came to get him. He did, but the walls were thin and he could hear his mother having sex with different men, many of whom were quite rough with her. He'd often been scared, but dared not cry out for fear of igniting his mother's wrath. She'd been a mean drunk.

Danny's father had been a burglar. He'd spent a lot of Danny's youth in jail and Danny hardly knew him.

It wasn't hard to imagine that with such lousy role models, he would be drawn to a life of crime, just like his old man. Rodriguez had come into Flores' life at a critical time and Danny had responded to the mentoring. He'd been looking for direction, guidance, and for someone who actually cared about him. Rodriguez did, and Danny would never forget the role the police captain had played, stepping in where his absent father never could or would.

Captain Rodriguez arrives and takes command, as the crime scene investigators and medical examiner scurry around and complete their respective tasks. The captain's protocol is to set up a command post and have the various teams at a crime scene report to him, as they gather evidence or form theories or hunches about what has transpired.

He carries a leather briefcase in which he keeps several lined pads, a thick spiral notebook and a collection of sharp number two black and blue pencils. He has a very orderly and consistent way of doing things and has no interest in heading into the electronic age, as many of his fellow officers had. He is fine with pencils and paper. He would take notes on a yellow pad, adding his own comments in blue pencil, and later that day, he would transcribe the key points into the spiral notebook. He would repeat this process throughout a case until it was solved. Not all cases were solved, of course, and when enough time elapsed on a case where a decision was made to drop it, he would make a note in his notebook to that effect—but would always keep all the old notebooks, just in case.

Rodriguez sets up shop in the bedroom at the suggestion of Flores, takes out a pad and a few pencils, and waits patiently as his team continues to collect and catalog evidence.

He is collecting his thoughts when Devin walks into the kitchen. As always, she is a vision of efficient sexiness. She is stunning in her dark blue, just a little too tight skirt and blouse, with her trademark black stiletto pumps, the ones with the red soles. He looks up, surprised to see her.

"What are you doing here?" he asks.

"Your guys can't keep a secret and are trying to make points with me."

Devin comes over and gives him a kiss on the cheek and a hug. She smells great and she leaves a hint of her perfume on his suit where her wrist touches his shoulder, as she hugs him just a little longer than necessary.

The captain takes the opportunity to enjoy the smell of her thick, perfumed chestnut hair. It is intoxicating and very distracting. Devin knows the effect she has on men and on the captain, in particular. She lingers and brushes against him just enough to really get his attention and then takes a seat next to him on the office couch. He watches as she crosses her sexy legs and can't help wondering what it would feel like to have them wrapped around him. She smiles as she sees the lustful and slightly dazed look in his eyes. Finally, he snaps out of it and refocuses on the crime scene investigation.

"We've got to stop meeting in these romantic locations," Rodriguez says. "People could talk."

"Yes," Devin says. "There's something about a dead body that gets my heart racing."

"Sick," Rodriguez says. "Sick, but amusing."

"So what do we have here?" Devin asks.

"Not sure, yet," Rodriguez replies, "but at first glance, it appears to be a deal among friends, or should I say, thugs gone bad."

"You think?" Devin says.

"You don't?" Rodriguez replies.

"Not sure," Devin says. "I'd like to stick around and see what the crew comes up with."

"Fine with me," Rodriguez says. "I'd rather look at you than at these mutts," he adds, laughing, glancing at the various detectives and technicians scurrying around.

As each team finishes up, its members come to Rodriguez and give him their report – what they found, what they didn't find, and what they think. The general consensus is a deal between two criminals gone bad. Rodriguez takes copious notes on his pad as Devin looks over his shoulder, sitting just close enough so he can smell her and feel her breath on his neck. It is intoxicating and very distracting.

In the meantime, Detective Flores is conducting his own tour of the apartment and surrounding areas. Daniel always likes to do his own crime scene investigation and form his own opinion, in addition to finding out what the teams found or thought. He spends more than an hour walking around inside and outside, thinking, measuring, and looking at the scene from different angles. After a long while, Flores comes into the bedroom/office. He is the last to finish and when he comes in, everyone is gone except for him, the captain, and Devin.

"What you got?" Rodriguez asks.

"Well," Flores says, "we found a window open in the bathroom. That could be where the perp got in, or he could have had a key, or the victim could have let him in."

"So, nothing," Rodriguez says.

"I'm not finished, Captain," Flores continues. "We found a business card from that guy, Ridgefield, who we've been looking at and it says '10K – Craig Andersen' on the back. On the surface, it appears that it could be as simple as a reminder that 10K would be coming Caputo's way – as payment for dealing with Andersen. It could have been payment for a beating that went too far, or maybe it was payment for a hit on Andersen. I doubt it's the latter. These guys weren't hardened criminals. They were just dirty, corporate types used to getting their way, with the use of a little muscle, sometimes. Either way, perhaps Ridgefield hired Caputo, things didn't go as planned, and he came here to discuss the situation. We do have the wine glasses in the kitchen. They both have prints on them and possibly DNA." He continues, "If the prints end up matching Caputo and Ridgefield, that would support my working theory. You know, Cap, we've been looking at Ridgefield and Caputo for the Andersen murder. You remember the tip we got from Louie the baker?"

"Yeah," Rodriguez says. "It's looking a lot like a disagreement between conspirators. Perhaps Ridgefield was paranoid about leaving loose ends around, since the beating turned into a murder. Perhaps Caputo was a loose end."

"It makes sense to me, Cap," Flores says.

They both nod.

"How about you, Devin?" Rodriguez asks. "This make sense to you?"

"Sure," Devin says, "it makes sense. I just don't believe that's what happened."

"You spooks are always looking for some complex labyrinth of intrigue, but sometimes, it's just a simple deal gone bad," Rodriguez says.

"Ex spooks," Devin says. "Sometimes, it is as simple as it

looks, but sometimes it isn't," Devin continues.

"How profound," Flores says. "Sometimes it is and sometimes it isn't. I'll have to remember that. Well, cap, I'm done here. See you back at the precinct?" Flores asks.

"Yes, Flores, I'll be back in a while. I need to confer with my colleague first," Rodriguez says.

"I'm sure you do," Flores says and leaves.

Devin and Rodriguez sit for a while. Devin is unconvinced that this is a Caputo-Ridgefield deal gone bad, but keeps any further thoughts to herself. She thinks things are just too neat – the fingerprints, if they match Ridgefield, the business card. It just seems too neat.

"I've got to go," she says to Rodriguez.

"Always a pleasure," Rodriguez says.

"Could be much more pleasurable if you wanted it to be," Devin says as he gets up and leans over to kiss her for real. They enjoy a moment of passion and then, Devin disconnects. "Very unprofessional, captain, but that was nice," she says. "Perhaps if the surroundings were different, it could lead to something," she says with a slightly devilish smile. Devin starts to head out, but stops. "I have a question," she says to Rodriguez. "Were there any footprints found leading to the door, or back behind the open window? It rained a few days ago and it's pretty muddy. There should be some footprints somewhere."

"I don't know," Rodriguez says. "Let me ask Flores." He reaches for his cell and calls. While it's ringing, he says, "Here's a bonus – I get a few more moments to gaze at your sexiness."

"Very unprofessional," Devin says, "but much appreciated." She winks. "Maybe one day, you should do more than gaze."

They sit looking at each other, the sexual tension increasingly palpable, as Flores answers. Rodriguez relays Devin's question.

"Interesting about the footprints," Flores says.

"How so?" the captain asks.

"There are no footprints on the front steps at all, but in the mud outside the window, there are foot-shaped marks."

"What does that mean – foot-shaped marks?" Rodriguez asks.

"Like someone was wearing galoshes or something. No tread marks, though. Smooth marks."

"Interesting. Thanks, Flores," he says and disconnects. He relays this information to Devin.

"Very interesting," she says. "I've got to go."

"That's it?" Rodriguez says. "Very interesting?"

"That's all I've got for now. I need to think about this. I'll call you if I come up with anything, or perhaps if I get lonely later."

She leaves, with Rodriguez wondering about many things.

After she leaves, Rodriguez heads to his car, calls Flores, and tells him to send two uniforms, Williams and Johnson, to pick up Ridgefield for questioning. He is comfortable with the theory of a beating for hire gone bad and he wants to investigate it further. He gives Flores the address of Triangel and suggests they go there to find Ridgefield.

The uniforms arrive at Triangel, but no Ridgefield. Williams radios in to Flores and Flores patches in Captain Rodriguez, who tells them to ask for Goelner. He should know where Ridgefield is.

"Back in a moment," Williams says. There is some static and then Rodriguez hears, "No Goelner either and no one here knows where either one is."

"Thanks, Williams," Rodriguez says. "Head back to the station. I'm going to turn this over to Detective Flores."

"Roger that, Captain," Williams says and signs off.

CHAPTER 32
SWIMMING WITH THE FISHES

It's 11 p.m. and Rodriguez is preparing to watch the news and enjoy a scotch, some honey roasted peanuts, and a few slices of summer sausage. His cardiologist would probably be horrified, but after getting out of the service years before, having seen things no man should ever see, he'd vowed to himself that he would enjoy his life—even if it ended a little sooner than it could have, had he taken care of himself like his doctor had advised. So far, it was working out fine.

This late night TV, scotch and snack ritual is something he enjoys as often as his crazy schedule allows. Rodriguez lives in a nice two-bedroom condo in Jersey City, overlooking the Hudson River and the New York City skyline. The condo is on the 9th floor of a luxury high-rise building which Rodriguez normally couldn't afford; however, it was his dream to live in a place like this, so, when it became available pre-renovation, he borrowed from friends and bought the place. He'd worked all kinds of security type side jobs to pay back his friends, but in his eyes, it was well worth it. He loves the place, which turned out to be an excellent investment to boot. Overall, it's clearly been the best financial and joy producing move he'd ever made.

Being a confirmed bachelor, his condo is decorated like a traditional man cave. The focal point of the apartment is the living room, or rather, the TV room. One wall is mostly windows to capitalize on the view and the other consists of a sixty-inch plasma TV with all the high fidelity and surround sound accoutrements to make the room as close to a private theatre as possible. Other than the TV and sound system, the room is sparsely furnished.

There are, however, dog toys scattered around the room and Rodriquez's eighty-pound pit-bull, Rocco, is laying in the middle of the room enjoying a huge bone the neighborhood butcher had dropped off as a thank you to Rodriguez for handling some unpleasantness with local toughs looking to sell the butcher some insurance that he didn't need. The butcher had offered the straight arrow, Rodriguez, a monetary gift as thank you for his help, but the captain told him an occasional bone for Rocco would be fine. That occasional bone had turned out to be a Friday tradition and neither he nor Rocco is complaining.

The captain sits in his plush leather recliner chair, turns on the elaborate TV system, and settles in for a relaxing end to a brutal day. He takes his first sip of scotch, the first sip always being the sweetest, as his phone rings and jars him out of his relaxed state. "Shit," he says out loud when he sees who's calling. It's Flores. This can't be good at 11pm.

"Captain," Flores says, "we found Ridgefield."

"Great," Rodriguez replies. "And I need to know this at 11 p.m. on a Friday—why?" he asks.

"Well," Flores says, "he's dead."

"Shit," Rodriguez says. "Who found him and where?"

"A longshoreman down at Pier 11 spotted a strange black object floating near the shore. He hooked it with one of those towing poles and dragged it to the boat ramp out of curiosity.

He ripped open the bag and threw up when he saw the contents. He called 911 and Johnson responded. He's working a double today. He recognized the victim as Ridgefield."

"Crap," Rodriguez says. "I'm on my way."

"See you there, cap." Flores says and hangs up.

When Rodriguez arrives at the pier, the same crew that had spent the afternoon at Caputo's apartment is already there.

The ME, Brian Paterson, comes up to Rodriguez. "Amateur body dump," he says. "The clown's weighted down by cans filled with concrete, but they weren't heavy enough to keep it down once the body started to decay and swell with methane. Must have been their first time disposing of a body this way."

"Hey," the captain says, "you're always looking for extra money, Paterson. Maybe you should produce a seminar on how to properly dispose of a body."

"Good idea," Paterson says.

"I was joking," Rodriguez says.

"Seems like a solid idea to me," Paterson says.

"You're a sick fuck," Rodriguez says.

"Perhaps," Paterson replies.

"Anything else I should know?" Rodriguez asks.

"Yeah," Paterson says. "Mr. Ridgefield had two .22 caliber holes in the back of his head, his hands were bound behind him with nylon ties, and his balls were cut off and stuffed into his mouth."

"This just keeps getting better and better," Rodriguez says. "I may never get to sleep tonight. Was the castration performed pre or post mortem?"

"Judging from the amount of blood pooled near the victim's groin and in his throat, I would say the victim was alive when they cut his balls off."

"My God," Rodriguez says. "Someone was very pissed off."

"Indeed," Paterson says, "I'm used to seeing a lot of sick shit, but this will definitely give me nightmares. This guy must have fucked with the wrong guy."

"Or the wrong woman," Rodriguez says.

"Don't even go there, cap," Paterson says. "I'm just getting back into the dating world after my divorce. Your idea could keep me home whacking off to 'net girls who can never reach out and touch me."

"Sorry to slow your roll," Rodriguez says, "but it could be a woman."

"Shit, captain," Paterson says and walks away, absent-mindedly holding his dick.

Rodriguez realizes that he also, is holding his dick. It seems to be the natural reaction when a crime like this is committed. He still has his hand on his dick when he turns and literally runs into Devin. He is surprised and a little embarrassed.

"What are you doing here?" Rodriguez asks. "And don't tell me some lame story about your scanner. It's after midnight and either you're stalking me, which I probably wouldn't mind, or something else is going on."

"As charming as I find you, captain," Devin says, "it's the something else. Although the sight of all you macho cops walking around holding your dicks is a sight to see," she continues. "I assume this victim had an injury to his dick?" she asks.

Rodriguez tells her about the pre-mortem castration theory espoused by Paterson.

"Wow," Devin says. "I can understand why you are all holding your dicks and I am becoming more and more interested in this case."

"Care to tell me why?" Rodriguez asks.

"Perhaps," Devin says, "in due time. Any thoughts?" she asks.

"Not sure," Rodriguez says, "but we need to figure out

what is really going on here. This is turning into an epidemic. In this case, I think maybe Caputo had this hit arranged before Ridgefield killed him. They did each other in," he tells Devin. "It makes sense to me. What do you think?" he asks her.

"Good theory," Devin says.

"And?" Rodriguez asks.

"I'm not buying it," Devin says.

"I'll ask again, care to share?"

"Not yet," Devin says. "You mind if I look around?" she asks.

"Not at all," Rodriguez says. "I always welcome your involvement."

"Thanks," Devin says and heads off towards the pier and the team of investigators.

CHAPTER 33
FAT AND HAPPY

Wesley Goelner is on his second day of extreme partying with his favorite woman of the night, Marlena. They are shacked up at the Four Seasons Hotel, in the Presidential Suite. Between hotel bills, room service, champagne and Marlena, Wesley is burning close to $10,000 per day, but he doesn't give a shit. After all, it's not his money. It's money stolen from duped investors and when it runs out, he will steal some more. He is feeling like the King of Wall Street! He has no idea that his cronies, Ridgefield and Caputo, have been murdered. All he is thinking about is doing another line and having more sex with Marlena.

Wesley had not always been the contemptible pig he is, today. He'd grown up in the privileged Five Towns section of Long Island, the son of disinterested, but wealthy parents, truly a latch key kid—albeit, the key and lock were made of gold.

Nonetheless, Wesley had raised himself. Schooled by a nanny when he was young, he'd soon enough outgrown her influence and learned from the spoiled rich kids he hung out with. His clique had a lot in common—too much money, too much unsupervised time, and lousy role models. Most of the parents had considered their kids more as possessions than as family, taking them out when it suited them, but most of the time, leaving them under the care and tutelage of others. These kids had grown up thinking that they could buy their way out of anything and/or call Dad's lawyer to 'fix' things. The group, and Wesley in particular, had grown up with entitled, self-serving values.

Wesley had learned from watching his dad, albeit from a distance, four core values:

- The pursuit of money is everything;
- Take what you want and vanquish your enemies,
- Surround yourself with good lawyers and fall guys,
- Fuck every woman who is even remotely intriguing.

Wesley lives his life by these "values." The result is a lifetime spent creating wealth, destroying lives and disrespecting his family, most notably, his devoted wife, Emily. Many wonder why Emily stays with a pig like Wesley, but it's probably due to fear of losing the luxurious lifestyle in which she lives, so she is willing to look the other way, while Wesley fucks everything in a skirt.

Wesley lives the life of a second-generation rich kid. He has developed a commonly held rich kids' opinion—that the ability to buy your way out of things actually makes you tough. Truth be told, in that regard, Wesley isn't half the man his father had been. His dad had actually fought his way up from the streets and, although a contemptible pig, at least he'd been as tough as he'd seemed. Wesley, on the other hand, believes that he's tough because he's grown accustomed to winning. His school days consisted of confrontations with kids he consciously picks because they're weaker than he—easy to bully and control. He never really had a fight where he stood a chance of losing.

All grown up, he enters the realm of expensive lawyers and political influence, playing golf with elected officials, supplying them with drugs and hookers, as requested, always creating enough evidence to blackmail them—should he need to, one day. The innocent looking selfies he takes are really well-thought out documentation of his associates' bad behavior. It's so easy for him to entrap them in a web of drug-induced, illicit, and inappropriate behavior, because he understands the allure all too well.

In addition to his contrived political clout, Wesley's legal team is adept at crushing adversaries by abusing the discovery process, a key element in the legal process. Most people who don't understand the law think that if you are in the right, you sue, and then, a judge or jury sets things right. Unfortunately, that is seldom the case. The road between filing suit and getting in front of a judge or jury is called the discovery process. Here is where lawyers can cause endless, expensive delays and impediments through countless motions, depositions, interrogatories, and case management hearings. The more complicated the facts surrounding the suit, the longer and more expensive the discovery process, and Wesley's deals are always very complicated, by design. If one of his duped investors makes the naïve mistake of trusting the process to give them justice, Wesley's legal team teaches them a lesson about the flaws in the system and spends them into submission.

Wesley's view of the world, thus far, is colored by these experiences and by those of his youth. He'd never really lost a battle and has thus gained a sense of invulnerability. That's about to change! He is a fierce adversary in his world. He is about to be dragged into a world where he doesn't understand the rules. He will soon feel what his victims feel—helplessness.

For now, however, all he can feel or think about is Marlena. Although he has had so many experiences with prostitutes and party girls, Marlena is different. She seems to understand him in a way no others do. He feels that he and Marlena have a special connection, that he is not simply another client, but that in a different time and place, he and Marlena could actually be a couple. He sometimes envisions the *Pretty Woman* scenario, where he whisks her away from a life of prostitution and makes an 'honest woman' of her. So now, he looks at her—as close to lovingly as his damaged mind can muster—her beckoning him to climb on top of her and enter her once again. He feels a euphoria that he imagines she is feeling, also. He couldn't be more wrong.

Marlena is adept at making men like Wesley fall for her. At $1,000 an hour, she is no less a professional than any of Goelner's lawyers or accountants. She knows her craft and she knows it well. She's come up hard, soon learning that her natural sexiness can and will take her out of her poor surroundings and into a life of luxury that few can afford.

Her mentor, Anna, a much sought after courtesan in her youth, her handler in the old country, has trained her well. Running a very successful escort agency in Columbia catering to the business and political elite, Anna discovers Marlena working in a hotel bar. She watches the lowlife patrons trying to play grab ass with the beautiful girl, who struggles to maintain the fine line between protecting her dignity and collecting the tips she lives on. Anna decides that Marlena will be an excellent recruit for "the life" and she sets about saving Marlena from her life of poverty, taking her to a place where grab ass gets her thousands of dollars and expensive gifts, rather than a crumpled twenty with the phone number of some drunk pig scrawled on it.

Anna does just that. She recruits Marlena and teaches her the ways of an expensive call girl. She teaches her how to dress and apply make-up skillfully. She teaches her how to walk in heels properly, how to stand and sit seductively, how to make powerful men lust after her. Marlena is an excellent pupil. She learns Anna's lessons well, and soon she becomes Anna's most requested companion, entertaining professional men, the power brokers in Columbia. After Marlena perfects her craft, Anna suggests that Marlena move to America and she arranges for Marlena to transition to her friend's agency in New York. Anna does the right thing by Marlena and Marlena will always be grateful for all that she's given her.

Marlena enjoys her chosen profession and the life she leads. Most of her clients treat her exceptionally well, lavishing praise, money and endless compliments on her. They are, for the most part, very well-groomed and dressed. Most of them are in their 50s and 60s and mostly married to women who'd lost interest in sex with their husbands for one reason or another. They'd lost both their desire to please and to be pleased, sexually. They either don't realize that powerful men are, for the most part, driven by sex—or they do, and don't care.

Marlena understands powerful men and how to give them what they need. She is very attentive to their specific likes and dislikes and keeps a journal about each client, so she knows exactly how to dress, what shoes to wear, what to say and how to smell, in order to excite them to the highest degree. She loves the power she has over her clients and how she can make even the most accomplished industry leader or wiseguy tremble like an awkward teenager when she works her magic.

She knows the effect she has on Wesley, and she knows he feels they have something special. She uses it to cause him to become addicted to her. When he'd first come to the agency, he'd gone from girl to girl—for variety, he'd said. Over the last year, it had been only Marlena. She'd cast her spell on him and like the fly to the spider, he'd got caught in her web of lust and seduction.

What he doesn't realize is that she is simply an excellent actress, playing the part of the girl of his fantasies. She takes what he divulges in moments of vulnerable pillow talk and gives it to him in ways that he interprets as genuine affection. The truth is that Wesley is one of her least favorite clients. She hates what he stands for. She is repulsed by the stories of victimization of innocent naive people that he brags about post-coitus, and when he isn't in a cocaine-induced stupor. She is a consummate professional though, using Wesley's secrets against him to encourage his growing schoolboy-like crush and enticing him into extremely expensive multi-day encounters, where thanks to the cocaine, Marlena does very little and makes piles of cash. The only thing she enjoys about Wesley is taking so much money from him over and over. To her, he is a contemptible man, more a coward than the warrior he professes to be. She thinks about how short a career he would have in Columbia, where men don't and can't hide behind lawyers, and where the system won't stand in the way of righteous revenge.

CHAPTER 34
ATCHINSON'S FOLLY

Wesley Goelner has exhausted himself with Marlena. To her delight, he dismisses her with a huge tip and promises to "do this again, soon!"

What a pig and an idiot! Marlena thinks, as she leaves. *He actually thinks that I enjoy his cocaine-laced slobbering attempts at lovemaking? My God—he must be delusional, or I must be quite good at my job!* She leaves the hotel and goes home to take a very long shower, before taking a run to sweat the smell of him out of her system—and then another shower. Hopefully, after that, she will feel clean again.

Wesley sleeps for the next eighteen hours. He is completely out of touch, and unaware of what's happening and how his world is about to change. He gets up, orders one last abundant breakfast in his room, scatters tips around and heads to the office. The hotel is glad to drop him off in the hotel limo. After all, he'd dropped about $50,000 dollars there, over the last few days. It is the least they can do.

He gets off the elevator and walks down the marble hall to his decadent office. It is strangely quiet and there aren't the usual number of employees milling around interacting with each other. He heads straight to his office through the back entrance, so no one sees him enter. He buzzes for Carolyn, his secretary, and moments later, she appears. She looks terrible, which is odd for her—since he'd hired her for her good looks and sunny disposition, certainly not for her typing skills.

"What's with the long face?" he asks her. "That's not like you. Pretty girls should always smile," he says, trying to be piggishly flirtatious.

"How can I be happy amidst all this tragedy?" she says.

"What do you mean?"

"You don't know?"

"No."

"Ben Ridgefield has been killed and Mr. Caputo also. The police have been here every day, also some investigator woman, named Devin. They've been questioning all of us."

Wesley tries to keep his composure, but he is breaking out in a cold sweat. He stares at Carolyn in disbelief and is about to continue his incredulous conversation with her, when Captain Rodriguez appears at his door with Cary Devin right behind him.

"I need to ask you a few questions," Rodriguez says, "probably more than a few."

The questions come fast and furious. Rodriguez doesn't want Wesley to have time to think about his answers. He wants to elicit a revealing stream of consciousness. The captain is focused on his belief that Caputo and Ridgefield are responsible for each other's deaths. He feels the motive is a combination of greed and fear. He is searching for some agreement or validation from Goelner, but he gets none.

Goelner theorizes that they're both wannabe mobster types, so they'd been hanging around with a dangerous crowd. "Who knows what they were into?" Wesley asks. "It probably got them killed! I often warned them to choose their friends more carefully. It looks like not taking my advice may have gotten them killed."

Devin jumps into the inquisition. "What, exactly, do you mean by a 'rough crowd?' Who were they associating with who would want to kill them? Rough crowd or not, a double murder would have to be provoked in a big way. Any idea what they were into, that would make someone angry enough to kill them?"

"I think they were messing with women who were spoken for—and by guys who didn't respond well to that kind of thing. They spent a lot of time partying in Brighton Beach at some of those private social clubs—lots of cocaine and hot women. Brighton Beach can be a dangerous place for outsiders. Perhaps my deceased friends paid the ultimate price for leading with their dicks and their false sense of toughness."

Devin brushes off the answer. "That sounds like a load of crap!" she says to Rodriguez. "You're not buying this, are you?"

"The guy is just giving us his theory," Rodriguez says.

"Sure," Devin says, "that must be it."

The two of them spend another half hour grilling Goelner, but they get nowhere and finally give up. They walk out together, Devin musing, "That was a colossal waste of time—either he doesn't know anything, or he's a good liar. I'd go with the latter."

"Of course you would," Rodriguez replies.

Goelner is gripped by a paralyzing fear after Rodriguez and Devin leave. His typical feelings of invulnerability are gone. Ridgefield and Caputo are dead! They didn't lose a lawsuit or make a bad investment. They're dead! He has no one to turn to about this and even if he did, he wouldn't know who to trust, and he really doesn't know what is going on. All he knows is that his world suddenly seems to be falling apart and he is clueless about what to do next. It is an awful feeling! Perhaps, he is feeling just the way that the people he'd victimized over the years did. In a moment of humanity, he feels for them. But in an instant, he is back to worrying about the only person who ever really matters to Goelner—himself.

While Goelner contemplates his situation in his office, unbeknownst to him, another nightmare is unfolding in his warehouse.

Mitchell Atchinson has agreed to accept a sample shipment of the new coffee product from Colombia, and is anxious to test a roast. He is at the loading dock when the truck pulls up to deliver the coffee. Four men unload the hundreds of sacks of Arabica Coffee, he signs for it and they drive off in an empty truck. Atchinson takes out his knife and is about to cut open one of the bags to sample the beans, when he hears shouting.

"Freeze! Hands on your head!"

Atchinson looks up to see the warehouse suddenly swarming with law enforcement personnel in black SWAT gear, DEA clearly stenciled on their vests, assault rifles in their hands.

"On your knees!" the team leader shouts.

Atchinson does as he's told. The agents surround him and shortly thereafter, Captain Rodriguez arrives, walking with Devin, DEA's SAC Billings, and FBI Special Agent Tobias. The three men are all in business suits and smiling the pleased smile that comes from a joint operation, well executed. At this point, Devin is just an interested observer.

"Do you want to do the honors?" Tobias asks Billings.

Agent Billings asks one of his men for a blade and receives a six-inch serrated assault knife. He walks over to one of the bags.

"You need a warrant!" the now-terrified Atchinson yells.

"Indeed," Billings says, retrieving the warrant from his

inside jacket pocket and showing it to Atchinson. Billings takes a pair of surgical gloves from his pocket, puts them on and cuts open one of the bags. He roots around with a gloved hand for a while and comes up with a wrapped key of cocaine, hidden deep within the bag of coffee—just as the informant had indicated.

Atchinson is horrified when he sees Billings come up with the bag. "What the fuck?" he screams. "I had no idea, I swear!"

"Check the other coffee bags," Billings says, handing the knife to one of his men.

Several agents take out their knives and begin a methodical search of the coffee bags. Overall, they come up with small but bragable take of 50 bags of cocaine, with a street value of about $250,000 dollars. One bag of cocaine is hidden inside each sack of coffee.

"Read him his rights and take him downtown!"

The agents do so and they drag the belligerent and defensive Atchinson out of the building and into an unmarked DEA cruiser.

"I had no idea, I swear!" is the last thing they hear before an agent puts Atchinson into the car, protecting the suspect's head as he's doing so, and shuts the cruiser's door.

While all this is going on, a clueless Goelner is pacing about his office. He sends all the employees home, so he has the place to himself. He needs to think, but he can't think straight. He is frantic—way out of his comfort zone.

In a panic, he calls Marlena. "I need you!" he says. "I need you, now! Please come?"

Marlena is surprised to hear 'please.' She hadn't known that Goelner knew that word. "Okay, Wesley," she says. "Calm down! I'm on my way."

Marlena puts on one of Goelner's favorite outfits, retrieves a small gold box from her jewelry box, and puts it into her pocket. She arrives to find a pacing and sweating Goelner—a far cry from the arrogant prick she is accustomed to seeing! "Relax, sweetie," she says. "Whatever is troubling you, I'm sure I can make you feel better."

He is momentarily calmed by her sexy voice and slumps into his chair. She comes close and pulls his head to her chest. His senses, as always, are struck by her intense sexiness and the intoxicating scent of her perfume. For a moment, the stirrings in his pants disconnect his brain from the events that are torturing him.

"We need some really special happy dust today!"

"I'm here, *mi amore*," she says, choking on the words. "Relax, I'll be right back!"

Marlena goes to the bar in Goelner's office, takes a glass and fills it with some ice from the small refrigerator. She turns her back to Goelner, so her body is blocking what she is doing. She removes a small golden container from her purse, secretly slips the contents into his drink and turns to present his cocktail to him.

Goelner smiles and pulls her close to him.

"Is it really good?"

She stares at him for what seems likes minutes. He mistakes her longing gaze as affection, but Marlena is always amazed by his greed and narcissism. She caresses his face and tells him: "It's the best, I saved it for you."

CHAPTER 35
ALL THE KING'S HORSES AND
ALL THE KING'S MEN

All entrances and exits to the Brickman's Bistros building are closed off. Police cars decorate the front and side streets of the large old building. The scene is right out of a *Law and Order* episode where someone gets busted, with the public forming spectator lines alongside each roped-off area. FBI Agent Tobias and Police Specialist Devin are inside comparing notes and questioning employees. Tobias orders her team to track both the shipment origin and anyone connected to the cocaine sale and delivery, as DEA people pile in through the rear entrance and play their roles in the sting.

Tobias moves with independence and swagger as she barks out orders for a laundry list of things she wants tracked. Devin is smug and says little, but the two women respect each other for accomplishments in male-dominated organizations. Devin tugs at Tobias's suit jacket and suggests they head over to the Triangel building and find Goelner.

"Jenay, I think we've got all we want here. Perhaps it's better we chase the mouse and not the cheese?"

As Tobias looks to answer, Rodriquez marches up and interrupts. "Listen, the feds may have made a nice bust, but we've been on this case since the beginning. It's obvious the Triangel people have set up a nice front for this investment banking scheme and are the only parties responsible here. I still have several murders on my hands, if you recall. I'm sure you thought this was strictly a racketeering case, maybe with some mob influence, but I see it as strictly Triangel taking advantage of the little guy and having muscle with the mob."

Devin looks up for a moment and clenches her lips, holding back her own observations and what she perceives as another strong possibility. Every action and every thought sequence in her mind points to the three Marines and their clever positioning.

She is about to offer another clue, when Tobias interrupts to say, "I don't care who followed whatever, but I'm going to Triangel and put a cage around my mice."

Devin smiles and offers her companionship. "Mind if I come along—woman to woman?"

"Yeah, sure, why not?" Tobias answers, then mumbles, "woman to woman."

As they stride toward the exit, Tobias is met by another assisting agent, who informs them that their own DEA people in Colombia say the shipment warehouse is empty and hasn't been used in ages. Also, there was no inspection at Port Newark, and the phone number and email on the business card Atchinson has is no longer in use—it must have been a throw away. As for the address on the card, Atchinson should have done his homework—it's the address of the police academy in Seagirt, New Jersey.

"Are you kidding?"

"I wish!"

Tobias continues: "What about the check they issued?"

"A cashier's check cashed in Colombia by a small coffee company that we can't locate. I think it was a set-up."

"Well, keep questioning everyone here. I don't care how long it takes."

Frustrated and with clenched teeth, Tobias marches out the exit, with Devin close behind.

★ ★ ★

Driving with lights and siren in full throttle, the two women make it to Manhattan. Once there, Tobias is met by a small contingent of FBI and DEA agents. Tobias storms through the front entrance, showing her shield, with Devin following. They promptly make it to Goelner's office and demand to see him. His secretary is flushed by the intrusion, noticing more agents and police entering the waiting area.

"I want your boss, Goelner, here now!" Tobias points her finger to the floor, staring at her for maximum impact.

While waiting for an answer, Rodrigues enters and winks at Devin.

Tobias wastes no time protecting her turf. "Rodriguez, you're a little out of your jurisdiction, don't you think?"

"I'm just passing through and you could say, if it wasn't for our guys, you wouldn't have much to work with." Rodriguez frowns and winks again at Devin.

"Let's just say I want to finish my case in my jurisdiction and it's not just drug related. I'm getting to the bottom of this and you stay out of my way!"

"Of course, Agent Tobias, I respect the law." He smiles and puts his arms behind his back in a military at-ease position.

The clamor of police radios and people filing around makes it difficult to hear requests and conversation. Goelner's secretary tells Tobias that Goelner is not in his office.

"Then call his cell phone and find him. I'm sure the Wall Street King likes to be available!"

As his secretary dials his number, another agent comes to interrupt. The agent is visibly nervous as he approaches Tobias, who is focused on the whereabouts of Goelner.

"Agent Tobias, we're getting a report from the local police that they've located Goelner."

Tobias lights up. "Good! Where is my fat mouse?"

"They found him dead in an old hotel in the Bronx. He OD'd."

Tobias yells, "WHAT?"

"They say he was so full of cocaine, his heart stopped. The shit he was using must have been pure nitroglycerin. There seems to be no robbery or foul play, because he had almost $12,000 in his pockets and he was still wearing his gold Rolex." The assisting agent tries to hold back a smile.

Tobias is quick to question. "What are you smiling about?"

"Well, the Wall Street King must have gone out in style— he had a pocket full of condoms."

Tobias quietly turns to Devin with a look of bewilderment.

Devin turns to Rodriquez, who grins and declares, "Well, if you lie with dogs, you get fleas."

Devin answers quickly. "Oh, really? That simple?" Her tone is somewhat mocking, as she chuckles.

Rodriguez, surprised by her answer, sarcastically responds: "Oh, excuse me, Master Detective and Police Professor, you don't agree with my narrative and conclusion?"

In that very moment, Devin flashbacks to all of the evidence she developed leading to the three Marines. She remembers the triangle her friend Andersen left in his blood as a clue and how DeAngelo made light of it, even avoiding it. He must have made the obvious connection, so why not share his convictions with the investigating police? Then there were the set-up murders of the security people from Triangel. They would never ruin their own dirty work or make the implications so obvious. And what about the force of the kill? It could only have been inflicted by a giant of a man who knew how to kill. And finally, Ridgefield and Caputo—what a kindergarten set-up that was to draw attention to each other as the obvious murderers and away from the real assassins. Yeah, obvious, too obvious!

She paints a perfect picture of the murders, but at the same time, she remembers a destroyed crippled hero lying in his own blood from the merciless beatings of a greedy organization. She remembers the dedication and love shared between the three valiant Marine veterans and the widow of a fallen hero and friend. All of them had put their trust in the system—each time to be cheated, broken and devastated. She smiles, runs through her own conclusions, and then turns to Rodriguez.

Connecting the dots, she must choose to either follow the oath of her calling and bring the case to its real conclusion, or to remember a friend who'd saved her life, along with three heroes and a hero's widow, who'd only hoped for a chance at life.

Reluctantly, she feels her instinct swell with a commitment to principle, as she answers: ***"Yeah, you're right—there's a lot of gold in those coffins!"***

CHAPTER 36

"FIRST THEY IGNORE YOU, THEN THEY LAUGH AT YOU, THEN THEY FIGHT YOU, THEN YOU WIN"

—Mahatma Gandhi

Sonny, Lou, Connie and Donnie are at one of their favorite hangouts—DeRosa's, far from the chaos and calamity of New York and the Triangel implosion. It's a late Friday afternoon and happy hour is in high gear. There's a bittersweet silence between the four friends, as they nurse their drinks and remain contained.

Finally, Lou breaks the silence. Looking over his shoulder, in his baritone voice, he directs a question to Sonny: "Why were you so sure Zalenko would take out Ridgefield?"

Sonny takes a sip of his bourbon, grins sheepishly and points his drink at Lou. "I know Victor, and his jealousy is only bigger than his ego. I knew it wouldn't take long for him to react. He loves Irina and would never hurt her, but I pity the man who tries to take her away!"

Lou chuckles and turns to Donnie. "Your old buddy, Don

Vito, came through for you on that phony cocaine set up with his *amigos*—but where did the money come from for that?"

DeAngelo smiles again. Taking a sip of his vodka martini, he looks at each one of his friends, then nods at Sonny to respond.

"Well, Uncle Craig had some life insurance and guess who he remembered?"

They all laugh and Lou chimes back. "But, now you're out a lot of cash!"

Sonny smiles,and looking into his drink as if to find a diamond, remarks, "Well, it seems Ridgefield returned some money for an x-rated film he purchased – and not a very complimentary one, at that!"

They laugh again and DeAngelo adds: "Yeah, and my good friend and loyal counsel, Jim Fredericks, says he's working on what they call a "CLAWBACK" with the SEC, because Triangel screwed us, knowing full well about the building and what it's worth. You see, they made this Ponzi scheme to get rich on our backs—even taking our assets and making *mucho* millions on the sale of our building and home. I will be more than glad to complete the transaction in short order, and make all that booty for us."

He puts his arm around Lou and Sonny, who flank him on both sides. He shakes their shoulders and pulls them close to him and tells everyone: "Then we can get Ole Big Lou here, the treatment he needs, and new 'digs' for him, Brickman's Bistros, and even a nice, new place for Connie." He winks at her and she blushes with happiness.

Big Lou speaks up again, this time more anxious and excited. "Donnie, I got to ask you one last thing—Goelner, he got his, huh? Guess he won't be ruining any more lives?"

There is another moment of pregnant silence as DeAngelo

takes another a sip of his drink and remarks, "Oh, well, I forgot to tell you, my old friend, Don Vito, owns Fleur de Nuit escorts and Marlena is his niece."

The four friends survey each other with incredulity, and then laugh.

They toast their glasses and look up at the big screen TV in DeRosa's, as a breaking news flash begins:

> Today, police raided a coffee shipment at one of Triangel Brothers Corp's companies, BRICKMAN'S BISTROS, and found a shipment of cocaine hidden in their coffee bags, with a street value of over $250,000. They are launching an investigation of the venture capital giant on the heels of a murder and suicide overdose investigation involving three of their top executives, including CEO Wesley Goelner. The large investment banking firm offered no comment, but the police and FBI are launching an investigation into the activities of the firm and expect to file criminal charges.

.